This is a novel. Except where they can be historically identified, the characters are not intended to depict real persons, living or dead.

'We are brothers all in honour.'
William Wordsworth

Contents

Part One

End of an Era

'The grim wolf with privy paws daily devours apace.'
John Milton

One

Happy Days

'There,' Captain Harry Watson said. 'See what I mean, James?'

Captain James Barron bent over the table and studied the photograph. 'A lot of vehicles,' he commented. 'Could be tanks. Certainly motorized infantry.'

'Well, sir?' Watson turned to Colonel Barrett.

'We know they're there,' Barrett pointed out. A short, heavy-set man who wore a moustache, he was inclined to bristle. 'We have known they were there since Christmas.'

'Yes, sir. The point I am making is that three days ago they were *there*, about twenty miles further back.' Watson was thin and pallid; James sometimes wondered about his health. But he was always prepared to argue his point. Now he prodded another photograph, and then indicated the relative area on the map underneath. 'Now they have moved, twenty miles nearer the border. And their place has been taken by another armoured division. Look here, sir.' He offered a magnifying glass. 'Those are tanks. That is a panzer division.'

Barrett studied the photo. 'You could be right. They are obviously expecting an attack.'

Watson looked over his superior's head at James, eyebrows arched, clearly seeking support. James was prepared to give it, but he was anxious to have the meeting close: he had more important things on his mind than odd German troop movements. A big, ruggedly good-looking man, who had played rugby for the army and come close to an England trial, he had thoroughly enjoyed being seconded from his

3

regiment to the staff, if only because it had removed him from the boring business of maintaining the health and morale of his men while they had had absolutely nothing to do save change guard and square bash, as they had done for the last eight months, ever since landing in France in October 1939. That he was now serving in Military Intelligence he regarded as a justifiable tribute to his own intelligence. But he had resolved, last September, that he was not going to allow the war to interfere with his enjoyment of life, and right now that enjoyment was centred on Madeleine de Gruchy. So he contented himself with saying, 'Perhaps his lordship might be interested.'

'I'm sure Lord Gort has more important things to do than look at odd photographs,' Barrett remarked. 'These are not even of our section of the front. The Ardennes! Ha!'

'Then you entirely discount their importance, sir.' Watson was not about to give up.

'I discount their importance to us. If you wish to send them along to General Billotte, by all means do so. But I imagine he has his own aircraft taking snaps.'

'You do not consider that this steady build-up of enemy forces suggests that they are going to attack *us*?'

'I consider that to be highly unlikely at this time, or in the immediate future. I will tell you why, Captain. Firstly, Hitler is fully committed in Norway. No sane soldier is going to fight two campaigns at the same time. Secondly, I don't believe he intends to attack here in the West at all. He is looking for a negotiated peace. He has made this quite clear. The fact is, he dare not attack us. He's got himself up against the best and strongest army in Europe, probably the world. The French have ninety-nine divisions. Add in their garrison troops and we're talking about five million men. Add us in, and you have twenty-six more divisions, getting on for another million men. That is six million troops under arms, Harry. What has Hitler got? A hundred and three divisions, maybe three and a half million men, but quite a few of those are in Norway or on his eastern front. The French have two and a half thousand tanks;

we have more than a thousand. Hitler has maybe the same. No superiority. The French have eleven thousand guns; we have two and a half thousand. Hitler has seven thousand. The French have more than two and a half thousand planes; we have nearly two thousand. Hitler has about four thousand. Again, no superiority there. I won't talk about the fleet strengths. Hitler doesn't have a fleet. Facts are facts, laddie. And Hitler can understand facts as well as the next man. He thought our declaration of war was a face-saving device and that we'd accept the fait accompli after the fall of Poland. Now all he can do is make a loud noise and pray for us to climb down.'

'That chap who came down in Belgium in January . . .'

'When a German staff officer happens to crash land in a country supposed to be a target, carrying a complete set of plans for the invasion of that country, it has to be a plant. And that proves my point. Those captured plans clearly stated 17 January as the date of the attack in the West. Here we are, 9 May, and hardly a shot fired.'

'You don't think the attack was postponed, and maybe the plans altered, just because those original plans were captured?'

'It doesn't take five months to redraw a set of plans. No. No, that little escapade was an attempt to make us *think* we're going to be attacked.'

'Yes, sir,' Watson said doubtfully.

'And even if he did mean to attack, this apparent build-up of forces behind the Ardennes . . . My dear Harry, no one in his right mind would attempt to invade France through the Ardennes. It simply is not tactically possible to wage modern war in such wooded and uneven country. Send these photos along to Billotte and let us get on with our job.'

'Yes, sir.'

'Ah . . .' James ventured. 'If there is to be no war this weekend, sir, may I have it off? The weekend, I mean.'

'You are not due for Blighty leave.'

'I am not going home, sir. Just as far as Chartres. If I left this afternoon, I'd be back on Monday.'

'Today is Thursday. If you wish the weekend off, you should leave tomorrow.'

'Yes, sir. But you see, the wedding is tomorrow.'

'Whose wedding? Not yours, I hope?'

'No, sir. I'm a guest.'

'These are English people?'

'No, sir. They are French.'

'And they're friends of yours? From before the war, you mean?'

'No, sir. I met them— well, her, the last time I was in Paris. At Christmas.'

'Good heavens! Are you speaking of the bride?'

'Her sister, sir.'

'Hm. Well, you can have three days off, starting now. But I want you back here by Sunday night. Now, I have a lunch engagement. Good morning, gentlemen.'

The door closed. 'Only a madman would do this, only a madman would do that,' Watson remarked. 'I thought it was pretty well established that Hitler *is* mad. And if all he wants is peace, why did he start this show in the first place?'

'The old man has a point about our numerical superiority,' James suggested.

'Oh, he had the facts and figures, but not the reality. We may have nearly two thousand planes, but only a quarter of them are in France. And we have only a couple of hundred tanks over here. Anyway, numerical superiority is meaningless. It's morale and leadership that counts. Didn't Alexander the Great beat the Persians at Arbela when outnumbered by more than three to one?'

'You're not suggesting that Hitler is an Alexander the Great?'

'I'm suggesting that we're going to look a right set of fools if we sit back and take no notice and it turns out that he *is*.'

'Well, I'm not going to worry about it until Sunday night. I have to move. There's transport to the station in an hour.'

'What's this girl's name?'

'Madeleine de Gruchy.'

'Sounds up-market.'

'Very. So is she.'

'And you met her in Paris, at Christmas. That's damn near five months ago. You must have had an effect if she remembers you well enough to send you an invite to her sister's wedding, five months later.'

'Oh, she said she was going to. And she sent it two months ago. It just got misdirected, so I only received it this morning.'

'Any sisters? Apart from the one getting married?'

'I think there's another one.'

'Hm. And when you say up-market . . . ?'

'Wine. You must have heard of Gruchy wine. They own half of the claret country.'

'But they live in Chartres?'

'They have houses all over the show. Even one in England. And apparently getting married in Chartres is a family tradition. There's a whacking great cathedral.'

'Well, tell them that you have a devoted friend.'

James grinned. 'Do you want the bad news, or the good news?'

'Oh, the good news.'

'I'll mention your name.'

'And the bad?'

'The third sister, the one who is not getting married, is the oldest.'

'So?'

'We're talking about thirty plus.'

'Ah.' Watson was twenty-three. 'I thought, in these aristocratic continental families, any chap who goes knocking has to take the daughters in strict order of seniority.'

'This appears to be a liberated aristocratic family.'

'Still strange that the eldest shouldn't be married. Or is she the ugly one?'

'I have absolutely no idea,' James said. 'I'll tell you on Sunday night.'

*   *   *

To reach Chartres James had to change trains in Paris. The last time he had made the journey to the capital, in December, it had been an exhilarating experience, certainly for an officer in British uniform. If most people even then had seemed to hold the same opinion as Barrett, that Hitler wasn't coming for a while, if at all, they all appeared happy to see one of their allies in their midst.

But this time he begrudged every moment of the journey, and not only because he had to wait half an hour for his train. This time there were no smiles, and even, he felt, some derogatory remarks; he didn't know enough French to be sure. But he was seriously concerned when, while he sat on his platform waiting for the train, a company of *poilus* arrived to wait for *their* train, and were booed by the other waiting people. 'Is that a punishment company?' he asked the stationmaster, who he had discovered spoke English when he had asked for directions and train times.

'No, no, Captain. They are off to the front.'

'And for that they are being booed?'

'Well, they are going to fight. Who wants to fight? Why should we fight? We fought the last time, and where did it get us? A million dead. A million widows. Several million orphans. Would it not be better to let the Germans get on with it?'

'Because then Hitler would take over Europe.'

'What can Hitler do to us that can be worse than a million dead? Do you want to fight, Captain?'

'It happens to be my profession.'

'Yes,' the stationmaster said grimly, and wandered off.

As an officer in Military Intelligence, James felt he had to make a mental note of what he had seen and heard. Not, he supposed, that Barrett would be any more interested in French morale, or the absence of it, than he was in German troop movements.

At least the weather was fine, but apart from the attitude of the people – James could not imagine English soldiers being booed on Waterloo Station – Paris contained too many memories, which in turn contained too many uncertainties.

He was no longer absolutely certain what Madeleine de Gruchy looked like. On pre-Christmas leave in the most exciting city in the world, he had felt utterly lonely as he was surrounded by people enjoying themselves with the hysterical awareness that they were trembling on the brink of an abyss. His sense of isolation had been heightened by *his* awareness that when the abyss opened, if these people were to find themselves tumbling in – in the event of a German victory, for instance – he would no doubt find himself on a ship back to the safety and sanity of England. Certainly neither his mother and father, nor his two sisters, would be at any risk.

In desperation he had attended a tea dance being held at the embassy, and found himself chatting, and then dancing, with the most entrancing woman he had ever met – not that in the hectic seven years since he had left Sandhurst, both soldiering and playing rugby, there had been a lot of time for meeting women, apart from his sisters' friends, and they had all been too much of the china doll variety to interest a romantic brought up on such classics as *Beau Geste* and *Captain Blood.*

Madeleine de Gruchy had suggested a comparable amount of spirit, in her flashing eyes, her athletic movements. About five feet six he estimated, slim without being thin, with upswept dark hair, her features had been handsome rather than beautiful, but were dominated by her utterly delightful smile, as if she could switch on a brilliantly lighted bulb in her brain. She wore a printed brown calf-length georgette dress, fronted by a huge floppy bow on her bodice, matching court shoes and small hat, and grey gloves.

As usual with him as regards women, he had got off to a bad start. 'Is this a duty, or a pleasure?' he had asked when they had been introduced.

She had considered for a few moments, perhaps trying to

decipher his French, before replying, in perfect English, 'Why should it be a duty?'

'I would have thought you would have more interesting things to do than entertaining British officers.'

By then he had been holding her quite close as they danced, inhaling her scent, and when she had turned her head to look into his eyes their noses had almost touched. 'Do you not find yourself interesting?'

It was time to start again, even more disastrously. 'What I meant was, how did the embassy get hold of you?' He had looked around the room at the other well-dressed and attractive young women. 'All of you.'

'Do you suppose they dragged us in off the street? Or raided a few brothels?'

Her directness as well as her use of a word not considered polite in mixed company in England made him feel at once foolish and excited. 'Of course not. I . . .'

'My father and your ambassador are friends. I cannot say the same for all the girls here, but most of them are friends of mine. Yes, I suppose it is a duty. But it is a pleasure also, to entertain the officers of our gallant allies.'

Was she being sarcastic? 'I owe you an apology.'

'And I accept your apology.'

At which moment the music had stopped. 'Will you have a glass of champagne?'

'Thank you.'

He waylaid a passing waiter, and they seated themselves. Then he tried to regroup. 'If my history is correct, Napoleon had a marshal named de Grouchy.'

She sipped. 'There are some who say he cost us the Battle of Waterloo by blindly pursuing the Prussians instead of marching to the sound of the guns.'

'He was obeying orders, with which, perhaps, he did not agree. That can be the hardest part of soldiering, for an officer.' She had given another sharp turn of her head, as if she had not expected him to have considered his profession so deeply. 'Would he have been an ancestor?' he asked.

'We spell ours without the O. My family has always dealt in wine rather than bullets.'

'Claret or burgundy?'

'What you call claret.'

'Of course! Château Gruchy.'

'Do you like it?'

'I've never actually tasted it. It's a bit pricey.'

'That is because it is the best. But it is terrible that you should never have tasted it. Our estate is close to Paulliac. Do you know it?'

'I'm afraid not. I'd never been to France until last October. Do you know England?'

'We have a flat in Sloane Square. Do you know that?'

'Ah . . . I've passed it. Do you go there often?'

'Only for shopping, really. Have you been a soldier all your life?'

'Since leaving school. I went straight to Sandhurst.'

'Your Saumur.'

'Ah . . . yes, I suppose you could say that.'

'Pierre went to Saumur.'

'Pierre?' The last thing he wanted to hear was that she had a boyfriend tucked away.

'My brother. Do you have a brother?'

'No. I have two sisters.'

'Why, so do I. What does your father do?'

The temptation to lie, or at least exaggerate, was enormous. And what the hell? He would probably never see this gorgeous creature again. 'He's a schoolmaster. A headmaster. Of an English public school.'

'A headmaster! That is very important.'

'Do you know what an English public school is?'

'Of course. I went to Benenden.'

She could slap him down on almost every subject. 'With your sisters?'

'Well, not all at the same time; Liane is six years older than I. I liked it very much. Better than Lucerne.'

'You went to school in Lucerne as well?'

11

'Finishing school. It was all right. But when I went, we had a bad reputation. Liane had been expelled. So Amalie and I were very carefully supervised.'

'I can see that would be tiresome. May I ask why your sister was expelled?'

Madeleine de Gruchy gave one of her enchanting smiles. 'You may ask, Mr Barron, but I am not going to tell you. You will have to ask Liane herself.'

'I should love to be able to do that.' He spoke without thinking, and flushed as she arched her eyebrows. 'I mean . . . if I were in a position to do so, it would be because I would be seeing you again.'

She gave him another of her considered looks, then said, 'I have always been told that Englishmen are very slow. But you are very fast.'

'Then I apologize again.'

'No, no. Friends should never apologize to each other.'

'Are we friends?'

The music had started. 'Would you like to dance again?'

'I would rather talk with a friend.'

Another quizzical look, then she said, 'Why, so would I.'

It was just getting dark, and was extremely cold, but Madeleine, predictably, was wrapped in a mink. They found a café on the Champs Élysées where they were out of the wind, ordered coffee and cognac. 'Is it not uncanny,' she remarked, 'that there is a war on, and yet Paris is still Paris, and the Champs Élysées is still the Champs Élysées. Do you think if we both closed our eyes, held hands, and wished very hard, it would all go away? The war, I mean. Hitler.'

'I should love to close my eyes and hold your hand, but I don't think it would make a lot of difference to Hitler.'

'That is because you are a soldier. You *want* to fight.'

'Do you know, I did, up to half an hour ago. Now I would rather spend the rest of my life talking to you.'

'A romantic soldier! But that is a very nice thing to say.'

'I have a confession to make.'

Again that delicious arch of the eyebrows. 'To me?'

'My father is not a headmaster. He is a housemaster.'

'Well, what is wrong with that? He will be a headmaster one day.'

'I wouldn't bet on it. But if you forgive me, I would like to take you out to dinner.'

She made a moue. 'I have a dinner engagement.'

'Of course. Well, then . . .'

'I am free tomorrow.'

'And I am due back at camp tomorrow morning.'

'The Fates are against us. When will you next be in Paris?'

'I have no idea.'

'I hate the Fates.'

'Would you give me an address, or a telephone number, so that I can contact you next time I get leave?'

'That would do you no good. We go back to Paulliac the day after tomorrow, for Christmas, and we shall be spending the winter there. It is warmer than here.'

'Hell! I beg your pardon.'

She shook her finger to and fro. 'No apologies, remember. Listen, we will make a date. My sister Amalie is getting married in May. Give me the name of your regiment and I will send you an invitation, well in advance. Surely they will give you leave to attend the wedding of a family friend?'

'Am I a family friend?'

'You are now.'

'But . . . May?'

'I know. It is a long time away. You will have forgotten all about me by then.'

'I was thinking that you will have forgotten about me. But . . . Paulliac? That's also a long way away.'

'Not Paulliac. Chartres. De Gruchys always get married in Notre-Dame in Chartres. Listen. I will send you an invitation, and you will come to the wedding. You will stay with us. We have a house in Chartres. We will get to know one another better, and I will give you some of our wine to sample.' She gave a little giggle. 'You will be able to ask Liane why she was expelled.'

He had put the whole thing down as a dream, until this very morning, when the invitation had arrived. It had been mailed in March, and that it had taken so long to reach him had been because on that December evening he had still been a line officer, and as he had not had an address for her he had been unable to inform her of his change of status. Thus the envelope had spent several weeks moving around army sorting offices until he had been located. The thought that it might never have got to him, or at least not until after the wedding, made his blood curdle. As was the thought that she might be offended, or have struck him off the guest list, because he had never replied. But he was here at last. 'De Gruchy?' he asked the ticket collector.

'Ah, de Gruchy.' A volume of French.

'You wouldn't happen to speak English? I'm looking for their house. Maison de Gruchy?'

The ticket collector came to a decision. '*Fiacre*,' he said, and summoned one. James accepted that it might not be a bad idea to turn up in a taxi, but it took a very long time. Not that the streets were crowded, but they were extremely narrow as they slipped down to the River Eure, while the driver insisted on making a detour to show him the cathedral, which was certainly striking with its spectacular twin towers – although he reflected that he would be taking a closer look at it tomorrow – but the front drive of the de Gruchy mansion was packed.

The house stood on the banks of the river, the gardens reaching down to the water. The long entry drive also made its way through clustering flower beds, and was crammed with delivery vehicles of every description. The taxi driver considered the situation, and made a remark. James couldn't understand what he said, but his meaning was obvious enough. 'I'll walk the rest,' he volunteered, and held out a sheaf of notes. The driver selected two of these, and James picked up his valise and made his way through the throng. People cast curious glances at his uniform but did not appear to comment. However, when he went up the huge wide front steps to the open double doors, he encountered a formidable-looking individual in a frock coat, who looked him up and down, identified his khaki uniform, and inquired, in English, 'Your business, sir?'

'I'm a guest at the wedding,' James explained.

The butler looked sceptical, but then a voice said, 'You must be James.' In its quality, low and musical, yet clear and resonant, James thought it the most attractive human sound he had ever heard. He turned, not knowing what to expect, and was for a moment rendered speechless. Here was another Madeleine, only the handsome features were overlaid with a crisp softness which made for real beauty, dominated by the eyes, huge and blue and wide set, the whole framed in wavy yellow hair, worn loose and unfashionably long, well past her shoulders, kept in place by a bandeau. She wore a white silk blouse and loose black pants. He never doubted that she had a splendid figure: her blouse was full and her hips slender, and although she was no taller than her sister, her legs were also long, and her bare feet, thrust into high-heeled sandals, were exquisite.

'Do I pass muster?' she inquired.

He flushed. 'I am most terribly sorry. I . . .'

'Was expecting Madeleine, perhaps. But you will have to do with me, for a while.' She held out her hand. 'I am Liane.'

'Madeleine's elder sister.'

'That is correct. And you are Captain Barron. Madeleine has told me all about you.'

'I must apologize for not having sent an acceptance. The invitation only reached me this morning. It got lost in various regimental post bags.'

'But you came anyway, and at such short notice. That was sweet of you.' Men carrying boxes of glasses hurried by. 'Shall we get out of the line of fire?' Liane suggested. 'It is all right, Antoine, he is not going to steal anything.' She led the way down a vast hall, with a chandelier hanging above their heads, and a grand staircase mounting on the right, and turned into a drawing room, as spacious and luxurious as everything about this family. 'Champagne?'

'I haven't missed the wedding, I hope?'

'We always drink champagne. Don't you?'

'I'm afraid it's not always on offer in an army mess.'

'I know. Soldiers have a difficult time. Laurent!'

An under-butler hurried forward with a tray and presented two glasses. Liane raised hers. 'Welcome to Chartres. My brother is a soldier.'

'Madeleine told me. About Madeleine . . .'

'She is having a last fitting. She did not like her gown for tomorrow, and it had to be altered. You will see her at dinner.'

'About tomorrow . . . and dinner. I have only my uniform.'

'You look divine. Should a man not always be in uniform?'

Thank God for that, he thought, remembering Paris.

'Mama, this is Madeleine's friend, Captain Barron.'

The woman who had just entered the room offered him her hand, in such a manner that she clearly expected him to kiss it, so he hurriedly put down his overnight bag and did so. She was not a day under fifty, he estimated, but he could tell immediately where the sisters had got their looks. 'Welcome, Mr Barron,' Madame de Gruchy said, her accent establishing that she was as English as himself. 'Would that be the Devon Barrons?'

'Ah . . . we come from Worcestershire.'

'Of course.' Laurent was back, and she took a glass. 'I must apologize for all the fuss and botheration. Weddings are such tiresome things, and this is our first.'

'Where are we putting Captain Barron?' Liane asked.

'The list is in the study. You will have to check with Antoine as to a room for the Captain's man.'

'Ah . . .'

Liane put down her glass and held his hand. 'Come along and I'll sort you out.'

16

James picked up his bag. 'If you'll excuse me, Madame de Gruchy . . .'

'Don't let her bully you. Laurent! I really do not like that vase on that table. Kindly move it.'

Liane led James out of the room and down the hall to another door. 'You don't have a man, do you?'

'I have a batman. But I didn't bring him with me. Do you think I should find an hotel?'

'Certainly not. We would be insulted. *I* would be insulted,' she added, leaving no doubt that that was far the more serious consideration. She opened the door. 'Papa! This is Captain Barron, of the . . . I don't know the name of your regiment.'

'I'm in Intelligence, Monsieur de Gruchy. I hope you don't mind my barging in like this.'

Albert de Gruchy was seated behind a large desk, in the centre of another enormous room, lined with bookshelves. He made James think of a St Bernard dog; even his bow tie, as large as everything else in this house, suggested a flask of brandy strapped to his neck. He didn't get up, but extended his hand to be shaken. 'Intelligence, eh? Do you know what the Boches are up to?'

'Ah . . . I'm afraid it's all theory at the moment, sir.'

'Intelligence!' Liane said. 'How terribly exciting. You must tell me all about it. Papa, do you have the list?'

'Which list? I have twelve lists. I have a list for the wine, a separate list for each course of the wedding banquet, a list for the dinner tonight, a list of car parking places, a list of the children's positions at the ceremony, a list of who leaves the cathedral with whom . . . Do you know what our army needs, Barron? And probably your army as well. My wife as chief of staff.'

'I want the list of sleeping arrangements,' Liane said.

'It is here somewhere.'

She went round the desk and sifted through the papers. 'Here we are. Let me see . . . You're not here!!'

'I would say I was not expected, as I did not reply.'

'We'll have to put that right.'

'I think Marengo is still vacant,' Monsieur de Gruchy suggested.

'Marengo! But that is on the third floor. Who is in Wagram?'

'I imagine it is Pierre.'

'Then he will have to move. He isn't here yet, anyway.' She picked up a pen, stroked out the name, and replaced it. 'There. Now you are next door to me. We will share a bathroom.' James cast a hasty glance at M de Gruchy, but he was already studying another list. 'And you'll have Joanna on your other side,' Liane said. 'What fun. Come along. I'll show you.'

James's head was spinning. 'If you'll excuse me, monsieur . . .' M de Gruchy waved his hand. James picked up his overnight bag and followed Liane into the hall. 'I can't share your bathroom.'

'Why not? You can lock the door when you want to be alone.'

He watched the black slacks moving in front of him as she climbed the stairs, and tried another tack. 'Is Joanna another of your sisters?'

'No, no. Joanna is a friend. Like you. We were at school together.'

'And she's English?' Oh, what he would give to encounter an average Englishwoman, educated to his own middle-class code of conduct, in this den of aristocratic eccentricity. Except that he supposed any friend of the de Gruchys would probably be an aristocrat in her own right.

'Joanna is American,' Liane explained. 'Well, half American.'

'And the other half?' He remained optimistic.

'Her father is Swedish.' They reached the top of the stairs, and James found himself in another hallway as long and as high as the one below, this one with doors to left and right at regular intervals. 'They're split up. Americans are always splitting up.'

He followed her along the hall. 'And she was at Benenden?'

'No, no. She was at Lucerne with me.'

'Oh. Lucerne.' He wondered if he dared ask about that.

'Here we are.'

The name, Wagram, was in gilt over the door. To the left was Austerlitz, to the right Borodino. 'Are all the rooms in the house named after Napoleonic victories?'

'Napoleonic *battles*. Papa is very broad-minded.' James had already deduced that. 'He and Mama sleep in Waterloo. Well, Mama is English. I suppose you saw that.'

James followed her into a luxurious bedroom. 'Yes,' he said absently.

'She was a Howard. Do you know them?'

'Not the . . . ?'

'She's a cousin of some sort. We were taken to Arundel once, but I don't think the duke knew who we were.' She gave a tinkle of laughter. 'I don't think he wanted to. Will this be all right?'

'This is stupendous. But if it's your brother's room . . .'

'It isn't really. Only when we happen to be in Chartres. We only come here once a year as a rule, and he isn't always with us. Mama only put him here this time because we haven't seen him since Christmas, and she thinks he is a good influence on me.'

'Well, then . . .'

'I hate good influences. Especially Pierre. He lectures me. You aren't going to lecture me, I hope? In fact, I'm rather hoping you'll be a bad influence. I do like bad influences.'

'Ah . . . what time do you expect Madeleine home?'

'Oh, she's home. In the housekeeper's apartment, being fitted. You could be a good bad influence on her as well. She's terribly strait-laced.' Liane opened an inner door. 'This is the bathroom. And that door leads to my room. If you want to come in, do knock first. I may be doing something you shouldn't see.'

'Don't you think it would be more proper to lock your door?'

'Good heavens, no. I hate locked doors. Come in when you're ready, and we'll go down together. Or would you rather I sent Madeleine to you?'

'Well, I suppose, as I am her guest . . .'

'You are the guest of all of us. But I'll tell her you're here.'

She went through to her room and he regarded the door for some seconds. He wanted to use the bathroom, but he didn't want to offend her. He had never before been so swept off his feet. Carefully he turned the key, then unlocked the door again when he was finished. Then he unpacked, a matter of seconds, as he had only a single change of shirt, socks and underclothing and his toiletries. He hung up his tunic and took off his boots, then carried his wash bag into the bathroom, and arrived before the sink to gaze at toothbrush and toothpaste, and a razor, and several tubes and bottles. What to do? He had never shared a bathroom with a woman before, and he was not even supposed to be interested in her. But how could anyone not be interested in Liane de Gruchy?

He arranged his things a safe distance from hers, then returned to his room and lay on the bed, which was a tester, and gazed at the canopy. He actually was quite tired, having been travelling all afternoon after poring over maps and photographs all morning. And there was so much to think about, so much to savour over the next three days. Could he possibly fit into such a society? Did he want to? Oh, he wanted to. But he simply could not envisage himself taking Madeleine, just for instance, back to Worcester to meet his parents. Liane, perhaps. He suspected that she would take anything in her stride. But he wasn't supposed to be thinking about Liane.

He woke up with a start when there was a knock on his outer door. He hadn't intended to fall asleep. Now the afternoon was drawing in; his watch told him it was just past six. 'May I come in?' Madeleine! He leapt off the bed, looked desperately left and right, but he didn't have a dressing gown, and the door opened. 'Or were you asleep?'

'I was. I do apologize.'

She wagged her finger at him. 'There you go again.'

'I mean, well, I'm not dressed.'

'You have pants on.'

'But I should be downstairs. Shouldn't I?'

'Come down whenever you wish. Dinner isn't until eight thirty.' She closed the door behind herself as she came into the room, and he realized she was wearing a dressing gown, and her hair was loose. He also realized that while she was every bit as attractive as he remembered, she was not Liane. Who, apart from any other consideration, had to be at least four years older than himself. 'I'm so glad you made it.' She continued to approach him. 'Do you like the room?'

'It's fabulous.'

'And next door to Liane. That can be wearisome.'

'She put me here herself.'

'I know she did. My sister believes that everything in this world, but especially every man to whom she takes a fancy, has been put here for her delectation. But you're *my* guest. Do you agree?'

'Well, of course. I can't thank you enough.'

'You can thank me by kissing me.' Her arms went round his neck and her body became wedged against his. Her lips were moist, her tongue eager. James had never been kissed like that before. And Liane considered her strait-laced? 'Now,' she said, 'I should try to avoid kissing Liane.'

'Is she dangerous?'

'Very. To the man involved. And anyone else who may be involved. I would like to have you to myself this weekend. You don't object?'

'I'm flattered. But I don't want to cause trouble between you and your sister.'

'There won't be any trouble. Now, how long are you staying?'

'I must be back on Sunday evening.'

She made the moue he remembered so well. 'That is not very long.'

'Well, there is this war business . . .'

'It is a nuisance. Now, tomorrow is a write-off, at least until the evening. The Catholic ceremony is at ten, then we have to go to the synagogue at eleven, then there is the reception

21

and the banquet, which is unlikely to break up much before
eight . . . We could go off on our own then.'

'I beg your pardon. Did you say synagogue?'

'Henri is a Jew. Do you have anything against Jews?'

'Of course not. It's just that . . .'

'I know. This is the first time a de Gruchy has married a Jew.
But Amalie is so in love. And he really is very nice. He's in
Pierre's regiment. They are best friends. That's how they met,
when Pierre brought him down to Paulliac for a visit last year.
Amalie fell in love at first sight.'

'Do you believe in love at first sight?'

Another moue. 'It is risky. Second perhaps.' She kissed him
again. 'Now you get dressed and I will see you downstairs.'

She closed the door behind herself, and he remained staring
at it for several seconds. I fell in love at first sight, he thought.
But that was before he had met Liane. So was he setting
up to be the most unutterable cad? He simply couldn't let
Madeleine down. But when he went into the bathroom to shave
he deliberately did not lock the door to Liane's room . . . and
then realized he was too late; the bathroom was heavy with
her scent. She must have used it when he had been asleep.

Maybe he had had a lucky escape, at least from himself.

He dressed and went downstairs, to a drawing room filled
with people. To his great relief several of the men were in
uniform, even if French uniforms managed to look so much
more glamorous than British.

Madeleine was waiting for him, stunning in a dark green
evening gown cut low both front and back. She tucked her
arm through his and led him into the throng. 'I want you to
meet Pierre.'

He looked left and right, and spotted Liane, talking to
someone with her usual animation. She was wearing pale
blue, and had her back to him, but he could tell that her
décolletage was quite as deep as her sister's. 'Ah,' Pierre
said. 'The usurper.' He was every bit as handsome as his
sisters were beautiful, and wore the uniform of a lieutenant

in the Motorized Cavalry. 'But like a good soldier, you were obeying orders, eh? This is Henri.'

The man beside him, slight and dark, wearing the same uniform and displaying the same rank, shook hands. 'Liane tells me you are in Military Intelligence. Do you have any idea when the enemy will attack?'

'I'm afraid only Herr Hitler knows that,' James said.

'And he will not tell us. But he will come one day. We are looking forward to encountering these famous panzers, eh?'

'No apprehensions?'

'Should we have? We are not the Poles, with their outmoded equipment. Our Sommas are the biggest and best tanks in the world. We each command one. The Germans have nothing to match us.' Something else, and much better, to report when he got back.

'We are not discussing the war tonight,' Madeleine said. 'Come and meet Amalie.'

James had been doing some mental arithmetic. He had placed Madeleine's age at about twenty-four, or two years younger than himself. If Liane was about six years older, as suggested by what Madeleine had told him, she was probably thirty. Pierre had to be younger than Madeleine, as he was still a lieutenant. Probably he was around twenty-two. Thus Amalie could hardly be more than twenty, as was obvious in the immaturity of both face and figure when compared with her sisters, although that she would at least equal them in time was obvious. But what had accounted for the six-year gap between Liane and Madeleine? Or was there yet another sibling tucked away somewhere? He needed to concentrate on the present. 'How very good of you to attend my wedding,' Amalie said, in faultless English. Like Madeleine she had dark hair, and like both her sisters the most enchanting voice; she was actually the tallest of the three, by a couple of inches, with an elegant slenderness of body, and even more lively eyes.

'It is very good of you to invite me, mademoiselle.'

'Oh, Amalie, please.'

'And this is Joanna.'

'Well, say,' Joanna remarked. 'You mean you don't speak too much French either? You could be a gift from the gods.'

If entirely different in appearance from the Gruchys, the Swedish-American woman was no less striking. Her features, softly rounded rather than crisp, were framed in long, straight yellow hair; again, it would have been quite unfashionable in London, or, he suspected, New York, but perhaps not in Stockholm, and definitely not in the de Gruchy drawing room. Taller than Amalie, and in fact only an inch or two shorter than himself, her figure was definitely voluptuous, amply displayed by the apparently de rigueur low-cut evening gown. If James hadn't already been overwhelmed by the female pulchritude with which he was surrounded, he would have been again rendered speechless.

'Actually, she speaks perfect French,' Madeleine remarked. 'She just likes to pretend. This is Aubrey. Now he doesn't have a word of French. Aubrey is Joanna's brother.'

'Hi.' Aubrey shook hands. He did not bear the slightest resemblance to his sister, as, although he was fair-haired, he was short and slender, as well as obviously younger.

'Aubrey is my half-brother,' Joanna corrected. 'Mom married again. Are you really in Military Intelligence?'

James was regretting having confided that fact. 'Yes, I am.'

'You and I must have a get-together.'

'Eh?' He cast Madeleine an anxious glance, but she was deep in conversation, in voluble French, with another guest.

'Well, you might be able to tell me something I could use.'

'Use for what?'

'I'm a journalist,' she explained. 'Oh, I'm on holiday right this moment, visiting Pa and attending this wedding, but my boss did say he'd be happy if I could pick up anything kind of confidential we could maybe use while I'm in the war zone, you could say.'

'And you seriously expect me to give you classified information?'

'Oh, don't be all stuffy.' She fluttered her eyelashes at him. 'I could maybe make it worth your while.'

To his great relief Madeleine turned back to them, and the conversation became general. James could not stop himself continually glancing at Liane, and eventually she did drift across the room towards him. 'You are a heavy sleeper,' she remarked.

He gazed at her in consternation. Could she possibly have come into his room while he had been asleep? But before he could think of a riposte, the dinner gong went. James was required to take Madeleine in; he found himself sitting between her and another woman, with Liane at the far end of the long table. 'Monsieur Moulin, I would like to introduce you to Captain Barron, British Military Intelligence. I'm afraid Captain Barron does not speak much French.'

Jean Moulin was seated opposite him, and gave a slight bow over his soup plate. He was a handsome man, not very old, with intelligent features. James braced himself for the inevitable question, but he merely said, in English, 'We are flattered by your presence, monsieur.'

'Monsieur Moulin is the prefect of Chartres,' Madeleine explained.

James all but choked on his soup; he had never before moved in this social class. 'You have a beautiful city, monsieur,' he managed.

'It is old, and venerable, and needs looking after,' Moulin observed.

'But it is not so beautiful as Bordeaux,' Madeleine declared. 'As you will see, James, when you visit us in Paulliac.'

'When you can see it,' Moulin agreed, with easy humour. 'That is, when the morning mist clears off the Garonne. That is usually about noon, is it not?'

'I hate you,' Madeleine said, with one of her flashing smiles.

James waited for the conversation to drift away from them, then asked, 'Is the prefect a friend of your family?'

'Of course, or he would not be here.'

'Quite. I really must get out of the habit of asking stupid questions. But . . . am I going to visit you in Paulliac?'

'The next time you have leave. Only you must come for a fortnight. When will that be?'

James considered. He would be due for Blighty leave in August, and duty required him to go home to his parents. But could duty possibly compete with desire? 'Will that also be a family gathering?'

'I doubt it, unless Mr Hitler has given up and gone home by then. Liane hardly ever comes down: she finds it boring. She prefers Paris. She has a flat there. And Pierre will be with his regiment. And Amalie will be living in Dieppe with Henri's parents. But that will be perfect, don't you see? We'll have the place all to ourselves.'

The party broke up about eleven; everyone knew that the morrow was going to be a long and hectic day. 'You can walk me to my room,' Madeleine suggested, after they had said their goodnights, and held his hand as they climbed the stairs. 'Did you enjoy the evening?'

'It was a bit overwhelming.'

'I know. I shouldn't have sprung it on you. Did you like our friends?'

'Ah . . .'

'Be honest. I shan't be offended.'

'That American creature . . .'

'Joanna Jonsson? Isn't she gorgeous?'

'I suppose she is.'

'But you didn't like her.'

'Is she a close friend of yours?'

'Not really. She's Liane's friend. They were at Lucerne together.' She gave one of her little giggles. 'They were expelled together.'

'Are you going to tell me why?'

'Haven't you asked Liane yet?'

'Well, no.'

'I'll tell you the whole story when you come down to Paulliac. How did Joanna upset you?'

'She wanted me to give her some secret information to publish in her newspaper. She said she was a journalist.'

'She is a journalist. But I agree, that is a bit naughty. Never mind. She goes home on Saturday.'

'Back to the States?'

'Not right now. To Stockholm, to be with her father. Anyway, we'll be rid of her.' She paused before a door named Moscow. 'Here we are.' Her arms went round his neck. 'Would you like to come in?' she whispered.

'I'd like to. But . . .'

'You're a gentleman. I'm glad of that. I'd like to ask you in, but I'm a lady. Well, I suppose I am.'

A last squeeze, and she closed the door behind herself. James slowly retraced his steps to Wagram. He had had a great deal to drink, both champagne and the family brew, and lacking the steadying influence of Madeleine's arm, found the hallway inclined to sway. Fortunately there was no one about and he gained the room without mishap.

He stripped off his clothes, trying to focus on what had happened this evening, and what might happen were he to visit Paulliac, if he was going to visit Paulliac. He opened the bathroom door and blinked, as the light was already on, and gazed at Liane, wearing only a pair of knickers, bending over the basin as she cleaned her teeth. 'Oh, my God!' Hastily he stepped back through the doorway as she turned to face him.

'I don't think you can rush off now,' she remarked.

'I . . .' He tried to do absurd things with his hands. 'I completely forgot we were sharing. I'll just . . .'

'Come here.'

'I need to put something on.'

'I like you better the way you are.' He stepped back into the bathroom while she rinsed her mouth. As he had known would be the case, she was superbly built, the breasts high, the belly flat, the legs long and strong. Liane dried her mouth. 'You have the advantage of me,' she said. 'I'm a great believer in equality.' She slipped her knickers down her thighs and allowed them to slide down her legs to the floor, thereby redoubling her beauty.

'Listen . . .' he tried.

'You need to use the toilet. I'll wait in the other room.'

To his consternation she went through his doorway, not hers. He cleaned his teeth and followed her. 'We must be mad.'

'It's the best way to be.' She lay on the bed, one leg up.

'Madeleine . . .'

'Are you the confessing kind?'

'Well . . .'

'Neither am I. What she doesn't know will never harm her.'

'She's your sister!'

'Sisters are supposed to share. Even if they don't know they're doing it.' She stroked his thigh. 'I'd say you're about ready. I know I am, but take your time.'

He lay beside her, kissed her mouth – he had wanted to do that from the moment he had seen her – then tentatively stroked her breasts – something else he had never supposed he would ever be allowed to do – and could not suppress a little convulsive jerk when her hand slipped down to find his manhood.

She frowned. 'You *have* done this before?'

'Well . . . not with . . . well . . .' He knew he was blushing.

'You mean you've only ever been with a whore? You poor boy. Come to mother.'

When James awoke she was gone. But her scent was everywhere. My God, he thought. What have I done? What she had wanted. Because she had been as drunk as himself? Or simply because it was something she had wanted to do. He remembered Madeleine's warning. But Madeleine! He sat up. How could he face her? And she had all sorts of plans for the rest of the weekend. He had to face her. He had to face all of them, including Monsieur and Madame de Gruchy! And it was clearly going to be an early start. Although it was only half past six the house was filled with noise.

James frowned. The noise was random, and very loud. And not at all joyous; he was sure he could hear a woman screaming. More than one. He swung his legs out of bed, and his door crashed open. Pierre stood there, fully dressed. 'Have you heard?'

'Heard what?'

'The Germans have invaded Holland and Belgium. They are through Luxembourg. They are about to enter France. The battle has begun.'

Two

Blitzkrieg

J ames sat on the bed. Of course they had always known
this was going to happen. But to have it happen just at
this moment . . .

'What's happening downstairs?'

'You could say all hell has broken loose,' Pierre said.
'Henri and I have to rejoin our regiments immediately.'

'But the wedding . . .'

'That's it. Amalie is having hysterics. I have to get down
there. Come as quickly as you can.'

James nodded, watched the door close, and dashed into the
bathroom . . . and encountered Liane, fully dressed in her shirt
and slacks. 'I was listening. Will you have to go?'

'Well, of course I must go.'

'Have you had orders as well?'

'Not yet.'

'Well, then . . .'

'The reason I have not had orders is that no one knows
exactly where I am. Only that I am in Chartres.' He began
to shave.

'Then if you stayed here, no one would ever know where
you are.' She was standing behind him, and he looked at her
in the mirror. 'I know,' she said. 'You would be a deserter.
Oh, fuck it!'

He blew her a kiss. 'I'd rather fuck you.'

'Listen . . .' She checked as the bedroom door opened
and closed.

'James?' Madeleine asked. Liane darted back into her

30

room and closed the door. 'James?' Madeleine came into the bathroom. 'I could swear I heard Liane's voice just now.'

'Yes. She came in, saw I was here, apologized, and left.'

Madeleine looked him up and down. 'She saw you like that? Do you always sleep in the nude?'

'I forgot to bring any pyjamas. And now you've seen me like this as well. You told me I shouldn't apologize.' He stepped past her and began to dress.

'What are you going to do?'

'Rejoin my unit.'

'Shit!' She sat on the bed. 'Will you be coming back?'

'If I'm invited.'

'Of course you're invited. Now and always.' Her shoulders hunched. 'There was so much I wanted to do with this weekend.'

He stood in front of her while he knotted his tie. 'Madeleine . . .' She raised her head, and he realized that now was not the time. Why cause grief and anger when he might never see either of them again? 'Don't be afraid,' he said. 'I'll see you downstairs.'

She left the room, shoulders still hunched, and he finished dressing, repacked his valise, and hurried down the stairs, to find the hall filled with people. Henri stood with his arms round a weeping Amalie. His parents, whom James had met after dinner, stood behind him, looking absolutely shattered. Pierre had his arm round Liane. Joanna Jonsson stood with her half-brother, eyes gleaming; no doubt, James deduced, she was mentally composing a report for her newspaper. Aubrey looked bewildered.

Only Albert and Barbara de Gruchy appeared quite calm, and Monsieur de Gruchy was clapping his hands for silence. 'So the Boche has acted,' he said in a loud voice. 'He will have to be taught a lesson. We must all do our duty. Those of you who are soldiers must return to the colours. The rest of us must preserve the home front. But . . .' He raised his voice as a combined rustle and murmur spread round the throng. 'We have some unfinished business. Today was to be the happiest day of my daughter's life. I am resolved that it will be as happy a day as is possible. I have sent for Father Jerome, and the ceremony will take place now, here, before any of you depart.' He gave a grim smile. 'I promise you it will be a short one.' He looked at the Bursteins. 'The second ceremony will be held as soon as possible. Now . . .' He looked past them at Antoine, standing in the outer doorway and signalling. 'Father Jerome is here. Will you kindly take your places in the drawing room.'

Madeleine had joined them, like her sister, wearing slacks. 'We are the bridesmaids,' she said. 'Dressed like this! I have no hat.'

'At least Amalie will remember her wedding.' Liane was wearing a silk scarf, and this she tied over her head. Madeleine used a handkerchief, placing the square on her crown.

The two sisters took their places. Joanna stood beside James. Incongruously, he thought, she was wearing a dress and court shoes, and a broad-brimmed hat. 'Will you beat them?' she whispered.

'Do you care?'

'Temper, temper.'

'I was merely under the impression that the Americans want no part of this. Nor do the Swedes.'

'Some of them,' she remarked, and fell silent as the service began.

The service, as promised, was brief; James got the impression that Father Jerome was as anxious to be attending to other duties as anyone. Then Henri said goodbye to his bride, his parents, and his in-laws. Amalie was again weeping. 'You'd think they'd give them an hour together,' Joanna said. 'I mean, is the marriage legal until it's been consummated?'

'I'm sure this one will stick.' James left her side and sought Pierre. 'Where is your regiment?'

'At Conde on the border. Or it was yesterday. Our orders were to move into Belgium the moment the Germans crossed the frontier.'

'Conde isn't all that far from Lille.'

Pierre shrugged. 'Fifty kilometres, maybe.'

'Will you go through Paris?'

'By train, you mean? The war could be over before we get to the border. The trains are going to be absolutely clogged.'

'My own thought. So how *do* we get there?'

Pierre looked at Liane, who had joined them. 'I am going to drive them,' she said. 'You can come as well, if you like.'

James gazed at her in consternation. 'You are going to drive up to the front line?'

'Who is going to stop me? And it isn't the front line. Our people are moving forward to meet the enemy. Where do you want to go?'

'Well, Lille. That is where our HQ is.' Or was, he thought. Like the French, the BEF was under orders to move into Belgium the moment that little country was invaded.

'Lille is fine. We leave in five minutes.' She squeezed his arm. 'I am so glad you're coming with us,' she whispered.

There was so much to be thought about, and no time to think about anything. James ran upstairs, collected his bag, and ran down again, encountering Madeleine at the foot. 'You are leaving now?'

'I am going with Pierre and Henri. Liane is giving us a lift.' He didn't specify to where.

'Well . . .' She embraced him. 'Come back to me when you have won.'

He kissed her to save replying, and hurried down the hall to where Barbara de Gruchy was saying her goodbyes. 'I am so sorry,' he said.

'There is nothing to be sorry for, Captain Barron. You are going to beat the enemy. That is a great and glorious thing. Give Amalie a kiss.'

Amalie had stopped crying, although there were tear stains on her cheeks. She put her arms round him and held him close. 'Kill them, kill them, kill them,' she whispered.

He kissed her forehead, nodded to Antoine, and went down

the outside steps. There were cars everywhere, shunting back and forth, but the one at the foot of the steps was, predictably, a Rolls Royce, into which various footmen were loading a case of champagne and an enormous hamper from which emanated the most delicious smells. 'The wedding breakfast,' Joanna explained. 'Aren't we the lucky ones.'

James looked past her to watch Aubrey climbing into the back of the car. 'Oh, no,' he said. 'And you?'

'I am beginning to think you don't like me,' she remarked. 'Of course we're coming. You don't think we'd miss the start of a war? Besides, there may be something in it I can use.'

Liane arrived, pulling on a pair of driving gloves. 'You're in front with me,' she said. 'You too, Joanna. James in the middle.' She waved at her brother. 'You three can sit in the back.'

There was no time to argue. And besides, although James had no wish to spend a couple of hours rubbing hips with Joanna, he certainly wanted to stay as close to Liane as possible for as long as possible. Albert de Gruchy joined them. 'You have a full tank. That should get you to the border and back. But here is the ration book, just in case. Please drive carefully.'

'Don't I always, Papa?'

'No. And I do not wish any scratches.'

'How about bullet holes?' Joanna asked, and received a glare. 'Sorry. Just a joke.'

'I promise to take good care of it,' Liane said, and kissed him. 'We'll be back tomorrow.' She started the engine, waved out of her window, and drove away. Everyone cheered and clapped. James presumed that Madeleine was there, but he didn't see her.

'Did you say tomorrow?' Aubrey asked.

'We'll never get back tonight.'

'But we have no things. No toothbrushes!'

'We'll spend the night at my flat. You'll enjoy it.'

'You don't have a gun,' Joanna exclaimed.

'We don't usually wear them to weddings,' James explained.

'*They* have guns.'

James looked over his shoulder and Pierre winked. 'Who did you want to shoot?'

'Well . . . we could run into a Nazi.'

The roads outside Chartres were reasonably clear, but the traffic was steadily building. 'Are we going through Paris?' Aubrey asked.

'Good God, no,' Liane said. 'If we got into Paris we'd probably never get back out. I'm making for Beauvais.' The traffic continued to increase, until their speed was down to twenty miles an hour, bumper to bumper, with frequent halts. James looked at his watch; it was just coming up to ten. 'We'll make it,' Liane said. 'Will your people wait for you?'

'I doubt it.'

'Where are they going, anyway?' Joanna asked.

James didn't suppose it mattered now. 'Our orders are to advance into Belgium and then wheel to our right and take up a position along the line of the River Dyle.'

'You mean if the Germans don't get there first.'

'They won't. The Belgian army is going to hold the line of the Albert Canal – that's further to the east – until we're in position.'

'Wouldn't it have made more sense,' Aubrey asked, 'to have occupied the line of this river *before* the Germans started something?'

'It would,' Pierre agreed. 'But the Belgians wouldn't let us in until Hitler fired first, just in case that encouraged him *to* fire first.'

'That seems a bit short sighted.'

'They were afraid,' Henri said. 'Everybody is afraid.'

'Is that the right mood in which to fight a war?'

'Now we have to stop being afraid,' Pierre said. 'Is anybody hungry?'

'Yes,' everyone said at the same time; no one had had the opportunity to eat any breakfast. The hamper was opened, and two of the bottles of champagne; there were even glasses.

'Some way to go to war,' Aubrey commented.

*   *   *

As noon approached, with everyone sated, the car grew silent. Liane, who had had only a single glass to go with her chicken leg, drove with relentless concentration, revealing a side to her character James had not suspected . . . but which made her still more attractive.

He was having difficulty staying awake himself, and every time he nodded off his head drooped towards Joanna's shoulder. She was also half-asleep, her skirt disconcertingly pulled up above her knees; her hat had come off, and as the windows were open for coolness, her yellow hair kept drifting across his face. He sat up. 'What happens after you drop us?'

'I will go back to Chartres. Via Paris.'

'With Joanna and Aubrey?'

'Of course.'

'Will you be all right?'

'I am always all right.'

'I shall dream of you.'

She glanced at him. 'There are some cards in my purse in my handbag with my Paris address. Look me up when next you are in town.'

'You will let me open your handbag?'

'It's the only way to get inside.'

He opened the bag, found the red leather purse, with the name Liane de Gruchy in gold, took one of the cards. 'Won't you be going down to Paulliac with your family?'

'I prefer Paris. Shit!' The civilian traffic had largely ceased as they drove north, but now they saw in front of them a military convoy, a good twenty trucks, proceeding very slowly and occupying the entire road. Liane drove up to the back of the last truck, both car and driver arousing considerable interest amongst the *poilus*. She put her head out of the window and shouted, 'Will you let us through?'

'We are going to fight the war,' someone replied. 'You should not be here.'

'You're an officer,' Aubrey pointed out. 'Why don't you order them to get over?'

'I am not *their* officer,' Pierre said. 'They would ignore me. Our best bet would be to go round them. Down there.' He pointed at a lane leading away from the highway.

'It is too narrow,' Liane objected. 'It will scratch the car.'

'Fuck that. We also have a war to fight.'

'You will have to explain it to Papa.' She swung the car off the road and a moment later they were driving between high banks from which vegetation drooped, as she had feared, constantly scraping along the sides of the big car.

Joanna had woken up. 'You reckon this is a one-way street?' she asked. 'Holy shit! What's that noise?'

'Aircraft,' Pierre said. James squinted through the windshield.

'Are they ours?' Henri asked.

'No.'

'Oh, my God!' Joanna muttered.

'They're not interested in us,' James assured her. 'But those poor buggers . . .'

They were now nearly a mile distant from the column, although from time to time they saw the trucks where the hedges thinned; the highway was raised above the surrounding countryside. Now they watched the Stukas peeling off to go plunging down, and saw the plumes of earth and flame rising to meet them. 'Those guys don't stand a chance,' Aubrey said. 'Don't you guys have any planes?' Nobody answered him.

The sense of adventure disappeared with the Stukas' attack. They drove through the lanes for about an hour, and then reached a village where there was a crossroads and a main highway. People came out of their houses to shout at them. 'We'll get some directions,' Liane decided and braked.

'We have directions. Lille!' James pointed at the signpost.

'Hallelujah!' She waved at the villagers and gunned the

37

engine. But within half an hour they were again in heavy military traffic, although this was British.

A redcap on a motorcycle pulled up beside them. 'You can't go up there, miss. That's a restricted area.' Then he looked further into the car. 'With respect, sir.'

'This young lady is trying to get me to HQ,' James told him. 'I'm on the staff.'

'You'll never make it in this wagon. Tell you what, sir. Jump on behind me and I'll run you up. It's only another twenty-odd miles.'

'You must go,' Liane said. 'I'll see you in Paris.' She kissed him, long and deep, which left him embarrassed.

'Have a good war,' Joanna suggested, and got out to make room for him.

'Thank you. Thank you all.' James saluted, and the redcap stopped the traffic to allow Liane to make a five-point turn.

'Friend of the lady, are you, sir?' he inquired as the Rolls disappeared.

'Yes.'

'Some car. Some brass, I'd say.'

'And you'd probably be right. Shall we get on?' He wondered if he'd ever discover why she had been expelled from finishing school. With Joanna.

'You and him got something going?' Joanna asked.

'We could,' Liane said.

'Bit young for you, isn't he?' Pierre asked.

'Why don't you mind your own business?'

'I thought he was Madeleine's guest,' Henri commented.

'The same goes for you,' Liane told him.

'Sounds like you *do* have something on,' Joanna muttered. 'You slept with him?'

'Could be.'

'You'll have to tell me about it.'

Liane concentrated on the road, which was no less encumbered going the other way, although they made better time. She didn't want to discuss James, not even with her oldest and most intimate friend. Because she was ashamed of what she had done? She had never been ashamed of having sex before. But those had always been people in her own social circle, artists and poets and would-be novelists who thronged the Left Bank cafés, and to whom sex was as casual as ordering a fresh cup of coffee. With her wealth and her beauty she had always dominated every gathering; with her intelligence she had always known that none of those people were her friends, merely hangers-on intent on cadging whatever they could from either her purse or her body. So what the hell, she had always thought. It beats masturbation.

But she had never indulged herself under any of her parents' roofs before. Apart from not wishing to upset them, it had simply not been feasible. To have seduced one of Pierre's friends would have created an impossible situation even had she been able to find any pleasure in it, and Mama had apparently accepted that her eldest daughter had no interest in marriage and had ceased seeking eligible men to entertain. And she seldom saw Joanna more than once a year nowadays. But last night she had allowed herself to become over-excited at the idea of the wedding. Little Amalie, the complete virgin, who so looked up to her big sister. Neither Amalie nor Mama and Papa had the slightest idea of the life she lived. Heaven forbid! Madeleine did, but Madeleine had never betrayed her. And now she had betrayed Madeleine!

Did Madeleine really have designs on a man so much her social inferior? She realized she actually did not know enough about her sister. They saw very little of each other. Madeleine liked life in the country; she found it unutterably boring. But did Madeleine also like to dominate men? That was *her* principal pleasure in life. And James Barron had been the perfect target. He was so innocent, had been so completely out of his depth, at once eager and uncertain. And yet . . . Her instincts told her that there had been something else, hidden in that so pedantically bred exterior, some coil of steel kept carefully under control. She wondered if she would ever see him again. Or even hear of him.

*   *   *

It was three o'clock before they made contact with the French forces, and Pierre and Henri were able to secure official transport to take them up to their regiment, several miles away.

The officers they met were in a state of high excitement. 'They are saying that the Belgian army is in full retreat, that Eben-Emael has fallen.'

'That is not possible,' Pierre declared.

'What is Eben-Emael?' Joanna asked.

'It is the strongest fortress in Belgium. It is impregnable. If it has fallen on the first day . . .'

'I suggest you go and get it back.' Liane kissed him and then Henri.

'Will you be all right?'

'We shall be back in Paris tonight, Chartres tomorrow.'

'Well, tell Amalie that I love her.'

'I will do that.' She turned the car.

'Do you think it is as serious as that man said?' Aubrey asked.

'There are always people who panic. What the shit . . .'

They had returned to the highway to see a solid mass of people on the road. They had earlier encountered several heavily laden cars and trucks heading south, but this was like an entire nation on the move. There were cars with mattresses strapped to their roofs, laden carts – some drawn by mules, others being pushed by hand – people walking, people riding bicycles, even one or two in wheelchairs, some driving cows or horses, others dragging wailing children beside them, barking dogs . . .

'Where are you going?' Liane asked one man.

'To the south. It will be safe in the south.'

'But *why* are you going?'

'It is the Boche. They will be here tomorrow.'

'That is not possible. The whole French army is between you and them.' The man pushed his bicycle away.

'How do we get through this lot?' Aubrey asked.

'We don't,' his sister told him.

'We have to find another way. Back to the lanes,' Liane decided. She reversed and turned down the first available opening into another maze of tiny, uneven tracks. There were people on these as well, but few vehicles, and most were willing to get out of the way of Liane's blaring horn.

The sun was now over their right shoulders as it sank towards the west. 'We're going east,' Joanna realized aloud.

'So?'

'Paris is south, isn't it?'

'Paris is south-east. We'll turn off as soon as we find a clear road. Listen, Aubrey, open a bottle of champagne. I need a drink. We all need a drink.'

'It's not going to be cold,' Aubrey warned, wrestling with the cork.

'It's liquid, and it's alcohol.'

Joanna was studying her map. 'According to this, we must be just about past Maubeuge. If you're not careful we'll be in Belgium.'

'I don't think anyone is going to worry about that today.'

'Yes, but isn't that where the Germans are?'

Liane glanced at her, as if realizing for the first time how close the fighting might be.

'Thunder,' Aubrey said. 'That's all we need, a rainstorm.'

'Those are guns, stupid,' Joanna snapped.

'Shit!' Liane muttered, and then shouted, 'A road!'

They emerged at a crossroads, and found themselves looking at a regiment of *poilus*, tramping by. An officer came up to them. 'Mademoiselles? What are you doing here?'

'Trying to get away from here.'

'We want to get to Paris,' Joanna said.

'That is a good idea. I will clear a space for you to cross the road, then drive south. There is a highway only a few kilometres away.'

'You are very sweet,' Liane said. 'Will the highway be crowded?'

'I am afraid so, mademoiselle. We have told the people

it is best to remain, but they will go. Too many of them remember 1914. But you must stay with them. Two so handsome women . . . It is best to have company, eh?' He regarded Aubrey for a moment, but clearly saw no reason to alter his advice. 'Good fortune.'

The march was stopped, and the Rolls crossed the road. The *poilus* cheered. 'What did he say?' Aubrey asked.

'He said we won't do better than following the mob,' Liane said.

'For how long? You looked at your gasoline gauge recently? You're under half.'

'It'll get us to Paris, if we don't find a service station first.'

As the captain had suggested, in half an hour they came to another crossroads, at a village, and encountered another moving wall of humanity; the people in the village had caught the contagion and were also packing up. 'It's going to be a long way back to Paris,' Liane remarked.

'Will we make it tonight?'

'I shouldn't think so. It's going to be dark in a couple of hours, and finding our way through this mob in the middle of the night without hitting somebody will be next to impossible. Open another bottle, Aubrey. Now is no time to be sober.'

Gently she eased the car into the stream, to the accompaniment of much comment and some abuse. 'Are you scared?' Joanna asked.

'Should I be?'

'Well, these people. They're hostile.'

'They are poor; I am obviously rich. They'll get used to us.'

They accepted glasses of champagne from Aubrey. 'I only came to be with you,' Joanna said. 'I never really knew Amalie. Are we . . . well . . . going to get together?'

'I don't think this is the time.' Liane jerked her head at the back seat.

'He has to grow up some time.'

Liane shot her a glance. 'He doesn't . . . . ?'

'For Christ's sake, of course not. We only see each other a couple of times a year as a rule. Whenever I'm home he's at college. This is a one-off.'

'I wish you two would stop whispering,' Aubrey said. 'There's some guy trying to attract our attention.'

Liane realized there was someone knocking on her window; when they had joined the throng they had rolled up the glass. Now she rolled the glass down a couple of inches. 'Can I help you?'

'You have a big car.'

'That's true.'

'It is empty.'

Liane considered him; they were only moving at walking pace anyway. He was poorly dressed and hadn't shaved for a day or two. 'There isn't room for everyone.'

'My wife is pregnant. And she is very tired.'

Liane looked at Joanna. 'Okay by me,' Joanna said.

'Make room, Aubrey.' Liane braked. The door was opened, and the woman – who was certainly pregnant – and her husband got in, bringing with them a strong scent of unwashed humanity. But then, Liane thought, they were pretty unwashed themselves.

'You are very kind,' the woman said.

'Have a glass of champagne?' Aubrey invited.

There was more banging on the window. 'There is room for more,' someone shouted.

'Fuck off,' their new passenger suggested.

'I reckon we've got ourselves some protection,' Joanna said.

Progress remained impossibly slow, and by eight o'clock it was growing dark. Many people were by then so exhausted they simply lay down on the road; others sought the fields to either side. 'I'm pretty tired myself,' Liane said. 'All right if we stop for the night, monsieur?'

'I think that is good. You have food, eh?' He was looking at the hamper.

'Yes, we have food. Supper, Aubrey.'

'I need to go,' Joanna said. 'How do we go?'

'Just open the door. But stay next to the car.'

'But those people . . .'

'They're all too busy doing it themselves to worry about you. Anyway, it'll be dark in half an hour.'

They ate, and then settled down for the night. They were surrounded by stealthy noise, while in the distance they could still hear the rumble of gunfire. But the night itself was quiet; inside the car the main sound was that of their male passenger snoring. Joanna slept with her head on Liane's shoulder. 'This is the weirdest situation I have ever been in,' she whispered.

'I seem to remember you were always looking for new experiences.'

'Not like this. What's going to happen, Liane?'

'Tomorrow we'll get to Paris.'

'I meant, the whole thing. Your guys don't seem to be doing very well.'

'Our guys haven't started to do anything yet. They'll get going tomorrow.' Now that she had stopped driving, her arms felt as if they were about to fall off. For all *her* many and varied experiences she had never slept sitting up in a car, even a well-upholstered Rolls Royce. But she did so now, heavily, to be awakened by someone shouting. Several people, she realized, opening her eyes and then using her hand to wipe the condensation from her window before rolling it down in consternation. Several black men were running down the road, waving their arms and shouting. They wore uniform, but it was not one Liane had ever seen before: a khaki tunic and short pants; then bare knees before leggings and boots. None of them carried rifles, although bayonet scabbards hung on their hips. '*Sauve qui peut!*' they shrieked. '*Sauve qui peut!*'

A gigantic rustle spread through the refugee column as people woke up to the cries of disaster. 'Hey!' Liane shouted. 'You! Why are you running? What has happened?'

'The Boche! They are over the river! The tanks! They

44

are coming! *Sauve qui peut!*' The soldier resumed running.

'What did he say?' Aubrey asked. 'Something about a river?'

'It must be the Meuse,' the man said.

'That can't be possible,' Liane objected. 'If they are across the Meuse already, then . . .'

'We have lost the battle, mademoiselle. France is lost.'

'Rubbish!'

'Then why are those men running away?'

'Because they are cowards. They should be rounded up and shot.' She started the engine. The entire column was moving, more quickly than on the previous evening, but most people were soon exhausted again and progress slowed as the sun rose out of a cloudless sky.

'It's going to be a great day,' Aubrey commented.

'You reckon that firing is closer?' Joanna asked.

'It's certainly louder,' Liane agreed.

'What happens if they catch us up?'

'What happens if the sky falls? Why can't these goddamned people get a move on.'

'They've caught us up,' Aubrey said, looking over his shoulder through the rear window. Others had seen the approaching squadron of planes, and a great wail was rising.

'Are they ours?' Liane asked, trying to avoid hitting people who had suddenly stopped to peer skywards.

'No.'

'Stukas!' said their passenger.

'I don't think so,' Joanna said. 'They look more like fighters. Shit! They're coming in.' The wail grew louder and people started to leave the road, throwing themselves down the parapets to either side.

'Out!' Liane shouted. 'Take cover.' She opened her door and half fell out of the car. Someone tripped over her and she found herself on her face. Now she could hear both the roar of the engines as a Messerschmitt passed immediately over her head and the chatter of machine-gun fire. She gained her feet, cast a hasty glance behind her, where there were already several bodies lying on the road, watched the surface breaking up as if cut by a jagged knife coming straight at her, looked up at the plane, then hurled herself to one side, right across the road, to go tumbling down the parapet. She came to rest in the midst of several people, men, women and children, pressing their faces into the earth and screaming. She hid her own face.

But the sound was already dying. Those sounds. She was surrounded by shouts and shrieks, groans and moans. It didn't make sense. No one could possibly have mistaken them for a retreating army. She got to her feet and had her ankle grabbed by the man next to her. She kicked at him, and he tugged harder. 'They're coming back.'

She realized he was right; the roar was growing again. She fell back to her stomach, pressed her cheek into the earth, still damp from the overnight dew, and heard a deep boom from immediately above her head. Shit, she thought. Papa will be *furious*. The aircraft were gone again; the sounds of distress were back.

Liane climbed up the parapet and fell over a dead body – her passenger, cut to ribbons by bullets. Her stomach rolled and she looked past him at what was left of the car. Bullets must have hit the petrol tank: the entire back of the Rolls had disintegrated; the front blazed.

She staggered forward. Someone attempted to grab her arm, and she threw him away with a sweep. But she could go no closer because of the heat. The pregnant woman! But she was not to be seen. Had she managed to get out? But then, Joanna! Her heart leapt when she heard a scream. 'Liane!!!'

She ran behind the car, looked down the other parapet. Joanna knelt at the foot, Aubrey in her arms. Liane slid down the slope, landed beside her. 'Is he bad?' There was blood everywhere.

'He's dead!' Joanna cried. 'Dead! My brother is dead!'

Liane crawled to her, and gulped; Aubrey's back seemed to have been opened in the same way as the road – she could see

his shattered spine. She sat down. For just about the first time
that she could remember in her entire life, she simply had no
idea what to do. For the dead or the living. Joanna continued
to kneel, rocking slightly, Aubrey's head hugged into her
breast, moaning. Liane had never known her so distressed,
either. She had never supposed that Joanna, always so brash
and boisterous, *could* be so distressed. There was movement
around her. Those people who were unhurt were resuming
their flight. They helped the wounded up, and carried them
where necessary; no one appeared to have any medical
supplies, and shirts and dresses had been ripped to make
rough bandages. They seemed to have accepted that nothing
could be done about the dead, and they were concerned with
saving their own lives. The children were mostly shocked into
silence. 'Jo,' she said. 'Listen. We must get on.'

'A church,' Joanna said. 'We must find a church.'

'I don't think a church will keep the Germans out.'

'We have to bury Aubrey.'

'Jo! That's not possible.'

Joanna looked left and right, at the other dead bodies; dogs
were already nosing about them. 'You want to leave him here?
My brother? To be eaten by dogs?'

'Jo, no matter what we do, he is going to be eaten, by
dogs up here, or worms under the ground.'

'I hate you! You are a filthy beast!'

'I am trying to save our lives,' Liane said patiently. 'You
must be real about this. I am terribly sorry about your brother,
but there is nothing we can do for him now. We have no
means of burying him. And if we don't move, we could be
overtaken by the Germans. That is going to be one whole lot
of shit.'

'I'm not going,' Joanna said. 'I can't leave Aubrey.' Tears
were streaming down her cheeks.

'Well, stay then.' Liane scrambled up the embankment. The
car had just about burned out, and the last of the refugees were
several hundred yards away. She looked back down. 'Joanna!
For God's sake.'

Slowly Joanna laid Aubrey on the ground and stood up. The entire front of her dress was soaked in blood. She climbed the slope to join her friend. 'I need a bath.'

'We both do. Let's go find one.'

'Where?'

'Paris.'

'How far is it?'

'We'll get there by this evening.'

'Like this?'

'I don't think we'll be unique.'

They walked for a while; the rest of the refugees had entirely vanished. 'Where do I join up?' Joanna asked.

'Say again?'

'I wish to join your army when we get to Paris.'

'You can't do that. You're not French.'

'What about the Foreign Legion?'

'They're men. Our whole army is male, apart from a few secretaries.'

'Look, all I want to do is kill Germans. Why should they stop me doing that? Isn't that the whole idea?'

Liane squeezed her hand. 'I know how you feel. Believe me. But killing is men's work. We just have to grin and bear it. Shit! Planes.' She forced Joanna off the road and they lay in the ditch, and waited for the aircraft to fly over. Then they heard the crump of bombs and even at a distance the wails of the victims.

'Why are they doing that?' Joanna asked. 'Killing civilians. Murdering civilians.'

'They're trying to break our morale.'

'Will they?'

'Of course not. We'll beat them.'

'But you won't let me help.'

'I told you, that's men's work.' They regained the road and walked in silence, passing another scene of desolation: dead bodies, human and animal, shattered belongings.

As if the sight reminded her of her own situation, Joanna

said, 'I'm starting to stink. Aubrey's blood! My God, Aubrey's blood. And I'm so thirsty. And hungry.'

She was on the verge of a breakdown. Maybe, Liane thought, she's already having one. And she didn't know what to do. Except . . . 'There's a loaf of bread.'

It had fallen out of the satchel of a man lying beside it, surrounded by a pool of blood. 'You can't be serious,' Joanna said.

'You said you were hungry.'

'I am. But I can wait until we reach Paris.'

'Paris is at least a hundred kilometres away.'

'You said we'd get there tonight.'

'That was if we could raise a lift. Now that doesn't look likely. So it could be a couple of days.'

'Did you say days?'

'Look, we just have to face facts.' Liane knelt beside the man, carefully extracted the satchel from his shoulder, avoiding touching any of the blood.

'Liane de Gruchy,' Joanna commented, 'robbing the dead.'

'Liane de Gruchy, staying alive.' She opened the satchel and found some meat wrapped in paper. 'Eureka!'

'You can't eat that. It'll give you diarrhoea.'

'It's smoked ham. Shit!' The planes were back.

They lay in the ditch while the aircraft droned overhead. They were flying very low, their black crosses clearly visible, but they obviously could see nothing worth attacking on this stretch of road.

'If I had a rifle,' Joanna said. 'I could hit one of those.'

'And five minutes later we'd be dead. Anyway, you don't know how to fire a rifle.'

'I do. I belong to a rifle club back home. I'm one of their best shots.'

'You learn something every day. Let's make a move.'

They walked through an empty afternoon. 'What happens when it gets dark?' Joanna asked.

'We wait until it gets light.'

'You mean, we sleep in the open?'

'It's not raining.'

They actually stopped well before dusk, utterly exhausted. More importantly, they had come to a stream. 'My feet hurt,' Joanna said. 'These shoes weren't intended for long-distance walking.'

'Join the club.'

'Mine are swelling.'

'Ditto. But we can at least bathe them.' She took off her sandals and dangled her feet in the water, then lay on her stomach to drink. And then scoop the water over her head.

'I don't think you should drink that,' Joanna advised.

'You'd rather die of thirst?'

Joanna made a face, but lay beside her to drink. Then Liane divided the last of the bread and ham. 'Are you going to tell anybody about this?' Joanna asked.

'About what?'

'Well . . . robbing that dead man.'

'He didn't mind.'

'How will you put it to the priest next time you confess?'

'So when do you reckon is the next time I'll be able to confess? Or feel like it?'

They slept in each other's arms. Living very separate lives, they had only done that on a couple of occasions since school in Switzerland, but even Liane wanted only comfort this night. 'Did you really fuck that Limey?' Joanna asked.

'He was a treat. Such a gentleman.'

'I thought he was rather a wimp.'

'He didn't go much for you, either. But I got the impression he was tougher than he looked.'

Joanna giggled. 'You mean harder. Say, what day is it?'

Liane considered. 'I think today is Sunday.'

'Holy shit! Won't your folks be worried?'

'My folks will be going mad. What about yours?'

'They don't know yet. I'll have to tell them. About Aubrey.

Oh, my God, Aubrey.' She burst into tears, and Liane held her close.

Next morning they drank some water and then resumed their walk, very slowly and painfully; their feet were now definitely swollen. Now they might have been the only two people left in the world; there were not even any bird calls to be heard. But the day was overlaid by the steady rumble of gunfire from behind them.

'That is definitely coming closer,' Joanna said. 'What are we going to do?'

Liane squinted. 'I see houses.'

'Oh, God! Do you think they'll have a bath?'

It took them half an hour to reach the village. It was difficult to determine whether it had been looted by the refugees or just abandoned in great haste; all the doors were open, some wrenched from their hinges, and various articles were scattered on the street. There were also several bodies lying about, which had been there long enough to be distressing; at least all the dogs had departed. Liane pointed to the two craters and the shattered roofs. 'The bombers were here.'

'There's the *pension*.' Joanna stumbled across the street, and Liane limped behind her. The inn door was open. Inside the chairs and tables were scattered about, but most of the bottles behind the bar seemed to be intact. 'No water!' Joanna exclaimed.

Liane located the pump, and filled two mugs. They drank greedily. 'Do you think there's a tub?' Joanna asked.

'Let's find out.' There was a tub upstairs, and another pump. 'This place is almost civilized,' Liane commented. 'You first.'

'Do you think they'll have any washing powder? I need to wash my dress.'

'That can keep until after I've had mine.' Liane went into a bedroom, sat on the bed, and with some difficulty took off her sandals. Apart from the swelling, her feet were blistered and bleeding in several places; her carefully manicured toenails were a mess. Her stockings were in tatters, so she took off her pants and removed them altogether. There was blood on her blouse as well. She took it off and stretched out on the bed in her cami-knickers. Never had she felt so tired, both physically and mentally.

The mental exhaustion was a combination of real tiredness, from the many hours of concentrated driving and then walking she had put in over the past two days, and shock, less at what had happened to her personally, her brush with death during the air attack, or even the death of Aubrey Brent – she had only met him for the first time three days ago, and she found it difficult actually to relate him to Joanna – or all the other dead bodies she had encountered and those sprawled on the street only a few yards away. It was the unbelievable suggestion that the army might have been defeated, on virtually the first day of battle. It simply could not be true.

She knew better than anyone, because of the life she lived in Paris, that France was by no means the boisterous, happy community it so often appeared to the outside world. In her artistic circle 'patriotism' was a dead word, and she also knew that Papa, and the business, had gone through a difficult time over the past few years, as the Popular Front government had been attempting to socialize the entire country. But whatever the social unrest, the absurd attitudes adopted in the cafés, there had been one rock on which the French state, French society, French confidence in the future, had been securely based: the army. The French army was not only the greatest in the world, it was also the finest. This fact had been drummed into her by her father when she had been a child in the twenties, when, whatever the catastrophic casualties and destruction of the Great War, France had emerged triumphant. It had been confirmed by Pierre and his friends during the last few years. And now . . .

It simply could not be true. Those colonial soldiers had simply deserted. They should be shot. They *would* be shot, when they were caught.

Joanna stood in the doorway, a splendidly naked figure. 'Do you think there'll be anything to eat? I'm starving.'

'We'll find something when I've finished.'

The water was a long way from clean, but she did not feel like emptying the tub and then refilling it. But as it was also distinctly cool she did not feel like hanging about, either. She soaked, soaped, and soaked again, then got out, watched by Joanna from the doorway. 'I've found some washing powder.'

'So let's have a go.' They scrubbed both the dress and Liane's blouse, reducing the bloodstains to several large but indeterminate blotches. 'At least they shouldn't smell so bad,' Liane said.

'Food,' Joanna suggested. They spread the clothes out to dry, went downstairs and found some cheese and stale bread. Liane opened a bottle of wine, and they sat at a table and had their lunch.

'What are we going to do?' Joanna asked.

'We are going to go to Paris.'

'How?'

'Walk.'

'To Paris? I have blisters.'

'Have a look at mine. We'll just have to grit our teeth.'

Joanna considered, and drank some wine. 'And then what?'

'We'll call Mama and tell her we're all right; then I am going to go to bed for a week.'

'But we're not all right,' Joanna said.

'So we have blisters and bruises. We'll recover.'

'Aubrey isn't going to recover.'

What to say? Liane wondered. What *could* she say, save meaningless platitudes. 'Listen, when we get to Paris and tell Papa what happened, he'll send out to find the body. Aubrey will have a proper burial.'

'There won't *be* a body by then. And Mom . . .' Joanna shivered.

'Would you like me to write her?'

'Shit, no. I'll have to tell her. As soon as we get to Paris I'll have to find a ship for the States.'

'Um . . .' Liane wondered how easy, or safe, that was going to be. 'This stuff is quite drinkable. Let's have another bottle.' She got up and checked at the distant sound of engines.

'Not more planes?' Joanna's voice was shrill.

'Those are car engines. Transport!' She looked down at herself, then grabbed a red and white checked tablecloth and wrapped it round herself. Then she went outside to wave her arms, and gulped. 'Tanks! Still, they can give us a ride. Oh, shit!' She squinted, and made out the swastika.

Three

Defeat

'Pack up,' Barrett said. 'We leave in an hour. What we can't take must be destroyed.'

His two junior officers looked at each other and then at him. 'We've only just settled in,' Watson protested.

'Well, now we have to get out of here. It looks like that report you filed on French morale, James, was one hundred per cent accurate. The front has collapsed.'

James looked out of the window of the house they had requisitioned as Intelligence headquarters. Through the trees he could see the waters of the River Dyle, and some of the considerable strength of the BEF consolidating their defensive perimeter. They had arrived here in a rush over the past few days, dismayed to learn that their Belgian allies had abandoned the line of the Albert Canal and were falling back towards them. Some Belgian units had already crossed the Dyle and were being redirected to the defence of Brussels. The Germans had been close behind, and there had been a fierce little battle, in which even the Intelligence unit had played its part. The enemy had then retired, and at the moment, they were not to be seen. It was a delightful spring morning, which, apart from the shell craters and bullet damage, made it difficult to believe there was a war on.

'Our front hasn't collapsed,' Watson objected. 'We've given them one bloody nose. We can give them another. We can certainly hold them.'

'I imagine we could hold them here,' Barrett agreed. 'But not if they're able to get round behind us, and that is what

55

could happen now they've broken through the Ardennes. Don't remind me, Harry. You were right and I was wrong. Now all we can do is get on with the job. And our orders are to pull out, in front of the army. The one thing the brass doesn't want to have happen is for their Intelligence unit to be overrun by the enemy. So let's get on with it.'

He bustled off, and Watson commenced putting papers into a satchel while various sergeants and privates scurried around the office. 'How do you think your friends will handle this? If the Jerries really have broken through, well . . . Chartres is only a few miles south of Paris, isn't it?'

'You don't suppose Gamelin is going to let the Germans take Paris, do you? Anyway, I shouldn't think the de Gruchys will hang about. They'll be off down to Paulliac. Miles away from any fighting.'

'And you never had the opportunity to get to grips with the fair Madeleine.'

'No,' James said thoughtfully. But Liane . . . Of course she would be back in Paris by now. But despite what he had just claimed, would even Paris be safe? And there was nothing he could do about it.

'There must be some way of getting news,' Albert de Gruchy said, twisting his hands together.

Jean Moulin had never seen his friend so agitated; he had always considered the wine grower the calmest of men. 'It was an incredulously dangerous thing to do,' he pointed out.

'Of course. But you know Liane . . . She wanted to be involved.'

Moulin scratched his ear. 'And you are sure she is not in Paris?'

'I have telephoned. It is difficult to get a line. But I have got her number three times, and there is no reply.'

'She could have been out each time.'

'If she was there, she would have called us, to let us know she was all right. She had that American woman and her brother with her. They would have wanted to be in touch with their parents. Anyway, I got through to the office, and they sent someone round. They reported back that the flat is locked and the concierge told them there is no one there. If she was somehow stranded in the north . . .'

Moulin nodded. 'I will see what I can do. But I cannot promise anything.'

'Surely there will be casualty lists? Just to know she is not on them would be a relief.'

'I do not think there will be any casualty lists of civilians overrun by the enemy. But I will do what I can. Now you must get out of here while *you* can. How long will it take you to reach Paulliac?'

'Depending on the roads . . . We will have to use two cars. Liana took the Rolls. God knows what has happened to that.'

'Then use two cars. Here is an extra ration book. But get down to Bordeaux as quickly as you can. I will telephone you there. Good fortune.'

'Well?' Barbara asked.

Albert sat down, looked around the anxious faces. 'Jean will do what he can. But it is all very confused. He says we must go down to Paulliac right away.'

'Why? We must stay here until Liane gets home.'

'My darling, our armies are defeated. The Germans are advancing very fast. Paris could well fall. They could be here in a week.'

'I cannot believe that,' Barbara snapped.

'What is the news of the BEF?' Madeleine asked.

'They are fleeing through Belgium.'

'Fleeing?'

'Retreating as fast as they can.' Albert looked at the Bursteins. 'My friends . . .'

'You must go,' David Burstein said. 'So must we.'

'Where will you go?' Barbara asked.

'Well, back to Dieppe. That is where the business is. And that is where the army will send news of Henri.' He looked at his daughter-in-law.

57

'I will come with you,' Amalie said.

'But . . .' Barbara bit her lip.

'That is Henri's home, Mama. Therefore it is my home too.'

Barbara looked at her husband, but Albert knew he could not interfere.

'We will take good care of her,' Rosa Burstein promised. 'Now we must pack.'

Albert stood up. 'So must we. Come along now.'

'I will stay here,' Madeleine said.

'Don't be absurd,' her mother told her. 'How can you stay here by yourself?'

'I will not be by myself. The house is full of servants. And here is where Liane will come, as soon as she can.'

Barbara looked at her husband. Albert shrugged. The continuing news of catastrophe seemed to have robbed him of the powers of decision. 'Well,' Barbara said, 'we will leave you the little sports car. Promise that if the war moves south of Paris you will leave immediately, and that you will do nothing stupid like trying to find Liane. She must come to you. You must stay in the house.'

'I will stay here, Mama. As long as it is safe to do so.'

What am I doing? she wondered as she stood on the steps to wave the two families off. Obeying her instincts. Chartres was where the family had exploded, and Chartres was where it would come back together, she was certain. Certainly her sisters. Dieppe was only a day's drive away, Paris a morning. Paulliac was too distant. And the men? She did not suppose there was much chance of hearing from Pierre for a while, but again her instincts told her that if he could get in touch, it would be to Chartres he would send, certainly in the first instance. Henri would no doubt do the same, and she would be able to tell him where Amalie was. By then Liane would be with her, and they could go down to Paulliac together. Oh, pray to God that Liane would be with her.

James? But James was surely already history, fleeing with

his army for the safety of the Channel coast and an evacuation to England. That was not his fault; it was a decision of his commanding officers. But that did not affect the reality that he was being swept by the tide of war outside of her orbit – after the briefest of acquaintances, which had promised so much.

General Erwin Rommel sat at the field table outside his tent and watched his batman pouring wine. French wine! It wasn't Gruchy Grand Cru, but it was very drinkable. The general was at once pleased and frustrated. If he had spent the past few years training and learning and becoming daily more excited about the possibilities of armoured warfare, and daily more confident of success when given the opportunity, he had never dared expect anything like this.

The orders given him by his superior, General Guderian, had been simple in the extreme. 'You will attack the enemy, you will force the crossing of the Meuse, and you will continue to attack and harass the enemy until further orders. Do not concern yourself with support or logistics. We will take care of that. Your only concern is the defeat of the enemy.'

Rommel had assumed that he was being launched into a vast battle which would be extremely costly, and had braced himself for an experience which would either make or break not only his division but his reputation. But the enemy, after a few abortive attempts to hold the line of the river, had simply melted away. He had expected a violent counter-attack from the French armour, which he knew, both in numbers and tank for tank, was more powerful than the Wehrmacht's panzers, but there had been none. His only problem was the one thing he had been told not to worry about: logistics. He had advanced so far and so fast he had been forced to halt his troops to await the petrol tankers. There was even a suggestion that the army commander, General von Kleist, had ordered Guderian to stop his panzers because they were advancing too fast! But he had been assured the fuel would be here in a couple of hours. Meanwhile . . . He frowned when he saw one of his aides-de-camp hurrying towards him, looking extremely anxious. 'You should try smiling, Willy. Join me.'

'Herr General . . .' Captain Eisner continued to look anxious. 'These women . . .'

Rommel put down his glass. 'What women?'

'A Mademoiselle de Gruchy.'

Rommel's frown returned. 'I know that name. The wine people.'

'Her father is one of the biggest wine growers in France.'

'Then what is she doing here? She's not hurt, I hope?'

'Ah . . .' Eisner preferred not to answer that. 'There is a woman with her. An American.'

'An American? Where?'

'They were taken in the village of Auchamps.'

'We passed Auchamps three days ago.'

'Yes, Herr General.'

'Eisner, you either have a great deal more to say or you have said a great deal too much. Two women, one a French aristocrat and the other a neutral, were in the village of Auchamps when it was taken by our people. Is that what you are telling me?'

'Yes, Herr General.'

'Three days ago. Why are you reporting it to me now?'

'I only discovered it this morning. The men holding them were only arrested this morning.'

Rommel gave him a severe look. 'I hope you did not state that correctly.'

'Sadly, Herr General . . .'

'You are saying that these women were held by our troops?'

'Half a dozen bad eggs, sir. From an infantry unit. They deserted as we advanced, entered the village, and, well . . . the women were apparently in bed. Naked.'

'My God!'

'They had been with a group of refugees. But they had been left behind after an air attack and had sought shelter in this village.'

Rommel's hand closed on his wine glass with such force that it snapped; his batman hurried forward with a napkin and a fresh glass, poured some more wine. 'You say these men have been arrested? Have a court martial convened immediately. Now, these women, where are they?'

'They are in hospital, sir.'

'You said they were not hurt.'

'They are not hurt in the sense of broken bones or open wounds, but their feet are in a bad state. I do not think they were accustomed to walking any distance, and, well . . . I don't think either of them had ever been raped before,' he added ingenuously.

Rommel stared at him. 'So what is their condition?'

'Fräulein de Gruchy seems fairly calm, although she is undoubtedly very angry. Fräulein Jonsson is hysterical. She is under sedation. Apart from what happened to her, her brother was apparently killed when the refugee column they were with was strafed by our planes.' Rommel sighed. 'She is also making all kinds of threats,' Eisner went on. 'It seems that her mother is friends with some big people in Washington, and her father is an official in the Swedish government.'

'What a shitting mess,' Rommel commented. 'Men under my command . . . Can these women be persuaded to keep quiet about what happened? If they are assured that their rapists are going to be court-martialled?'

'I think it is doubtful, sir. Perhaps, if you were to see them . . .'

'I will be resuming the advance the moment our fuel supplies catch up with us, which I expect to happen in the next hour. We have a war to win, Eisner. This could well become a political matter. Inform Colonel Kluck.'

'But sir . . .'

'I know. But the Gestapo have the time. I do not. Tell Kluck to interview the women, get their version of what happened, and then have them returned behind the enemy lines.' He pointed. 'There is to be no funny business and no threats, but if he can persuade them not to pursue the matter I will commend him.'

'Yes, Herr General. About the court martial . . .'

'We will deal with that ourselves, and now. I wish those men hanged. But the charges will be desertion in the face of the enemy, not rape. We do not want the sort of puerile propaganda used against us in 1914 to be raked up again.'

Eisner saluted.

'You understand, mademoiselle,' Hans Kluck said, 'that this could be a very serious business.' He was a tall, thin man, with aquiline features, and projected quite a formidable personality. But today he was nervous, not only because of the situation, but because he recognized that he was confronted by a personality as strong as his own, who, even if she did not know it, was in the stronger position because of her own background and thus the general's orders. He felt even more nervous at being virtually alone with her in the office provided by the doctor in charge of the field hospital, who he knew was right next door and would be able to respond to any untoward noise – he was not even sure that the fellow was a Nazi. To top it all, he was aware that his French, if fluent, was short on grammar, while her flawless delivery merely complemented her remarkable beauty.

His assistant, Werner Biedermann, who wore the black uniform of the SS, while less sensitive to either his surroundings or the reason for their visit, was clearly equally stupefied by the looks of the woman in front of them. He was a heavy-set, earthy young man, who, although by no means handsome, fancied himself as a ladies' man.

'Could be?' Liane asked. She wore a hospital gown, had been bathed – several times – and medicated where necessary: her feet were still bandaged and swollen. Both she and Joanna had been treated with the utmost care, segregated from the male patients in a separate room – it could hardly be described as a ward – and attended by solicitous nurses in huge starched white hats. As if by smothering them with kindness they could be made Nazi-friendly! In fact, her various aches and pains, if tangible evidence of her ordeal, she knew were transient, and would even be forgotten in time. The great emptiness in her mind might be there for ever. What had happened was outside both her experience and her comprehension. It was not so much the physical aspects: she had had sex with more than one man in her life that she had regretted long before he had even entered her. But those mistakes had been hers; even if she might have been unable to correct them on the instant, they had always been adjustable later, the cold look or word, the complete brush-off, the threat of the wealth and power of her family were the man to make himself a nuisance. And for those reasons she had never before experienced any physical violence.

In Auchamps the physical violence had been overwhelming, and there had been no end in sight. She remembered the panzers rolling by, their crews crowding the cupolas to wave and cheer at the two scantily clad women. She and Joanna had returned inside the bar, half relieved that the Germans had been too busy to stop, half disappointed that there was going to be no ride closer to their own people. But as there was no transport, and the countryside seemed to be full of Germans, they had decided to spend the night, where there was at least food and water and shelter, give their feet a chance to recover, and move on the next day. She had been quite confident that as she was Liane de Gruchy, and Joanna was a neutral whose mother played bridge with Mrs Henry Stimson, any German officer they encountered would be happy to give them a safe conduct through the lines.

They had not reckoned on deserters.

The soldiers had been a happy lot. Presumably like all of their comrades they were in a state of euphoria at the ease and completeness of their victory. But the euphoria had been mixed with bitterness and bloodlust; their unit had apparently been unlucky enough to encounter a French post prepared to resist them, and had suffered heavy casualties, including their officers and NCOs. No doubt after a few hours they would have rejoined the army and been restored to discipline. But in those few hours they had stumbled on Auchamps. By the time they had climbed the stairs they were already drunk, and when they had opened the bedroom door they clearly supposed they had stumbled into heaven.

Both Liane and Joanna had scrambled out of bed, reaching for their clothes, and had been seized and thrown on to the mattress, to lie shoulder to shoulder, on their backs and then on their stomachs. They had been dragged downstairs to amuse their captors while they ate and drank some more, and then dragged back upstairs again.

Joanna, being Joanna, had attempted to resist, and had been beaten. Liane, whatever her instincts, had had more sense. She knew that women only ever overcame men by the use of their brains, their charm and beauty, and their sexuality. Their mystery. There had been no opportunity to use her brains in Auchamps; because there had been six men and one was always awake, watching them. While their captors, if delighted with their beauty and their sexuality, had had no interest in their charm or their mystery. That had left only vengeance available to her. And that had demanded patience.

'It would be best for all if this matter could be, shall I say, brushed under the carpet,' Kluck suggested. Liane looked at him.

'The culprits are to be court-martialled,' he explained.

'And convicted?'

'Of desertion, certainly.'

'But not of rape.'

'Well, you see, Fräulein, they can only be convicted of rape if you testify against them in court, and frankly, my superiors do not feel this would be productive. The end result will be the same,' Kluck hurried on. 'They will be executed. Desertion in the middle of a battle is a capital crime.'

'And the world will never know that the mighty Wehrmacht is composed of men who rape defenceless women.'

'What happened to you was an isolated incident. No other case of rape has been reported. And I may say, Fräulein, that every army in the world, or ever known to history, has contained certain, shall I say, animal elements. It is the nature of the beast. When these elements are discovered, they are eradicated. This is what we are doing now.' He paused, hopefully. 'What is it you want, Fräulein? What will satisfy you?'

'I wish my friend and I to be returned to Paris.'

'We can arrange that. If—'

'No ifs, Colonel.'

Kluck regarded her for some moments, while Biedermann stood up and slowly walked round her chair. Kluck had no doubt they were sharing the same thought, that what a pleasure it would be to have this woman in one of his cells, beating the screams out of her naked body. But he also knew that when General Rommel gave an order it had to be obeyed. All he could do was try to keep the situation under control while reporting to his superiors and letting them decide what to do. 'I have said that you will be returned to Paris as soon as you are fit to travel.'

'We are fit to travel now.' She was carefully ignoring the presence of Biedermann, who was now standing behind her.

'Your feet are badly bruised and swollen.' Kluck allowed himself a smile. 'I assume you are not going to blame that also on the Wehrmacht?'

'It was the Luftwaffe that blew up my car and forced me to walk for two days. What you are saying is that you intend to keep us prisoners until every last physical evidence of what has happened to us is gone. And hopefully that our memories will also become distorted. Am I correct?'

Kluck stood up. 'We are doing everything we can for you, Fräulein. If you are sensible, you will bear that in mind. Good day to you.'

'I am sure we will meet again, mademoiselle,' Biedermann said.

'Perhaps you will hold your breath until that happens,' Liane suggested.

'Commanders assemble,' the radio said. 'On the double.'

Pierre de Gruchy climbed out of his tank and dropped to the ground. He had not shaved in a week or changed his clothing.

Henri Burstein was no different as he joined him. But at least they were still alive, which could not be said for a great number of their comrades. 'What happens now?'

There were only six tanks left out of the regiment. At least to be seen. 'It looks like we lose the war,' Pierre said.

They walked to the command tank. 'Well, gentlemen . . .' Major L'Orly's face was as stiff as ever, little moustache neatly combed, looking around the other five faces. 'The division has been destroyed. The enemy is now to the south as well as the east of us, and I have to tell you that this morning the Belgian army has surrendered.' He held up his finger. 'Now is not the time for questions or recriminations. Only for decisions. I have been informed that the British Expeditionary Force is withdrawing to the coast, where it is hoped that some of them may be evacuated. Again, it is not our place to comment or criticize. Their position, with the Belgian army no longer holding their left flank, is untenable.'

'And our position, Major?' someone asked.

L'Orly gave a brief smile. 'We still have an army in being, south of the German thrust. We still have all of France to fight for, and to fight with.'

'But we cannot get there.'

'Unfortunately, no. But we are still French soldiers, who will obey orders and do our duty. I have been ordered to assist the British retreat, acting as a rearguard where necessary. So, the first thing we shall do is make contact with the British and discover what their dispositions are.'

'Will they be able to provide us with gasoline?' Henri asked. 'I have only an hour left.'

'I also,' said another officer.

'We must hope so,' L'Orly said. 'Single file.'

The tanks moved off, clattering along a country lane well shaded by trees. But after half an hour they came to a canal. There was a bridge, but this was surrounded by sappers and was clearly about to be blown. 'Stop,' L'Orly shouted, standing in his cupola. 'Let us across.'

At the sight of the tanks the engineers had grabbed their rifles and gone to ground. Now their sergeant stood up. '*Parlez-vous Anglais, monsewer?*'

L'Orly turned round. 'Anyone speak English?'

Pierre was also in his cupola. 'I do.'

'Thank God for that, sir,' the sergeant said. 'Gave me a right start, you did. Thought you was Jerries. Then I thought, the Jerries can't be behind us yet.'

'We need to cross that bridge,' Pierre said.

'Right you are, sir. But make it quick.'

'And then we would like directions to your commanding officer.'

'Well, sir, I don't rightly know where he is. He told us to blow this bridge and then march west. Then he went off.'

'Then will you direct us to your nearest fuel dump?'

'There's a problem, sir. They're all being blown.' He gestured to the north. The Frenchmen had seen the clouds of heavy black smoke earlier, without taking in what they had to be.

'But your own tanks must have a supply,' Pierre said.

'Well, sir, they ain't going anywhere, you see. They can't be taken off. So, they're being blown too.'

Pierre took off his beret to scratch his head.

'What does he say?' L'Orly asked. Pierre translated. 'Shit,' the major remarked. 'Shit, shit, shit.'

The sergeant might not speak French, but he got the message. 'Tell you what, sir. I have some dynamite to spare. I can give you six sticks, one for each tank.'

'And what do we do then? We came to fight the enemy. We cannot do that without our tanks.'

'Well, sir. I'd say your best bet is to come along with us and make for the port. Dunkirk they call it. It's only about twenty miles away. That's where they're evacuating from.'

'That is where the English are being evacuated from. We are French.'

'Well, sir, they might give you a ride.'

They marched through the afternoon, twenty-four miserable

men, trying to forget the sight of their blazing tanks, their feeling of utter uselessness. Without their tanks they were helpless. They did not have a rifle between them; only the six officers had sidearms. Their depression was not lifted by the irrepressible cheerfulness of the engineers, their constant reference to their imminent return to 'Blighty'. They did not seem to realize that the war was all but lost. From time to time they saw aircraft, but their small group was not worth strafing. They saw sufficient evidence both of aerial attacks and of the demolitions being carried out by the retreating British – burned-out tanks and trucks, some dead bodies, shattered radio equipment – the completeness of the destruction, or the lack of it, being professionally criticized by their friendly sergeant. But they saw almost no discarded rifles. The BEF was still prepared to fight, no matter the odds.

It was near dusk when L'Orly called a halt. By then they were exhausted, and just fell where they stood. They had also accumulated several British stragglers, separated from their units. They exchanged food, and the British appreciated the wine ration carried by their allies. L'Orly sat with his officers. 'We will be in Dunkirk tomorrow morning. I do not know what will happen then. Perhaps we will be offered berths on the ships, perhaps not. But I must tell you that I can no longer consider myself in command. It is every man for himself, eh? Those of you who do not wish to go to England, well, the decision is up to you. If you decide not to go, you will have to surrender to the Boche.'

'Are you going to England, sir?' someone asked.

'The decisions must be individual, and private,' L'Orly said, and left them.

'Will you go?' Henri asked Pierre.

'If I am offered a berth, yes.'

'You will abandon France, abandon your family?'

'I can't do either France or my family much good in a German prison camp. Anyway, they will have gone down to Paulliac by now. They will be safe there.'

'My mother and father will have returned to Dieppe,' Henri said.

'That should be safe enough.'

'Do you not suppose that if the Germans win another battle they will move to the Channel coast?'

'I would think they'd go for Paris first. Anyway, who says they're going to win another battle?'

Henri looked at him, and he flushed. 'If I go to England,' Henri said. 'I may never see my parents again. Or Amalie. She will be with them.'

Pierre preferred not to comment on that. He had no doubt that Amalie would have gone south with her own family. 'You cannot see them either from a German prison camp,' he said.

'I am not going to a German prison camp. I am going to Dieppe.'

'How can you do that? You would be deserting. An officer does not desert. Anyway, you would have to go through the German lines.'

'There are no Germans on the coast yet. As for deserting, L'Orly has just said it is every man for himself. Once I have made contact with my family, I will rejoin the army. Will you not come with me?'

Pierre pretended to consider. But his decision had already been made. He had been horrified by the way the French army had just fallen apart, the errors of his commanding officers. He had known his tank was superior to any panzer. But not to two or three at once. The German armour had moved as a single immense and powerful force; the French had been split up into separate units, none larger than a regiment, most much smaller, and hurried to and fro as support for the infantry. While the infantry, with a few notable exceptions, had simply not wanted to fight. Even from his privileged position as a de Gruchy, Pierre had been aware of the political crises of the last few years, the increasing Communist infiltration of French industry, French thought. But the army had always been above that, he had supposed. Certainly in an elite corps like the Motorized Cavalry morale had always been high. But now it seemed that the army had also been infiltrated by Communists and pacifists, men who only wanted the war to be over, no matter what humiliation might follow.

If that were true, then the war was lost. But the British were showing no signs of collapsed morale or anxiety for peace. Listening to the sappers' conversation, if they discussed the war and their parlous situation at all, it was to remark that there must have been the most tremendous 'cock-up' somewhere, but their attitude was one of resignation, an acceptance that these things regularly happened, rather than either anger or despair, while there was utter confidence that somehow things would turn out all right and that 'Jerry' would be beaten. After all, the reasoning seemed to be, Great Britain had not lost an important war since long before it had taken the name – the American business was regarded as a colonial revolt, and even that had ended without any serious damage to Britain itself. He felt that if France was ever to regain its honour, much less its prestige, it would have to be with the help and at the side of men like these. And he had no fears for the safety of *his* family, tucked away down in Gascony. 'I'll go with the British,' he said.

Henri regarded him for several moments, but decided against offering an opinion on the decision. He held out his hand. 'Then I will wish you fortune, and hope to see you again.'

The Intelligence unit was taken off one of the Dunkirk docks by a destroyer. James and Watson stood on deck to look back at the town and the beaches, the sand crowded with men, and more arriving every minute. Lines were already stretching into the water as the soldiers reached for the tugs and destroyers that were nosing in as close as they dared, putting down boats to pick up the soldiers. But there were too many men, and so few ships. 'Poor bastards,' Watson commented. 'Do you think many of them will get off?'

'Doesn't look too hopeful,' James said. 'And those are fighting men. They should be here, and us there.'

'You don't suppose we're more important than they?'

'Not now, we're not. If we ever were. But now, what have we got to offer?' He had felt this increasingly during the retreat when they had been driven into the town, passing on their way lines of retreating soldiers, plodding onwards, being strafed by the Luftwaffe, but still not reduced to a rabble.

Watson scratched his head. 'Well, don't feel too bad about it. We haven't got there yet.'

He pointed at the row of planes swooping down on them. The sky was scoured by vapour trails, because the RAF was also up there, doing its best to protect the beaches, but it was outnumbered, and this squadron had broken through. The destroyer had just left the dockside and was still in the lengthy channel leading to the open sea. Thus there was no room to manoeuvre; its only defence lay in its anti-aircraft batteries, which opened up with everything they had. Streams of tracer bullets screamed skywards, and one of the attacking planes plunged downwards, smoke streaming behind it, far too low for the pilot to bail out. 'Poor bastard,' James said.

'For God's sake,' Watson protested. 'They're shooting at us. I'm going below.'

As the deck was crowded with men, that was not easy to do, but he pushed his way through. James preferred to stay on deck. He had been seasick when crossing back in October, and besides, he wanted to see what was going on. He stared at the three remaining fighter-bombers coming closer and closer, and suddenly realized that the destroyer was certain to be hit. For all his several years in the army, he had never actually felt in personal danger before. Even the strafing they had suffered during the retreat had been somehow distant. But these planes had him in their sights. Around him men were making a lot of noise, but there was nowhere to go, nothing to do. He heard a whistle blowing and the scream of a siren, and then there was an enormous *whoosh!*

He realized afterwards that he had lost consciousness for several seconds. Now he was in the sea, surrounded by men and by the remnants of the destroyer, which had settled in relatively shallow water; he reflected, irrelevantly, that she must have gone down very fast.

People were shouting at him, clawing at him, splashing all around him. He wondered if Harry was amongst them, and was amazed at the way his mind was working in such a detached fashion while he was swimming towards the town, slowly and painfully, already exhausted by the weight of his uniform and equipment. I should get rid of some of this stuff, he thought. But that would be deliberate destruction of army property. Well, then, at least the boots; they felt as if he had lumps of lead strapped to his feet. But how did he reach down to untie his laces without drowning? He could do without his cap. He put up his hand and discovered that the cap was gone. Instead, his hand came down covered in blood. Oh, shit, he thought. I've been hit.

His feet touched sand, and he managed to crawl a few feet before collapsing.

Noise! Nothing but noise. James opened his eyes and blinked at the light, and hastily closed them again. But the noise remained. It was inside his head. He forced his eyes open again, gazed at a nurse. A French nurse, he deduced, from her uniform. But she had a friendly smile. And she spoke English, after a fashion. 'You must try to lie still,' she said. 'I 'ave the sedative 'ere.'

'I don't want a sedative. Where am I?'

'You are in the 'ospital.'

'Hospital where?'

''Ere in Dunkirk.'

'That noise . . .'

'It is the Boche, monsieur. The planes and the guns.'

James sat up and blinked his eyes again as the room rotated. 'My head . . .'

'It is the bump.'

'Eh?'

'You 'ave a bump on the 'ead. I think it is when your ship goes down, eh? It is a big cut.' James put up his hand and

72

found a bandage. 'So you see, you must rest. I 'ave the sedative . . .'

He caught her wrist. 'How long have I been here?'

'You came in yesterday morning.'

'Yesterday?! What time is it?'

'It is four of the afternoon.'

'My God!' He threw back the covers. 'But we are still being bombed! They aren't here yet.'

'It will be soon.'

'Have all the British soldiers left?'

'There are still many on the beaches. I think they are waiting to be taken off, but I do not think it is possible.'

'I must get to them.' He got out of bed, clung to the post to wait for the room to settle down.

'No, no.' The nurse put her arm round his shoulders. 'You are not well. You must lie down.'

'Nurse, if you don't let go of me I am going to be very angry.' She retreated. 'Now tell me, do you know what happened to a Captain Watson? Or a Colonel Barrett? They were on the ship with me.'

'I do not know about this. I think maybe they were drowned. There were not many survivors. You were very lucky.'

I was on deck, he remembered. And out of the way of the direct hit. Harry had gone below, and Barrett had been on the bridge. Shit! 'There was also a Private Colley.'

'I do not know this. This ward is for officers.'

He looked left and right. None of the other three beds was occupied. 'You are a friend of this private?' the nurse asked, clearly finding that difficult to believe.

'Yes, he was a friend. He was my batman. My servant.'

'Ah.' She looked more puzzled yet, that an officer should be friends with his servant.

'Listen, where is my uniform?'

'It is in the cupboard. But you cannot go out. You are not well.'

'I'll be a lot worse if I'm in here when the Jerries come.' He opened the wardrobe. His uniform had been washed and pressed, and looked almost new. He dressed himself while she watched him, at last bestirring herself to tie the laces for his boots. He had no cap, but there was nothing he could do about that. 'You've been a treasure.' He kissed her on the forehead and went outside.

The outer ward was full, mostly of British soldiers – all seriously wounded – and nurses and doctors. One of these, a small man with glasses, stepped in front of James. 'You cannot leave the hospital. You are wounded.'

James held him by the arms and gently lifted him to one side. 'There are a lot of men here who need attention more than I.'

He hurried down a corridor. People stared at him, but no one attempted to stop him. He ran up a flight of steps – realizing for the first time that the wards had been underground – left the building, and checked in consternation. Inside the hospital sound had been muted, and the principal smell had been disinfectant. Out here he gazed at a destroyed and burning town, and the principal smell was that of scorching wood . . . and scorching flesh. He looked at the harbour, and gulped. There were several sunken vessels, half in and half out of the water; it was clearly no longer usable for embarkation. Then he looked at the beach north of the port, covered in men, and at the calm sea beyond, which was equally covered with ships of every size and description, from destroyers to launches and what looked like barges and even motor yachts closer in. To all of them there stretched lines of men, up to their chests in water, waiting patiently to be taken off.

For the moment there were no planes to be seen; James presumed they were away refuelling. He made his way through the burning streets and reached the open air, then climbed down to the beach. He passed several groups of soldiers, sitting or lying beside the road. 'Why aren't you on the beach?' he asked.

'There's time,' one replied, and added a belated, 'Sir.'

James went on, and passed a French group, staring at the

beach with sombre eyes. He saluted them, and was checked by a call. 'James Barron!'

James turned. 'Pierre? My dear fellow!' He went towards him and they shook hands. 'What are you doing here?'

'We have lost our tanks. So . . . But you are wounded.'

'Just a bump on the head. Now let's find ourselves a ship. Bring your men.'

'But . . . we are French.'

'We are allies,' James reminded him.

Part Two

The Conquered

'Honour was the meed of victorie
And yet the vanquished had no despair.'

Edward Spenser

Four

Occupation

Liane de Gruchy soaked in her tub. This was the third bath she had had in twenty-four hours; there were rumours of an imminent water shortage, but it had not happened yet.

It was not as if she any longer felt dirty in a physical sense. Her captors had been about the cleanest people she had ever met, and she had been given a bath every day during her stay in the field hospital. But they had been her captors. Today was the first time she had been free, and in her own flat. Her own private world.

Yet she was still a prisoner. All of Paris was now a prisoner. Perhaps all of France. She got out of the bath, towelled, wrapped herself in her dressing gown, and stood at the window to look down at the street. Sometimes she wondered if it was real. She could see the Eiffel Tower rising above the rooftops, so it was definitely Paris. But she had never known it so quiet. She reckoned about ninety per cent of the population must have been evacuated or just fled. The rest were staying indoors – today. It had been different yesterday, as the Wehrmacht had proudly marched under the Arche de Triomphe and down the Champs Élysées. Then it seemed that nearly all the remaining Parisians had turned out to have a first glimpse of their conquerors. Many had wept. Paris was now dead. For how long? she wondered.

She had almost been part of the march, following the army in an ambulance. There had been absolutely nothing the matter with her physical condition for over a fortnight, but she and Joanna had both been kept in hospital. Now, presumably, the

Germans felt there was no one left for them to tell their story to, to seek justice from. They had forgotten that Joanna was an American.

Her doorbell rang. She crossed the lounge and unlocked it. 'How did it go?'

Joanna headed straight for the sideboard and poured herself a cognac. 'He couldn't have been more helpful. Well, he had to be. Mom's been on the phone every day for the past month. And Dad's been raising hell with the Swedish embassy. So Bullitt's arranging transport to Switzerland, then Italy, then Portugal, then England. Then home,' she added as an afterthought. 'Did you get through to your folks?'

'The lines are down. I'm going to see if I can get down to Chartres when things settle a bit.'

'Are you going to tell them what happened?'

'When I feel up to it. When our business has been sorted out. What *about* our business? What did Bullitt say?'

Joanna sat on the settee, the glass held in both hands. 'In a word, forget it. That's two words, I guess.'

Liane sat beside her. 'You're not serious.'

'He said he's very sorry about Aubrey, but he wasn't sure anyone would believe me about what happened to us. I'm not sure he believed me himself. I had nothing to show him. Not even a bruise. Those bastards. Equally, I suspect he doesn't want to rock the boat right this minute. So your people got licked. Bullitt told me this new guy who's taken over, Petain, is asking for an armistice. That's surrender. So the war will be over as far as France is concerned, and he seems to think that Britain will then negotiate. So it'll all be done. And so far, apart from the strafing of civilians, it's been what he calls a clean war. He thinks it'd be best for everyone if it stays that way. Two silly women screaming rape when they were where they shouldn't have been in the first place might just stir things up, certainly when they can't prove their allegations.'

'So what are you going to do?'

'Get out of this goddamned country for a start. Sorry, Li, but as long as the Nazis are running it, that's what it is.'

'I agree with you. But when you get to England . . .'

'That's going to be a different ball game. Listen, you'll come with me. I put it to Bullitt, and he said he'd swing it.'

'France is my home.'

'Sure. But right now it's the shits. You just agreed.'

'We'll get it back. I want to be here when we do.'

'Could be a long time.'

'I have time,' Liane said.

'There are two men at the door,' said Bertha the maid.

'Do you think . . .' Rosa Burstein looked at her husband.

'It could be,' David said. 'It could be. Admit the gentlemen, Bertha.'

Amalie stood up, pounding heart turning her cheeks pink. Oh, if it could only be news . . . Even bad news would be better than not knowing.

The two men, both wearing trench coats and slouch hats, entered the drawing room. The Bursteins insensibly moved closer together. 'David Burstein?' one of the men asked. His French was good, but the accent was foreign.

'I am he.'

'You are under arrest. Frau Burstein, you are also under arrest.'

'What do you mean?' Amalie shouted.

The Gestapo officer looked at her. 'Your name?'

'I am also Frau Burstein, as you call it.'

He took a list from his pocket, studied it. 'There is only one Frau Burstein here. Come along, now. There is a train waiting.'

'A train?' Rosa asked, her voice high. 'I do not understand. We do not wish to go anywhere.'

'What you wish is irrelevant. You are being deported to Germany.'

'But why? What have we done?'

'You are Jewish.'

The Bursteins stared at each other in horror. The agent was looking at Amalie. 'You do not look Jewish,' he remarked.

'Of course I am not Jewish,' Amalie snapped.

'Then you are of no interest to us.'

'I am a member of this family. I am married to Lieutenant Henri Burstein of the Motorized Cavalry.'

'You have children?'

Amalie flushed. 'No.'

'Then we do not wish you. Come along now.'

'Bastard!' Amalie shouted, seizing a pewter vase and hurling it at him.

'You mean you are here alone?' Jean Moulin asked, looking from left to right as he stood in the centre of the huge drawing room. 'But . . . did not your parents go down to Paulliac?'

'Nearly two months ago,' Madeleine said. 'Champagne?'

Laurent was hovering. 'Well . . . that would be very nice. Thank you.'

'And you have news? Of Liane? Or Pierre?'

'I'm afraid not.'

'Oh.' The animation left her face.

'I have news of Amalie. Very grave news.'

'Amalie? She is in Dieppe.'

'She is under arrest.'

'Amalie?' Madeleine shouted. 'What are you saying?'

'The Bursteins have been deported to Germany. All Jews are being deported to Germany.'

'Oh, my God! But Amalie is not a Jew.'

'And they had no interest in her. But when her parents-in-law were arrested, it seems she lost her temper and hit one of the Gestapo agents on the head. He is in hospital.'

'Oh, Amalie! But I would have done the same. We must make them let her go.'

'I'm afraid they are not going to do that.'

'Not let her go?'

'Madeleine, I would like you to sit down.' Madeleine frowned, but did as he asked. Moulin sat beside her. 'I wish you to be very brave,' he said. 'Madeleine, under the laws imposed by our conquerors, striking a German officer while he is performing his duty is a capital offence.'

Madeleine clasped both hands to her neck. 'But . . . I must get in touch with Papa's lawyers. Do you have a phone? Ours is down.'

'A lawyer is not going to help. I thought of that immediately, but . . .'

'She has to be tried, hasn't she?'

Moulin sighed. 'The trial, if you can call it that, will be before a military tribunal, and will be held *in camera*. No lawyers will be allowed. And sadly, none of the lawyers I have spoken to wish to become involved. Amalie married into a Jewish family, and anyone convicted of helping Jews is likely to find themselves in prison, if not in a German concentration camp.'

'That is barbaric.'

'I'm afraid we seem to have entered a barbaric age.'

'There has to be something we can do.'

'I will continue to make representations. But I can promise nothing. What you must do is leave Chartres immediately. Otherwise you may find yourself caught up in this miserable business. Go down to Paulliac.'

'You mean, abandon Amalie.'

'There is nothing you can do to help her. And . . . well, you must consider that of your parents' four children, you could be the only one left.'

'You are saying that Liane and Pierre are dead? You know this?'

'I do not know this. But no word has been heard from either of them since the day of the invasion, and we know that the French army in Belgium was overrun and destroyed in the very first days of the war. I think you have a duty to your mother and father to be with them at this time. Now, it will be necessary for you to obtain a travel permit. This will be issued by the local commandant. His name is Major von Helsingen, and he appears to be a decent fellow. I suggest you visit him this afternoon. As soon as I get back to my office I will telephone and make an appointment for you. Please take my advice, Madeleine.'

Madeleine stared at him.

Poor girl, Moulin thought as he returned to his office. Poor family. Of course they were not the only family suffering tragedy, and at least with their wealth they were far better cushioned against adversity than most. But he felt *their* adversity more than any other. This was partly because he was a personal friend, and partly because they were so attractive, as a family. But more than any of those reasons, it was because their disintegration had been so rapid, and so complete. Two months ago they had gathered in that house without a care in the world. Now, Pierre was missing in action, as was Henri Burstein, who had to be considered part of the family. Liane had disappeared and could well be dead. Amalie was facing execution. Madeleine could indeed be the only one left.

He frowned as he got out of his car. Another car was parked just along the street. It flew the swastika from its bonnet, and there were at least two men inside, apart from the driver. He felt a quickening of his pulse as he entered the building. Up to now, apart from a formal visit by Major von Helsingen to inform him that Chartres was a military district, and requiring him to implement instructions as regards movement and rationing, the Germans had not interfered with his administration. His secretary waggled her eyebrows at him as he entered the outer office. He glanced to his right, where several people were seated, waiting to see him. Two of these were now rising to their feet: a tall, thin man with a hatchet face, and a shorter and more thickset, as well as younger, companion. Both wore civilian clothes. 'Monsieur Moulin?' asked the older man. 'We wish to have a word, in private.'

'Of course. As soon as I have seen those in front of you.'

'Ahem,' Marguerite said. Moulin looked at her. 'Colonel Kluck is from the Gestapo, sir.'

Moulin looked at Kluck, then at the other waiting people, who avoided looking at him. Having discovered Kluck's profession, they all seemed anxious to abandon their own interviews and get out of the office. 'You had better come in,' he invited.

The two men followed him into the office and closed the door. 'This is my associate, Captain Biedermann,' Kluck said.

'Captain.' Moulin did not offer to shake hands with either of them, but gestured them to chairs and seated himself behind his desk.

'You are a busy man, Monsieur le Prefect,' Kluck remarked.

'My people have a great deal to worry about. What can I do for you?'

'We shall not take up much of your time. We are going to ask a favour of you.'

'Yes?' Moulin's voice was cautious.

'We understand that you are friendly with the de Gruchy family. The wine people. They live in Chartres.'

'No. They have a house here, but they live mainly in the Gironde. That is where their vineyards are situated.'

'You mean they are not here now?'

'They left when the invasion started.'

'Leaving their daughter behind?' Biedermann asked.

Moulin frowned; this man could not possibly know about Madeleine. 'Which daughter are we speaking about?'

'You mean they have more than one? I am speaking of a hellcat named Liane.'

'You have news of Liane? She's not dead?'

'Unfortunately no,' Kluck said. 'She is in her Paris flat.'

'Thank God for that! And you came here to tell her family? That is very kind of you, Colonel.'

'That is not why I came here, Prefect. This woman found herself in the north of the country, in the path of our advancing troops. She had an American friend with her.'

Moulin nodded. 'Joanna Jonsson. They were delivering Mademoiselle de Gruchy's brother and brother-in-law to their regiment. That was on the day your people crossed the border. But that was two months ago. Where have they been since then?'

85

'Down to our occupation of Paris, in one of our hospitals.'

'You said they were not hurt.'

'They were in a very disturbed frame of mind. Obviously they had never experienced war before, and they were shocked at what they saw.'

Moulin nodded. 'I can appreciate that. Mademoiselle Jonsson's brother was with them.'

'So they say. But there is no evidence of it.' Moulin frowned. 'In fact,' Kluck went on, 'there is no evidence that anything they say is true. They were clearly traumatized, and have been making the most absurd statements of things they allege to have happened to them.'

Moulin continued to frown. He could not imagine Liane de Gruchy being traumatized by anything. 'They have even accused some of our soldiers of repeatedly raping them,' Biedermann said.

'That is a serious charge.'

'Of course it is,' Kluck agreed. 'And it is untrue. There is not a single shred of evidence to support their allegations.'

'Were they not medically examined?'

'Yes, they were. Neither was a virgin. But they admitted that they had both lost their virginity some years ago. We are not speaking of young girls.'

'But you still do not believe their allegations.'

'We know that they are untrue.'

'Then how can I help you?'

'Well, you see, Fräulein de Gruchy is not a problem. She is in Paris and, shall I say, under our control. Unfortunately, Fräulein Jonsson is not. We had hoped she would see reason, but the first thing she did on being released from hospital and returning to Paris was go to the American embassy. We could not prevent her from doing this,' he added ingenuously.

'And now they are raising the matter diplomatically.'

'They have not as yet. But the American ambassador immediately arranged for Fräulein Jonsson to leave the country. Now she has done so. She is in Switzerland and we believe on her way to England. This so prompt departure, one could

86

almost call it a flight, is very suspicious. It would appear that the Americans are intending to use her as a propaganda weapon against us. That would be unacceptable. It reflects upon the integrity of the Wehrmacht.'

'I can see that would be a serious matter,' Moulin agreed drily. 'But I still do not see how I can help you.'

'It is necessary that her story be utterly discredited before it is even made public. Of course we could bring pressure to bear upon Fräulein de Gruchy to say that her friend's allegations are entirely untrue, and we will do this if it becomes necessary. But it is a question as to whether the world, the neutral world, will believe her or suppose that she has been, shall I say, got at. We need the charge to be dismissed as nonsense by someone of spotless reputation and importance in the community, who also happens to know these women well, and can therefore confirm them as a pair of hysterics. You are the prefect of Chartres. Your integrity is widely accepted. You are also a friend of the de Gruchys. You have known these two women, or certainly Fräulein de Gruchy, for years. If you were to say, publicly, that you have no doubt that the charges are entirely the product of two overwrought female minds, it would carry a great deal of weight. As a matter of fact, what would suit us best is if you were to say that the women, or certainly Fräulein de Gruchy, had confessed to you that they were indeed raped, but by fleeing *French* soldiers. This would be very helpful in any future accusations that might arise.'

Moulin gazed at him for several seconds. 'You have just paid me the compliment of describing me as a man of integrity.'

'That is the public perception, yes. I would prefer to think that you are a man of sense. Your cooperation will be very beneficial for you, and for the people you serve. You must be realistic, Prefect. Most of France is now a German province. It will remain so for the foreseeable future. That being the case, does it not make sense to cooperate fully with us? I need hardly say that the personal benefits to you will be enormous.'

Moulin continued to gaze at him for several seconds. The temptation was certainly enormous, especially as he did not believe that the propaganda damage that could be done to the Wehrmacht by an unsubstantiated accusation of rape would be of the least importance to neutral, even American, observers compared with the shattering collapse of France. But to perjure himself, to dishonour himself, not only as a man but as a government official, not to mention letting down his old friends . . . So far there was nothing honourable about anything in this war from France's point of view, save for a few individual acts of heroism and determined resistance. And it was a very slippery slope that was being proposed to him. To lie for the Germans in this instance would mean lying for them again, as and when they required it. Because he *was* a man of integrity and people would believe him. 'Well?' Kluck demanded.

Moulin took a deep breath. 'I am sorry, Herr Colonel. I cannot assist you in this matter. As you say, I have been a friend of the de Gruchy family for a long time. I have known Liane since she was a girl. I know that she is neither a liar nor a hysteric. If she says she was raped by German soldiers, then she was raped by German soldiers.'

Kluck clearly could not believe his ears. 'You are defying me? You are defying the Reich?'

'Not at all. I am merely saying that I cannot assist you in this matter. In fact, it would be a disaster for you, as if you were to insist on involving me, I would have to support Mademoiselle de Gruchy's story.'

Kluck stared at him for several seconds, then looked at Biedermann, who drew a Luger automatic pistol from a shoulder holster beneath his jacket and presented it at Moulin's head. 'You are under arrest.'

Moulin refused to flinch. 'Am I allowed to know the charge?'

'In the first instance, the charge is of behaviour considered to be detrimental to the requirements of the Reich,' Kluck said. 'That is treason. Get up.' Slowly Moulin rose to his feet. 'Now walk before us down to my car. I do not wish to cause a scene and so will not handcuff you. And Captain Biedermann will pocket his gun. But should you make any attempt to escape, or should any attempt be made to interfere with us, he will shoot you dead, and anyone else who may become involved.'

'Am I allowed to send for my lawyer?'

'In due course. When you have discussed the situation further with us at Gestapo headquarters. If, for example, we manage to change your mind about cooperating with us, you will not need your lawyer.'

'Your business, Fräulein.'

Madeleine gazed at a bald head. 'I have an appointment with Major von Helsingen.'

The sergeant looked at her for the first time. Madeleine was wearing white slacks and a loose blue blouse and was well worth looking at, even if her hair was concealed beneath a bandanna. The soldier standing at her shoulder, who had escorted her into the building, rolled his eyes. 'Your name?'

'Madeleine de Gruchy.'

The sergeant checked his list. 'There is no appointment.'

'There must be. The appointment was made this morning by the prefect, Monsieur Moulin.'

The sergeant leaned back in his chair. 'Moulin, you say.'

'The prefect of Chartres,' Madeleine reminded him.

'He is a friend of yours?'

'Yes. He is a friend of my father's.'

'And where is your father?'

'He is in Paulliac. Why am I being asked all these questions? All I wish is a travel permit.'

'All you wish,' the sergeant sneered. 'Well –' There was a sudden flurry of activity, a clicking of heels. The sergeant pushed back his chair, and stood up, also coming to attention. 'Heil Hitler!'

'Carry on. Who is this?'

Madeleine turned, and gazed at a young man in officer's uniform. He was of medium height, but with good shoulders and chest, clean-shaven, his face crisply handsome. His hair was dark, although his eyes were blue. 'She says her name is

Alan Savage

de Gruchy, Herr Major,' the sergeant explained. 'Claims to be a friend of the prefect,' he added significantly.

'De Gruchy,' Major von Helsingen said. 'There are wine merchants of that name.' He spoke excellent French.

'My father, Herr Major,' Madeleine said.

'Good Heavens. Do you live in Chartres? I would have supposed –'

'Our home is in Paulliac, Herr Major. But we have a house here. Now I would like to go home, to Paulliac. Monsieur Moulin said I should apply to you for a travel permit. I would also like a gasoline allocation.'

'When did he tell you this?'

'We spoke this morning. He said he would make an appointment, but he seems to have forgotten.'

Von Helsingen regarded her for a few moments, then went to the foot of the stairs which led up from the hall. 'Come up to my office, if you will, mademoiselle.' Madeleine hesitated, then went to him. He stood aside to allow her to precede him. 'It is the door on the left.'

Madeleine opened the door, and a female secretary, smart and attractive in her white shirt, black tie and skirt, yellow hair in a tight bun on the nape of her neck, looked up in surprise, and then rose to stand to attention as the major also entered. 'I will take no calls for half an hour, Eva.'

'Yes, Herr Major.' She gave Madeleine an inquisitorial look.

Von Helsingen opened the inner door and allowed Madeleine to enter, then closed it behind them both. He gestured her to a chair before his desk, and sat behind it himself. 'You said you spoke with Monsieur Moulin this morning. Where was this?'

'He called at my house. Has something happened to him?'

'The prefect was arrested by the Gestapo late this morning.'

'Arrested?' Madeleine cried. 'But why?'

'The Gestapo do not confide their reasons. You say Moulin called at your house. Why?'

90

'He came to tell me to leave Chartres.'

'Why?'

'Because . . .' Madeleine sucked her lower lip between her teeth. 'My sister has been arrested.'

'Your sister? Here in Chartres? I have not been informed of this. What is her name?'

'Amalie. She lives in Dieppe. She hit a Gestapo agent on the head with a pewter vase.'

She felt sure Helsingen had to suppress a smile. 'That is a very serious matter. Are you saying this man is dead?'

'I do not think so.'

'Just angry, eh? That is fortunate. Did your sister have a reason for striking him?'

'She is very impulsive.'

'Apparently.'

'This man had just arrested her mother- and father-in-law.'

'Did *he* give a reason?'

'They're Jewish.'

'You're not Jewish?' He sounded positively alarmed.

'No, no. Amalie married their son.'

'Good Heavens! Why did she do that?'

'She was in love with him, Herr Major.'

'And he was also arrested?'

'No. He was serving with the Motorized Cavalry. He was reported missing after the Battle of the Meuse.'

'That was six weeks ago.'

'Six weeks in which she has not known whether he is alive or dead. She is distraught with worry.'

'She must be, to have hit a German policeman on the head.'

'Monsieur Moulin was going to see if he could help her. But if he has been arrested . . . Do you think that is why he was arrested?'

'I doubt it, unless there was something sinister about what your sister did.'

'Sinister? Amalie does not know the meaning of the word. She is only twenty.'

'Hm. Would you like me to look into it?'

'Would you? Could you? Oh, that would be splendid.'

'I happen to be a friend of the officer commanding in Dieppe. I will have a word with him. Are you in a great hurry to get down to Paulliac, mademoiselle?' Madeleine stared at him. 'It occurs to me, you see, that if I were to be successful in securing the release of your sister, it might be a good idea for you to remain in Chartres a day or two longer so that you can escort her down to Paulliac yourself. If she is as impulsive and hot-headed as you say, it might be unwise for her to travel by herself.'

'Oh. Yes. I see what you mean. How long –'

'I can be in touch with Franz this afternoon, and hopefully have things sorted out in a couple of days.'

'That would be wonderful. I should be eternally grateful. But . . . do you really think your friend will be able to help? We have been told that, well, the Gestapo is a law unto itself.'

'That is their reputation, certainly. And they do have extensive powers. But north-western France is under military occupation, and thus the Wehrmacht is the ultimate authority. The Gestapo usually find it convenient to cooperate with us. As we often cooperate with them.'

'Oh. Yes. I see. Well, as I said, I shall be eternally grateful to you.'

'Then perhaps you will do me the honour of having dinner with me tonight.'

Madeleine opened her mouth and then shut it again. But hadn't she always known there would have to be a price to pay? At least he seemed to be a very nice man.

'Tell me about this girl, Amalie de Gruchy,' Franz Hoepner suggested.

Captain Roess raised his eyebrows. 'You know her, Herr Major?'

'If I knew her, Roess, I would not be asking you to tell me about her. I gather she is well connected.'

'She is a daughter of Albert de Gruchy, the wine merchant.

That does not give her the right to strike one of my officers. Poor Moeller is in hospital and liable to remain there for at least another week. It was a very heavy vase, hurled with considerable force, and he was wearing only a soft hat. Had he been bare-headed, it might have killed him.'

'I am sure there was provocation.'

'There was none reported. Or claimed by her. She appears to have lost her head when her mother- and father-in-law were arrested. They are Jews.'

'So I have been told. Where are they now?'

'On their way to Germany.'

'And the son, this girl's husband, is reported missing in action. I would say there was provocation. Of circumstances. Sufficient to make a young bride lose her senses, temporarily.'

'That is still no excuse for striking one of my people.'

'So what have you done with her?'

'She is in a cell, awaiting trial. And conviction.'

'And?'

'Well, execution is the prescribed sentence. But she is very pretty. It may be possible to give her an alternative sentence.'

'In one of your brothels, you mean. You really are a detestable fellow, Roess.' Roess's head came up, sharply, but he decided against making a reply. 'So what have you done to her so far?' Hoepner asked.

'Nothing. Well, we had to search her.'

'Naturally. And what did you find?'

Roess grinned. 'That she was a virgin. After two months of marriage.'

'And is she still a virgin?'

'Well . . .'

'You are admitting that your men raped a prisoner who has not yet been convicted?'

'My men did not rape her,' Roess snapped. 'With respect, Herr Major. She was examined, searched. My men did not know she was a virgin as she was a married woman, and, well . . . fingers, you know . . .'

'I take back what I said just now. You are not detestable, Roess. You are downright disgusting. And your men.'

Roess's face stiffened. 'I resent that, Herr Major. My men were doing their duty.'

'No doubt. However, I would say that their *duty* inflicted something far worse than rape on Fräulein de Gruchy. I would also say that she has been punished sufficiently for a single impetuous act. I wish the charges against her dropped.'

'She is a prisoner of the Gestapo, not the Wehrmacht. You have no jurisdiction over us.'

'Have you ever met my uncle, the general? Or heard of him?' Roess swallowed. 'I see that you have. In view of his recent exploits, he is one of the Führer's favourite panzer commanders. I am having dinner with him next week. I am sure that you would like me to tell him what a good job you are doing, Roess. Or not, as the case may be.'

Roess licked his lips. 'If it is so important to you, Herr Major, the charges will be dropped.'

'Thank you, Roess. That is very good of you. Be sure that I will remember your cooperation. The girl will be delivered to me, personally.' Again Roess raised his eyebrows. 'Dismissed.' Roess left the room and Hoepner picked up his phone. 'Get me Major von Helsingen. In Chartres.' He waited, drumming his fingers on his desk until he heard the familiar voice. 'Good morning, Frederick. You owe me one.'

'Oh, well done. As you say, I owe you. Any problems?'

'I do not think so. Now perhaps you will tell me what it is all about.'

'This girl has a sister. The most entrancing creature.'

'I am told this young woman is very pretty, when she is not hitting policemen. So the sister inveigled you into a deal: her bed for her sister.'

'It is not the least like that. I offered to help her.'

'Just like that?'

'You haven't met her.'

'I look forward to doing so, certainly. But if you are going to fuck her, I recommend you do it right away. The baby sister may be in a trifle upset state.'

'She has not been interrogated?' Which was the standard euphemism for torture.

'Not in the Gestapo's books. But they searched her, as I'm afraid they were entitled to do.'

'And?'

'She was deflowered, by their fingers.'

'Good God! The bastards! But . . . deflowered? She is a married woman.'

'There is a mystery you may care to investigate. But as I say, have the first sister before the second is delivered to you, and you can tell her sibling what happened.'

'You do not understand, Franz. I am not going to *have* Madeleine at all, unless expressly invited to do so. I think I am in love.' Hoepner stared at the phone in consternation.

Madeleine stood on the steps of the Chartres house to watch the command car coming down the drive. As there were only half a dozen servants left, and a single elderly gardener, the grounds were starting to look somewhat wild, but she supposed it would get worse before it got better. Unless she stayed, and Frederick was as good as his word and found some help for her.

As good as his word! He was an enemy of her country and thus of herself. If some people were to be believed, he was an enemy of mankind. Frederick? He was certainly a Nazi. That was to say, he believed in Hitler. She could not accept he believed all of the Nazis' more grotesque theories, but he saw in his Führer the man to lead Germany back to greatness, the man who had already done so. It was difficult to argue with that.

At dinner the previous night, in Chartres' best restaurant, she had been a bundle of nerves. That had been partly because she had dined there so often before, and if there had been no more than a dozen other French diners, she was known to them as well as all the waiters. But it had mainly been because she had no idea what was going to follow the meal. Nothing had.

Frederick's manners had been impeccable, both during and after dinner; when he had driven her home he had done no more than kiss her on the cheek.

Now she was being offered a further example of his integrity: seated next to him in the back of the open car was Amalie. She ran down the steps. 'Amalie!'

The orderly sitting in front beside the driver got out and opened the rear door, and Amalie stepped down. She did not look at the man, or at Helsingen, who was seated beside her. To Madeleine's dismay, she did not pause to embrace her sister, but brushed past her and ran up the steps into the house. The orderly now came towards Madeleine, carrying a valise. Helsingen followed.

'What has happened?' Madeleine asked.

'Shall we go inside? I will take this.' Helsingen took the valise from the orderly's hand.

Madeleine led him up the steps. Antoine waited at the top. 'Where is Madame Burstein?'

'She went straight upstairs, mademoiselle.'

Madeleine looked at Helsingen.

'I think you should make sure she is all right. I will wait.'

Madeleine hurried up the stairs. The night before the wedding, Amalie had slept in Pyramids, so she tried that first. The door was locked. Oh, my God, she thought. She banged on the panels. 'Amalie! Let me in.'

'I am drawing a bath.'

Madeleine could hear the sound of running water. 'Then you will come down?'

'I do not know. Perhaps.'

'Amalie! Promise me you are not going to do anything silly. Listen, we are going down to Paulliac. Home to Mama and Papa. You will be safe there until Henri comes home. Please promise me you'll do nothing stupid.'

'I am not going to commit suicide, goose,' Amalie said. 'I am going to stay alive. So that I can kill Germans.'

'Ah . . . right. Come down when you are ready.' Slowly Madeleine went downstairs.

Helsingen stood in the drawing room doorway. Needless to say, Laurent had provided him with a glass of champagne. Now he hurried forward with a glass for Madeleine. 'Is she all right?' Helsingen asked.

'I think she will be. At the moment she's a little upset.'

'I am not surprised.'

Madeleine led him into the room. 'What happened to her?'

'She spent three days in a Gestapo cell. I . . . Well, perhaps you should wait for her to tell you herself.'

Madeleine sat down. 'I would like you to tell me, Frederick.'

He sat beside her. 'They seemed . . . interested in the fact that although she was married, she was still intact.'

'She got married on the morning your invasion started, and Henri had to rejoin his regiment immediately after the ceremony. But you mean . . . Oh, my God!'

'Technically she was not raped. But she had a pretty horrifying experience, certainly for one so young and inexperienced.' He held her hand. 'I am most terribly sorry, believe me. Can you ever forgive me?'

'You are not guilty.' Her voice was low.

'They were Germans. The ugly side of our society.'

'Will they be punished?'

'They committed no crime. By hitting one of them Amalie placed herself in their power.'

'From which you extricated her. I, my whole family, even Amalie in time, will be eternally grateful to you.'

'It is only your gratitude I seek.'

They gazed at each other. 'What do you wish me to do?' Madeleine asked.

Helsingen smiled. 'That is a dangerous question to ask a man who finds you as attractive as I do. However, in the first instance, what you must do is leave Chartres and take your sister down to Paulliac. And stay there until the war ends. It will not be long now. The Führer has invited the British to make peace. This they will almost certainly do, for all of Churchill's bravado; there is nothing left for them to fight and risk destruction for. If they do not, well, I can tell you that we have plans for that destruction, before the end of the year.'

'Oh,' she said. 'Yes. But Paulliac . . .'

'Is a long way from Chartres? You mean, if I wished it, you would stay here? Out of gratitude?'

'That would be part of it.'

'I would prefer to know about the other part.' He squeezed her hand. 'But not now. This is something we both need to think about, and you have a duty to take your sister to her home, where she can recover from her ordeal.'

'Oh. Well . . . if Henri were able to join us there, now that the war is over . . .'

'Henri?'

'Her husband.'

'The Jew. You told me he was reported missing in action.'

'Yes.'

'Then he is probably dead.'

'But if he were to be alive, and can join Amalie . . .'

'If he is alive, Madeleine, if he has any sense, he will never attempt to regain his wife, because the moment he does so he will be arrested and sent to a concentration camp.'

'Because he is a Jew. How can you permit such things?'

'I do not make the laws. I only fight the battles necessary to preserve them. Now you are angry with me.'

'Not with you, Frederick. Only with the people who—'

He laid his finger on her lips. 'Don't ever say it.'

She stood up. 'I do not wish to hurt you. I have said I am eternally grateful to you for what you have done. Now . . .'

He stood also. 'You must prepare to leave.' From his breast pocket he took an envelope. 'In here are travel permits for your sister and yourself, and train tickets to Bordeaux. I'm afraid there does not appear to be a train service from Bordeaux to Paulliac, but it does not look very far on the map. You have money?'

'Yes, I have money. But . . . train? I prefer to drive.'

'That would not be safe, for two unescorted young women.'

'Oh. Well, again, thank you. And goodbye. I don't suppose we shall meet again.'

'That is up to you. I have some leave coming up in a month's time. I was going to ask your permission to come down to Paulliac myself and call upon you. Would you permit me to do that?'

Madeleine stared at him in consternation. This man is a Nazi and stands for everything that is evil about that philosophy. But he is so charming, and so perfectly mannered, and he has saved Amalie from possible execution . . . And if the Wehrmacht is going to occupy at least western France for the foreseeable future . . . 'I would like that very much,' she said.

'The brigadier will see you now, Captain,' said the uniformed secretary. James stood up – he had been waiting half an hour – and followed her from the ante-chamber into an outer office, where there was another secretary banging away at a typewriter, and up to a pair of double doors. These she opened. 'Captain Barron, sir.'

She stood to one side. James stepped past her, came to attention before the desk, saluted, then removed his cap and tucked it under his arm. 'Take a pew, Barron.' James lowered himself on to the straight chair before the desk. Behind him he heard the doors close. The brigadier was a heavy-set man who wore a little moustache, incongruous against the background of his receding hairline. He studied the file before him. 'It says here that you are fit for duty.'

'Yes, sir.'

'It seems to have been a nasty dent. No repercussions? Headaches? Double vision?'

'There was some in the beginning, sir. Not now.'

The brigadier regarded him for a few seconds, then said, 'Two.'

It took James a moment to catch on. 'Four.'

'Eight.'

'Sixteen.'

'Thirty-two.'

'Sixty-four.'

'A hundred and twenty-eight.'

'Two hundred and fifty-six.'

'Five hundred and twelve.'

'One thousand and twenty-four.'

'Two thousand and forty-eight.'

'Four thousand and ninety-six.'

'Eight thousand, one hundred and ninety-two.'

'Sixteen thousand, three hundred and eighty-four.'

'Thirty-two thousand, seven hundred and sixty-eight.'

'Sixty-five thousand, five hundred and thirty-six.'

'One hundred and thirty-one thousand and seventy-two.'

'Two hundred and sixty-two thousand, one hundred and forty-four.'

'Five hundred and twenty-four thousand, two hundred and eighty-eight.'

'One million and forty-eight thousand, five hundred and seventy-six.'

'That's very good.'

'Actually, sir, it's a game I used to play with my sisters when we were kids. We could reach a billion.'

'Hm. You could have told me that when I began.'

'I assumed you were trying to prove something, sir.'

The brigadier gazed at him for several seconds, then grinned. 'And I have done so. Very good. You are passed here as physically fit, and you appear to be mentally fit as well. How about decisions?'

'I can make them, sir.'

'Unpleasant ones?'

'I believe so.'

'Ambition?'

'Right now, to be returned to my regiment.'

'You were in MI.'

'Yes, sir. But I do not believe there are any enemy POWs to be interrogated at the moment.'

'You won't find any of them handy to exchange fire with, either. We are not actually in contact with any enemy force at this moment, on land, save for a few shots to and fro across the Egyptian border. But the enemy are still there to be beaten. I would like you to remain in MI. Only this will be a special branch of Intelligence.' He indicated the file. 'You made a report, dated 10 May, in which you denigrated French morale.'

'Well, yes, sir. But—'

'That report turned out to be unpleasantly correct. Know the French well, do you?'

'I wouldn't say that, sir.'

'Please, Captain. I haven't the time to deal with false modesty. When you left Dunkirk, you brought out with you a French officer, Lieutenant de Gruchy. He says he was a friend of yours.'

'Well, yes, sir. He is.'

'His family are now in occupied France.'

'His family are the wine people, sir. They live in Paulliac. Only a few miles from Bordeaux.'

'Bordeaux is now occupied by the Germans. The whole Atlantic coast of France is under German occupation. Naturally, not all Frenchmen are happy with the situation. As you may know, there are quite a few of them in England, including your friend, who are anxious to do all they can to reverse it. That is going to take a long time. We could be talking years. But we have to start now. What we need is information. The fact is that the rapidity of the German victory has rather caught us with our pants down. All our agents in those countries now occupied have gone by the board, or have had to be pulled out in a hurry. Now, setting up agents is normally a matter of years. We don't have years to play with. We have got to know what is actually happening in France: German strengths and movements, civilian morale, the possibility of local physical resistance, etc. At the behest of the PM, we are setting up a unit to handle this. It will be called Special Operations. It seems to me that you would be ideal for a job in this new set-up. Would you like to volunteer? Believe me, you would be doing far more to bring down Jerry than aimlessly drilling an infantry company in the hopes of an early return across the Channel. Incidentally, acceptance of this posting carries promotion to major.'

'Well, sir . . .'

'Your first assignment would be to monitor your friend de Gruchy.'

'Pierre? I'm afraid I don't understand.'

'He, amongst others, has volunteered to return to France as a British agent.'

'Isn't that hellishly risky?'

'There is no reason why it should be. He went missing following the Dunkirk debacle. If he turns up in Paulliac with a suitable cover story of survival and privation, no one is going to ask any serious questions. And he is also an ideal man. The Germans appreciate their wine as much as anyone else. That means they will keep de Gruchy and Son in business. There is a Paris office, of course. Pierre will get his father to appoint him manager of that office, from where he will be rubbing shoulders with German brass every day. I think he is going to be invaluable.'

'Yes, but if he's found out . . .'

'If he's careful that should not happen. In any event, the risk is far less than that of stopping a bullet as a front-line soldier.'

'I was thinking of his family. His sisters.'

'He is confident that they will be supportive.'

'I was thinking of if *they* were arrested by the Gestapo. They are three most beautiful girls.'

'If everyone behaves according to the book, that should not happen. You said you were capable of making decisions, even unpleasant ones. I should also point out that as de Gruchy is determined to return as our agent, *someone* is going to have to monitor him, and his family, from our end. If you are as fond of them as you appear to be, wouldn't you rather be the monitor yourself rather than some complete stranger, who might regard them merely as names and pins on a map and not care whether they lived or died? Certainly if a situation arose where one, or even all, of them had to be brought out.'

'Is that possible, sir? Bringing them out?'

'It is possible, certainly. But the situation would have to be acute, and they would have to wish to come. In any event, such a decision would have to be taken by a higher authority. That is me. Do I understand that you will accept the posting?'

Time for that decision-making ability. He had never envisaged the war as more than a gigantic jolly. Not until Dunkirk, that is. And the horrors of Dunkirk had made him acutely aware that he should have been with his company rather than swanning around as a staff officer. All the time he had been convalescing his mind had been centred on returning to the regiment. Now . . .

But what other decision could he make? To hold the well-being, the very lives, of Amalie and Madeleine, and above all, Liane, in his hands was a frightening thought, but to think of the lives of those laughing, confident, happy women in the hands of someone else was quite unacceptable. 'Yes, sir. I accept.'

'You understand that as of this moment, your every action, your every thought, must be top secret, to be shared only with me. You will tell your operatives only what is absolutely necessary for them to know. Never, under any circumstances, unless authorized by me, will you divulge the existence or identity of one operative to another. You are, of course, beginning with a subject you know you can handle. I assume you trust this de Gruchy fellow?'

'Absolutely, sir.'

'Very good. However, in the course of time you will be handling other operatives, and we must accept that amongst them there may be a traitor, or potential traitor. Hence the necessity to limit their knowledge of what we are doing or seeking or who we are using to a minimum.'

'What happens if I do detect a traitor, sir?'

'I'm afraid such matters will have to be handled internally; calling in the police, with all the legal and political ramifications that could ensue, and even more, the resulting publicity, is not an option. Thus you may have to take what is termed executive action. Are you happy about that? I may say that no such action is ever to be undertaken without reference to me first.'

'I understand that, sir. And am grateful for it.'

'Yes,' the brigadier said drily. 'Very good.' He pushed a piece of paper across his desk. 'There is the address of your office, which will also be your quarters. It is not in a military establishment or in the most salubrious part of London, but your landlady and your staff know what you are about.'

'I have a staff, sir?'

'You have a secretary. You will need her. I may say that she is fully trained in this line of work.'

'May I ask how this lady fits into the secrecy set-up?'

'She is the one exception to the rule, apart from myself, of course. Obviously she will have to know what's going on. But as I say, she is utterly trustworthy. In addition to Sergeant Cartwright, you will find the office fully equipped. However, in the first instance, you will attend MI HQ for briefing, and you will have to take some special courses. I'm sorry there can't be more time. But you must do the best you can. Lieutenant de Gruchy will report to you in one week from today.'

'Yes, sir. Did you say Sergeant Cartwright?'

'Well, she holds a military rank, of course. Now, your cover. You are not in uniform because you are medically unfit for service. The medical certificate is at your office. Get yourself a civilian suit, today. You do not have a job, but are living on a small inheritance left to you by a doting grandmother. You are writing a novel.'

'Sir?'

'Don't you want to write a novel?'

'I have never considered it, sir.'

'Well, perhaps the idea will grow on you. Especially as you do not actually have to do it. Now listen very carefully. Your password is Sterling, which is also your cover name. Anyone who approaches you and does not use that word is to be treated as a potential enemy. Any communication from me that does not carry that word is spurious. And if you wish to contact me, you may, at this number.' Another piece of paper slid across the desk. 'Memorize that and then burn it. And remember that you will only be connected after use of the password. Questions?'

'You are suggesting that I am to be virtually incommunicado. What about my family.'

The brigadier glanced at the file. 'You're not married.'

'But I have parents. And two sisters.'

'In Worcester. Where you have just spent four weeks' convalescent leave. If you were to be returned to regular duties and sent overseas you would probably not see them again for a couple of years. You may see your family, whenever you are given leave. But as far as they are concerned, you have again been seconded to the staff, and your job is to assist in drawing up plans for the eventual return of a British army to the continent. That is actually not a lie. But these plans are necessarily top secret, as I am sure your parents will understand. There is one thing more. Do not buy your new suit in Savile Row. Remember at all times that you are a struggling unemployed author. Good day to you.'

James felt in a distinct daze. Everything he had been told in such a rush needed careful assimilation, and there were so many things he was sure he had not been told, or remembered to ask. But overlying everything was a sense of exhilaration, even if he was apparently going to be shacked up with a female NCO; the word 'sergeant' conjured up a vision of a large, formidable forty-year-old. This was to be real intelligence work, as opposed to interrogating prisoners who knew very little, or trying to draw accurate conclusions from indistinct photographs. And he would be 'handling' – what an evocative word – the three most attractive women he had ever met – even if at a distance.

He found himself humming a tune as he walked along the

street, and was taken totally by surprise when someone said, 'Holy shitting cows. You!'

He turned, sharply, to look at the woman who had suddenly appeared beside him. Joanna Jonsson!

Five

First Blood

'I thought it was you,' Joanna said. 'Couldn't believe my eyes. So you survived Dunkirk.'

'Along with more than three hundred thousand others.' Once again his brain was in a whirl. 'What are you doing here?'

'You know something? I'm asking myself that all the time. But seeing you . . . You're in Military Intelligence, aren't you?'

'I was,' James said cautiously.

'But you know people, right? Listen, we need to talk.'

'Ah. I'm afraid—'

'Okay. So you don't like me. But you like Liane, right?'

'Is she all right?'

'That depends on what you mean by all right.'

'For God's sake. What happened? Did you get back to Paris all right?'

'It's not something we can talk about on the street. Let's have lunch.'

James considered. He was under orders to report to MI HQ for briefing and urgent training, and then to disappear. He couldn't do that with this enlarged edition of Veronica Lake cluttering up his life. He should turn her down, and in such a fashion that she wouldn't come back. On the other hand, he was desperate to find out what had happened to Liane, and he could justify following this up: even if she didn't yet know it, Liane, as Pierre's sister, was already in what might be termed his control. If anything had happened to her he needed to know, before Pierre returned to France. And if he was going to disappear, finding out what Joanna had to say had to be done now, before anything else. 'Fine,' he said. 'I know a little restaurant—'

'I know a better one. The hotel where I'm staying. The Dorchester.'

James gulped. 'I can't possibly afford the Dorchester.'

'Don't be a drip. It's on me.' She waved at a taxi.

'You ever met Joe Kennedy?' Joanna asked as they had an aperitif, which, needless to say, was a champagne cocktail.

'I'm afraid American ambassadors seldom come into contact with junior British army officers. Or even senior ones. But you do, I take it.'

'He's a shit. Mom always said he's a shit. A pumped-up Irish nouveau riche, she always said. He reckons you guys are going to lose this war, you know.'

'Everyone is entitled to their opinion. Does Mr Kennedy have anything to do with Liane?'

'Let's order. What do you fancy?'

'My French isn't all that good. Why don't you choose for me?'

'Sure.' She did so. 'And do you have any Gruchy?' she asked the wine waiter.

'Of course, madam.' He opened the list.

Joanna ignored it. 'The '14.'

'Ah . . .' He looked dubious, and glanced at James.

'So we like good wine. We'll have two of them.'

'As you wish, madam.' He withdrew.

'Do I gather this is an expensive wine?' James asked.

'The '14 is the best. Something over a hundred pounds a bottle.'

'Did you say—'

'What the hell. If we don't drink it, someone else will. Quit worrying. I charge all my personal spending to Mom. She likes to know what I'm at. Where was I? Oh, yes, Joe Kennedy. Do you know what he said to me?'

'I'm afraid not,' James said, still trying to get his brain under control.

'He said the same thing as Bill Bullitt in Paris. You don't have a leg to stand on, he said. You shouldn't have been where you were, and you say the guys who did it were punished for something else. I'm sorry about your brother, but like you, he simply shouldn't have been there. The best thing you can do is go home and try to forget about it. He never did like Mom.'

'I gather the feeling is mutual. Will you please tell me what this is all about?'

They were called to the table, and got to work on their oysters. 'We were raped,' Joanna said. 'Liane and me. At least a dozen times each.'

James choked; he had never eaten oysters before, and it took several waiters several minutes to restore his breathing, while it seemed that every other diner had stopped eating to observe what was going on. 'Monsieur needs to be careful,' said the maître d'.

'Look, push off, will you,' Joanna suggested. 'You okay?'

James wiped tears from his eyes. 'No. Tell me what happened.'

Joanna did so. 'Hell,' she finished, 'it wasn't as if we were first-timers, but it was still a shitty experience. And coming on top of Aubrey . . .' Tears rolled out of her eyes and she dried them with her napkin.

'How did Liane take it?'

Joanna shrugged. 'She seems able to absorb everything. But underneath . . . I wouldn't care to be one of those soldiers if they ever ran into her again, when the odds were even.'

'You said they were executed.'

'For desertion, not rape. And then, those Gestapo thugs . . .'

'You were arrested by the Gestapo?'

'Not arrested. I reckon those guys had been told to talk us out of bringing any charges. Boy, were they the pits.'

'They didn't . . .'

'They didn't torture us, physically, if that's what you mean. But they sure put us under pressure. And the way they looked at us . . . That Biedermann, I reckon he's another guy who doesn't ever want to run into Liane on a dark night. So listen . . .' Joanna carved her rack of lamb with some power, while her drooping hair threatened to trail in the gravy. 'I want to do something about it. And don't give me any shit about being a neutral. My neutrality ended at Auchamps.'

'Just what did you have in mind?' James was still trying to accept the unacceptable: Liane being raped, again and again!

'How's about bumping off Hitler? He's the guy responsible for all of this, right?'

'He's a little difficult to get at.'

'Not for me. I have an American passport. I also have a Swedish passport. I can come and go anywhere in Europe. Anywhere in the world.'

James gazed at her. 'You're serious.'

'You bet. You ever been raped? Or seen your kid brother shot up before your eyes?'

'I don't have a kid brother,' James said absently. He couldn't believe what he was hearing. But of course she *was* serious. What she was saying was quite true. She did have access to German-occupied Europe. And she was dead keen. But that was the trouble: she was too keen, too brittle. She'd crack at the first setback. Or would she?

'So what about it? Will you guys give me a gun, or some gelignite to stuff in my knickers?'

'Do you have any idea what your Gestapo friends would do to you if you were found to be a British agent?'

'You don't reckon they've already done it?'

'What you suffered was kid glove stuff. But if you're really keen . . . How long are you staying in England?'

'How long do you want me to stay?'

'What about your mother and father?'

'I've written them. Kennedy thinks I should go home, but the day I take *his* advice I'll have my head examined. You mean you can help me?'

'I can't. But maybe there's someone who can.'

*   *   *

110

'You'll be Mr Sterling,' Mrs Hotchkin announced.

'Right first time,' James said, with more confidence than he actually felt. His new suit was definitely off the peg, and his new shoes weren't all that good a fit either; his uniform had been abandoned at his club. In addition, Mrs Hotchkin, short and stout with frizzy hair and a distinct moustache, was very far from his concept of a female MI operative.

She, on the other hand, was totally confident. 'You'll find everything you need up there,' she said. 'There's a gas ring, too. Only for heating water, mind. They told me you'd be taking your meals out.'

'Yes. There was something about a secretary . . .'

'She's up there now.' Mrs Hotchkin gave him an old-fashioned look.

'Is she, well, all right?'

Mrs Hotchkin sniffed. 'That's for you to judge.'

'Then I'd better go up. By the way, is there a Mr Hotchkin?'

'He didn't come back. From Dunkirk. You know about that?'

'I came back.' He couldn't be sure whether she was pleased or sorry about that.

He opened the door and there was a startled flurry of movement. The young woman had been sitting at the desk. Now she hastily stood up, falling over the chair as she did so. This caused her horn-rimmed spectacles to slide off her nose, to be retrieved after some disjointed fielding practice. 'Oops! Mr Barron? I mean, Sterling. Rachel Cartwright. Reporting for duty, sir! Only I'm already here.' She giggled.

James placed his two suitcases on the floor and closed the door. 'Simmer down. I'm not going to bite you.' Although he felt that might be a most pleasurable experience: with her fruity accent and her obviously expensive clothes she had to be about the most attractive female sergeant in the army. Rachel Cartwright was tall and extremely slender; she could almost be described as thin. This also applied to her features, although they were handsome enough; the glasses

111

actually suited her by creating an aspect of width. She had black hair, presently confined in a tight bun, although he got the impression that it might be quite long. He put her age down as early twenties, and felt extremely relieved that his brief but exciting acquaintance with the Gruchy girls had given him a certain immunization against upper-class chic, even if right now he did not dare think about the Gruchy girls, or at least one of them. But what this English equivalent was doing in a top-secret job would have to be discovered, just as rapidly as possible.

'I'm just trying to put things in order,' she explained. Her voice was breathless.

'Brilliant. Just what do we have?'

'Well, there's the desk, and the filing cabinet. There doesn't appear to be anything in it at the moment. And there's the telephone, and that typewriter, and the radio set.' She indicated the rather large piece of equipment on a table against the far wall. 'Do you know about radios, sir?'

'Some.'

'I am a qualified operator,' she said proudly.

'I'm told you're a sergeant. In the ATS?'

'Yes, sir. But seconded for special duties.'

'I see. How long have you been in the service?'

'I joined up last October, sir.'

'And were seconded?'

'In January, sir.'

A month before himself. 'You must have special talents. Tell me some of them.'

'They sent a circular round, asking for volunteers for the service, so I did.'

'And were accepted, just like that.'

'I had to go to training school for six weeks.'

'And passed with flying colours.'

'Well . . .' She took off her glasses, polished them, and replaced them.

'You'll have to do better than that. It is essential for me to be able to trust you.'

'Well . . .' She wrinkled her nose. 'I suppose Daddy had something to do with it.'

'Daddy being?'

'General Cartwright, sir. Sir Harold.'

'Good God!' He had actually met Sir Harold Cartwright, very briefly, when the great man had made a brief tour of Flanders the previous November.

'Sir?'

'I'm flattered. So you know all about it.'

'About what, sir?'

'What we're about.'

'I know nothing, sir. This is my first individual assignment.'

'Come again?'

'I was in the pool, sir. Then the day before yesterday, I was told to wear civvy clothes, report to this address, where I would be under the orders of a Mr Barron. Sterling.'

'Nothing else?'

'Well . . .' Her tongue came out and touched her upper lip. 'I was told that I should do whatever Mr Barron-ah, Sterling, required, without question.'

They gazed at each other. Then James said, 'So we appear to be jointly starting from scratch. However, we are both going to have a great deal to do in another week or so. What else have we got?'

Rachel considered for a moment. 'Well, that's about it, in here. Through here . . .' She crossed the floor and opened an inner door. 'The bedroom. It has its own bathroom,' she added, apparently surprised at that.

James stepped past her to inspect his domestic quarters, surveyed the single bed. 'Where do you sleep?'

'I'm in an ATS hostel. It's about half a mile away.'

'But you come in every day.'

'I come in whenever you require me, sir. Day or night.'

Once again they gazed at each other. 'Wearing civilian clothes,' James remarked. 'Don't your comrades ask questions?'

'They know I am on special assignment, sir.'

'I see. Well, it all looks very cosy. I'm sure we'll get along very well.' He looked at his watch: ten past six. 'I'd like you to unpack that suitcase out there. Use separate files for the codes, maps and references, countries, and have others ready for each agent.'

'Do we have any agents, sir?'

'We will, shortly.'

'Yes, sir.' She returned to the office, and he unpacked his personal gear. By the time he was finished she was standing in the doorway. 'All done? Then I think you can go home now. I'll see you in the morning. Eight o'clock.'

'Oh. Yes, sir. But . . . can't I do something for you now? A cup of tea? There's a gas ring.'

'Not tonight, thank you, Sergeant. I'll sample your tea tomorrow.'

'Very good, sir. Tomorrow. Eight o'clock.' She closed the door behind herself.

James wondered if she was going to be a problem in view of the difference in their social status, and again was grateful for his brief glimpse into how the other half lived. But this was different. He was not being thrown into her world; she had voluntarily entered his. Something to be considered. But he had work to do. He picked up the phone, gave the number. 'Hello,' he told the woman who answered. 'I'd like to have a meeting with the brigadier. Name of Sterling.'

'Miss Jonsson is expecting you, sir,' the reception clerk said. 'She said for you to go right up. Number thirty-seven. That's the third floor, sir.'

'Thank you.' James was wearing uniform, as he had worn uniform to lunch the previous week. At this stage there was nothing wrong in appearing as Joanna's boyfriend. But he felt uneasy, as he had done from the moment of their first meeting. She was such an unpredictable woman. On the other hand, it was now his business to make her predictable, at least for his purposes.

'James! You look a treat.'

'So do you.' She was framed in the doorway of what he realized at a glance was a suite, wearing a dress and looking as if she had just left a Buckingham Palace garden party.

'Do we kiss?' she asked. 'Or is that improper now you're my boss?'

He closed the door. 'I'm not your boss yet.'

'Oh, shit. Your people won't have me?'

'We have to talk about it.'

'Well, that's something, I guess. But say, if you're not yet the boss . . .' She put her arms round his neck and kissed him, very slowly and deeply. 'I've wanted to do that since the moment we met.' She peered at his expression. 'I guess English girls don't do things like that.'

'I didn't know American girls did, either. And . . . well . . .'

'You're in love with Madeleine, and you have the hots for Liane. She told me you'd had a session. She's quite fond of you, too. Drink?' James was speechless, which she took as a yes. 'I'm afraid it's only champagne. There doesn't seem to be anything else worthwhile to drink in this goddamned country. No one knows how to make a proper martini: they don't put any gin in it.' She sat beside him on the sofa. 'So what's the deal?'

'I've spoken with my boss. He thinks it might be possible to use you. But there are certain things you have to understand, and certain rules you have to obey.'

'I've never been too good on rules.'

'No rules, no way.'

'So tell me about it.'

'Rule number one: get rid of any ideas about killing Hitler, or anyone else.'

'Isn't that what it's all about?'

'Winning the war is what it's all about. Once we've done that, we can sort out the details.'

'So what do I do?'

'We can use you as a courier.'

'You have got to be joking. That's going to win the war?'

'Yes. We have certain agents within Nazi-occupied territory. These people are gathering information which is essential for our future victory. Their problem is how, safely, to get that information back to us. You are able to go in and out as you please. Your job will be to meet these people, collect what they have, and bring it back to us.'

'Big deal.'

'It may turn out to be a much bigger deal than you can possibly imagine. You want to remember that from the Nazi point of view you will be a spy, and that could turn out very badly for you if you were to be indiscreet enough to be caught.'

'So I'm discreet. How do I know these guys?'

'They'll know you. You, and they, will be given a password.'

'Real cloak and dagger stuff. When do I go?'

'Not for a few weeks. If you're going to work for us, you have to be trained. You'll spend the next four weeks at one of our training establishments.'

'Does that mean no booze? Four weeks? Shit!'

'You don't have to sign on.'

'Oh . . . okay. Suppose I go along with this. What am I doing in Europe, anyway?'

'Your job. Reporting for your paper.'

'Do they know about this?'

'Not yet. But your cover story has got to be impeccable. You will write to your editor today and tell him that you think there are some good stories to be had over here and you intend to have them.'

'What happens if he says no dice and tells me to come home?'

'We'll find you another newspaper. Maybe a Swedish one.'

She considered. 'You know, there's a hell of a lot more to this than meets the eye.'

'That's why we'd like you to consider very carefully before coming in.'

'Oh, I wouldn't miss it for the world. There's just one more thing. If I'm going back to France, can I look up the de Gruchys? They'd find it kind of odd if they discovered I was in the country and hadn't given them a shout.'

'By all means look them up. But—'

'Not a word about what I'm really at. Okay. I'm on board. When do I go to this training camp or whatever?'

'Tomorrow. I'll pick you up at dawn.'

'Dawn? That's a bit much.'

'You're in the army now. Oh, by the way, you realize you'll have to take oaths of allegiance and secrecy.'

'Allegiance? Mom'll throw a fit. She doesn't go all that much for Limeys.'

'She'll be proud of you at the end.'

'Yeah, well . . . You staying for lunch? Sounds as if it'll be my last bang-up meal for a while.'

'Sorry. I must be on my way.'

'You mean officers don't lunch with the GIs. How about sleeping with them?' He gazed at her and she pushed hair from her eyes. 'You can't blame me for being anxious,' she pointed out. 'You've managed to scare the pants off me with all that talk about how serious this is, so you may as well take advantage of the situation. I'm a better lay than Liane, too. She's too bossy.'

Suddenly she looked quite forlorn. He squeezed her hand. 'I'll see you tomorrow. Dawn.'

He had lunch at his club and changed into his civilian suit before returning to his rooms. 'First, agent files,' he told Rachel.

'Yes, sir.' She sat, notebook and pencil poised, and copied down what he had to say without comment until he was finished. Then she said, 'Forgive me, sir. But is this lady a friend of yours?'

'So is Pierre de Gruchy.'

'Do they know what they're risking?'

'De Gruchy does, certainly. Jonsson . . . well, I've told

her sufficient times. She suffers from an immortality com-
plex.'

'And how do you feel about using your friends in such a
business? Or shouldn't I ask that?'

'You shouldn't ask that. But if it's any comfort to you, I was
given the job of monitoring them just because they're friends
of mine. Now get those typed up and the files opened, then
lock them away.'

'Yes, sir.'

He wished he could be sure of the intonation in her voice.

'Do you know the last time I was up at this hour?' Joanna
asked as she got into the back of the car beside James. The
military chauffeur was squeezing her rather large suitcase into
the boot. 'What is this little thing, anyway?'

'It is known as a Wolseley. As for your first question, I
shudder to think. All set?' The car was already moving away
from the hotel forecourt to swing on to Park Lane.

'I'm scared stiff, if you must know. I would have called
you to say forget it, but I didn't have a number.'

'You can still say forget it. But this is the last time.'

'Oh, what the hell. Just tell me what they're going to
do to me.'

'The idea is to turn you into an ice-cold, emotionless,
efficient, and utterly ruthless British agent.'

'Do I want to be all of those things? Or any of them?'

'Do you want to survive to dance on Hitler's grave? Or at
least this fellow Biedermann's?'

She brooded for a few minutes as they left Westminster
behind. 'Just promise me there won't be any funny business.'

'I'm not sure what you mean.'

'Well, like cutting off my hair.'

'Good God, no. Your hair, your looks, are amongst your
principal assets.'

'You mean you actually think I'm good-looking?'

'I have eyes.'

'But you don't like me.'

'Personal feelings have nothing to do with appreciation of beauty. But I do like you. We got off to a bad start. Now you belong to me.'

'Say, I like the sound of that.'

'When you have been accepted,' he hastily added as she began to slide across the seat towards him. 'And what I mean is, when you have been accepted, I become responsible for you, at all times. We're going to be spending quite a lot of money making you into what we want. So we want you to survive, and make it all worthwhile.'

'You should have been a schoolmaster,' she remarked, sliding back across the seat, folding her arms, and appearing to go to sleep.

Joanna woke up when they swung through the gates of a large country house. 'Looks like a school.'

'Many a true word is spoken in jest,' he agreed.

'I hope you're kidding.'

The car stopped and the chauffeur opened the door for her. James walked at her side up the wide steps while the driver followed with her suitcase. The front doors had been opened for them by a trim young woman, hair in the required bun, wearing khaki with the three stars of a captain on her shoulder straps, and carrying a clipboard to which was attached a sheet of paper covered in notes. 'Major Barron,' James explained.

'Oh, yes. The commandant is expecting you. And this is . . . ?' She looked at her paper.

'Joanna Jonsson,' Joanna said.

'Jonsson, yes. Will you follow me, please.' The hall was wide and high-ceilinged, with a flight of stairs rising beside the right-hand wall, but their guide led them past the stairs to a door, on which she knocked before opening it. 'Major Barron, ma'am.'

She stood back to allow them to enter. The woman behind the desk rose and came round it to greet him. She was short and a trifle plump, but like her aide wore uniform, in her case with the crown and crossed swords of a colonel. Her face

119

was pleasant enough, and she smiled at them, but her eyes remained detached. 'Major.' She shook hands. Then she turned to Joanna. 'And you are an American, I believe.'

'That's right.'

The commandant took in the quality and cut of the dress, the expensive shoes. 'It is heart-warming to have our overseas cousins rallying to our aid,' she remarked. 'I am informed, Major, that this is a rush job.'

'We are a little pushed for time, ma'am.'

'What were you thinking of?'

'Well . . . four weeks?'

'That *is* a rush job. We have a lot to do. As I am sure do you.'

'Ah . . . yes, of course. I'll say goodbye, Jonsson. We'll meet again in four weeks. I hope.' He saluted, and followed the waiting captain out of the room.

Joanna stared after him, for the first time in her life utterly speechless. Her brain seemed to have solidified just as her knees were threatening to turn to water. She had been abandoned, in this . . . establishment. 'We're not actually going to eat you,' the commandant said, returning behind her desk and sitting down. Joanna cast a hopeful glance at the other chairs in the room, but she was not invited to sit. 'But to fulfil the major's requirements we are going to have to work you pretty hard. This we shall do, to the best of our ability, but you should know that we are a recent and still small establishment. This time last year, that a place like this might ever be necessary had not crossed anyone's mind. This means that we are still feeling our way, and that we have limited resources. That in turn means that we will require the utmost cooperation from you. Everyone here is a volunteer. There is no coercion. But there must be discipline and a desire to work, and succeed. Do you understand that?'

'Makes sense.'

'You will address me as "ma'am", and confine your comments to "yes" and "no", unless required to say more.'

Joanna gulped. 'Yes, ma'am.'

'Good. Now, I am not going to pry into your background, and whatever it is, I do not wish you to divulge it to any of your fellow students. You are about to engage in a highly secret occupation. Keeping your own secrets may mean the difference between life and death. So, your ability to do that starts now, and will be assessed as part of your course. Nor will you ask any questions of any of your comrades. No one is permitted to inquire into the background, or current status, of any other student. Breaking this rule can lead to instant dismissal.'

'Yes, ma'am.'

'Very good. Now, whatever your background is' – again she eyed the expensive clothes – 'I wish you to understand that every student here is regarded as equal. Any attempt to project superiority, whether by birth or wealth, will not only make you very unpopular with your fellows, but will be noted in your record. I don't know what you have brought with you, but I suggest that you leave it locked away for the duration of your stay. You will be provided with all the necessary clothes, and it goes without saying that we do not use either jewellery or make-up. Are there any questions?'

Yes, Joanna thought: how the hell do I get out of here? But she had volunteered, she really wanted to hit back at the bastards who had murdered Aubrey and raped her, and she was damned if she was going to be defeated by any bunch of Limey bastards. So she said, 'No, ma'am.'

'Very good. Captain Lennox will show you to your quarters and give you your schedule.'

'Yes, ma'am. Do I salute you?'

'In our army, Jonsson, no one salutes unless one is wearing uniform and a hat. You may close the door.'

'Yes, ma'am.'

Joanna stopped outside, closed the door, and faced Captain Lennox, who smiled at her. 'Her bark is worse than her bite, providing you don't step out of line.' Joanna looked at her suitcase, which had been placed in the hall by the chauffeur. 'I'm afraid you will have to lift that yourself,' Lennox said. 'Up those stairs.'

Joanna began the ascent. 'The boss said something about a schedule.'

'You will have one. But it's easy to remember. You rise at five.'

'Say again?'

'Five, Jonsson. That will be followed by a ten-mile run. Then showers and breakfast.'

'Don't tell me: the showers are cold.'

'Of course. This is not a hotel. Then three classes: politics, cyphers and survival. Then PT. Then lunch. After lunch, weapons training, followed by psychological assessments and unarmed combat. Then French.'

'I already speak French.'

'Then you'll find it easy. Then there is an hour's social gathering. Then supper. Then bed. Lights out, ten o'clock.'

'So that we can be up again at five.'

'That's right.'

'Holy fucking shit!'

'What did you say?'

'Sounds real fun. Ma'am.'

James returned to his club, changed into civilian clothes, and took a bus to within a quarter of a mile of his lodgings, then walked the rest of the way. He felt a remarkable sense of guilt as he wondered just what he had sent Joanna to. She had volunteered, of course, and if he was still not sure of either her commitment or her self-control, he had to believe that the training school would either dissolve those doubts or return her as unusable material. Besides, he reminded himself, he didn't even like the woman. He didn't like her flamboyant lifestyle, her confidence, her sexual projection, her wealth . . . Or were those all aspects of jealousy? Well, he could put her out of his mind for a month.

It was the thought of what had happened to Liane that was really upsetting him, as much by Joanna's careless comment that she had not been a virgin as by the event itself. Of course he knew she had not been a virgin when she had come to his bed on the night before the wedding, but that had been acceptable and even reassuring. The idea that she might somehow in the future devote herself to him had only developed on that crazy drive that had turned out so disastrously. Now the thought of her being savagely mistreated by several men made his blood boil. And there was nothing he could do about it, save involve her brother in yet more danger, which could well involve her as well. And Madeleine? But Madeleine had to be forgotten, on all of those counts. 'There's a visitor upstairs,' Mrs Hotchkin informed him. 'He had the password.'

'Is Miss Cartwright in?'

'Oh, yes. She's up there with him. What do you think of all them raids? Think Jerry's on his way?'

'Not if he sticks to bombing Wales.' James went up the stairs.

'James.' Pierre embraced him.

'You're early.'

'My training is complete and I am ready to go.'

'Excellent. I gather you have met my assistant?'

Rachel stood on the other side of the room. 'He had the password, sir.'

'Of course. He's the gentleman in your file. Sit down, Pierre. Rachel, perhaps you could make some tea.'

'Right away, sir.' She bustled off.

Pierre sat before the desk. 'Charming girl. So what happens now?'

'You have a passage on a ship for Lisbon, leaving Southampton on Friday night. Once there, you will find your way into France.' He opened the filing cabinet, took out various papers. 'Here is a list of people who will assist you on the way. This must be memorized and destroyed.'

Pierre nodded. 'What do I tell my family when I get to Paulliac?'

'They're your family. But you want to remember that everything you tell them about what you are doing may be dangerous for them. The important thing is for your father to appoint you to his Paris office. I don't know how much you will have to tell him to secure that position. For the rest, I recommend that you stick to your cover story that after the disintegration of the French army you went into hiding, got into Vichy, and have finally come home. You know, I suppose, that Bordeaux, the entire Gironde area, is in the Nazi-occupied zone?'

Pierre nodded, and regarded Rachel as she placed cups of tea in front of them, and then seated herself at the typing desk. 'I will handle it. And after I get to Paris?'

'Behave normally, do your job, sell wine to German officers, and if possible drink it with them, watch, listen and record. From time to time you may be contacted by other agents; accept them and their information, as long as they use our password.'

'I understand. How do I get this information back to you?'

'You have the radio equipment?' Pierre nodded. 'And you know how to set it up?'

'I have just been trained to do that.'

'Excellent. We wish you to listen to the radio at pre-arranged times on these frequencies. Rachel.' Rachel gave Pierre the slip of paper. 'That too must be memorized and destroyed,' James said. 'The calls will come from this office and be made by either Rachel or myself, but although you may recognize our voices, they must always be accompanied by the password.'

Pierre nodded. 'As I must use the word when I call you.'

'You must also use your number: GW1.' Pierre raised his eyebrows, and James grinned. 'Gruchy wine, right?'

'I see. Do I use English?'

'You are not to call us, except in the most dire emergency. The Germans will be able to trace such calls if they are too frequent or they are given sufficient time. If you have to call, yes, use English. But you must never use any name save Sterling.'

'But how do I get my information to you?'

'By courier. She will contact you. In about five weeks' time.'

'Did you say she?'

'Yes. I am going to break a rule here, Pierre, but I think it is necessary, because I don't want you to be so surprised that you may say, or do, something stupid. Your courier will be Joanna Jonsson.'

Slowly Pierre put down his cup. 'You will have to explain this.'

'Briefly, she came to England and volunteered.'

'Just like that?'

'We didn't inquire into her motives,' James lied.

'And you accepted her? My dear James, she is an absolute fly-by-night. She can no more keep a secret than she can fly to the moon.'

'We accepted her because she is a natural. She can come and go from occupied Europe without hindrance. As for keeping a secret, she is being trained now.'

'Does she know I am her contact?'

'No. She won't know that until she has completed her training and is ready to go into the field. Now listen. The information you give her will be in cypher. She is to bring it here, not understand it. Rachel.'

Rachel produced the book and a map. James unfolded the map.

'This grid covers all of France, including Vichy. When you wish to indicate any area, you just quote the cross-reference. The only matching grid in existence is in this office. It goes without saying that that book and that map are now your most valuable possessions. If at any time you feel you can no longer carry on, they must be destroyed. Hopefully you will be able to let us know you are doing this.'

Pierre placed the documents in his pocket. 'You mean I must do this if I am in danger of arrest by the Gestapo.'

'I'm afraid it is a possibility that must be considered. Should it happen, or should we ever suspect that it is likely to happen, the code and the map will immediately be replaced by a fresh set.'

'And if it turns out to be a false alarm?'

'The new material will be brought to you as rapidly as possible, by courier.'

'By Joanna, you mean.' He shook his head. 'I still don't like the idea of using her. How did she get to England, anyway?'

'As I said, as a wealthy neutral she can come and go as she pleases.'

'But she was with Liane. Did they get safely back to Paris? Did she have any news of the rest of the family?'

'No,' James lied again. 'Only that your mother and father are back in Paulliac.'

'Yes. Well . . .' He stood up. 'I will say goodbye, and hope that you are right in your judgement. Mademoiselle, it has been a pleasure.' He closed the door behind himself.

'What a handsome man,' Rachel remarked.

'You should see his sisters.'

'And they are all friends of yours? Aren't you the least bit worried about what may be going to happen to them?'

'What I would like you to do,' James said, 'is take this five-pound note, go out, and buy a bottle of scotch. Then bring it back here, and you and I are going to get drunk together.'

The sound of the doorbell awoke Liane de Gruchy. She had spent most of the past month in bed, and a good proportion of that asleep; she supposed the most important part of her life had been the bottle of sleeping pills that she kept always within reach.

She had only got up to prepare her meals, and once a week go to the bank, draw some money, and buy some food. For all that time she had not been in contact with her family; but she had called, once, at the Paris office, and old Henri Brissard, the manager, had told her they were all right and had gone down to Paulliac. At least, some of them. He had told her that Amalie, after a spell with her in-laws in Dieppe, had also joined the family in Paulliac. This was undoubtedly because both Henri and Pierre had gone missing after the rout of the French and British armies in the north. Poor Henri, poor Pierre. If they weren't dead they were prisoners of war.

Although she had not asked him to do so, she had no doubt that Brissard had informed her parents that she was all right, and the fact that her allowance was still deposited as regularly as always told her that the business also had to be all right. She knew she should obtain the necessary permits and go down to Paulliac. But she kept telling herself that could wait. She refused to accept that *she* might be suffering a prolonged nervous breakdown, perhaps the more prolonged because it had been delayed until she had returned to Paris. She had thought that of Joanna, but Joanna was far away by now, either in the States or Sweden, clear of anyone who could be associated with their ordeal. Perhaps she should have gone with her, after all.

But that would have meant abandoning everything she valued in life, every precious item that was here in her flat with her. Moreover, as Joanna had appeared determined to publicize what had happened, it would have meant reliving those horrible two days, over and over again, to slavering, prurient officials and newsmen. That was unacceptable.

But it was even more unacceptable to face her own family right now. Papa would be utterly bewildered, because emotional matters always bewildered him. Mama would be angry, because mishaps overtaking her children always made her angry – and in her anger she might well do something stupid. Pierre, if he was alive, would be critical, because Pierre was always critical – of her, at least. Madeleine would be shocked, but at the same time, curious, because Madeleine was always curious about things she had not yet experienced – she kept begging her to tell her what it was like to have sex with a man. And Amalie, so innocent in her love for her husband, would burst into tears. She did not feel she could face any of that at this moment.

So she was waiting. She did not know for what. But she felt she would know when the moment arrived, the day when she felt ready to face the world. Until then, here in her flat, she had her own private world, with no intruders. Until now.

She got out of bed, put on a dressing gown – in the July heat

127

she was naked – and went into the lounge. She stood against the door. 'Who is it?'

'A friend, Mademoiselle de Gruchy.'

Liane frowned. The voice was familiar, but it was not French. 'Identify yourself.'

'I am from Chartres. I have news for you.'

Liane slipped the bolt, opened the door, and gazed at Werner Biedermann. For a moment she did not recognize him, because he wore civilian clothes, and her memory totally associated him with his black uniform. Then she tried to close the door again, but his foot was in the way, and a heave of his shoulder sent her staggering backwards across the room; she needed both her hands to keep her dressing gown closed.

Biedermann came into the lounge and closed the door behind himself, carefully slipping the bolt. 'What an entrancing sight you are, mademoiselle.'

'Get out,' Liane said.

Biedermann took off his hat and coat, laid them on a chair. 'That is not very hospitable of you. Do you not wish to know what I have to say to you? It concerns your family.'

'Then say it, and leave.'

'You are so brusque. Will you not offer me a drink? Cognac. I should like a glass of cognac.'

Liane stared at him for several seconds. Her brain was a jumble of conflicting emotions, of which hatred predominated. But she knew she had to keep herself under control. This man held all the high cards. Besides, he might have something of interest to tell her. She went to the sideboard and poured, gave him the glass, feeling his gaze scorching her legs as they slipped in and out beneath the dressing gown.

'Aren't you going to join me?' he asked.

'I do not drink at four o'clock in the afternoon. Perhaps later. If you will excuse me, I will get dressed.'

'But I like you the way you are, mademoiselle. Liane. You do not mind if I call you Liane?'

Liane shrugged. 'It is my name.'

'So, sit down, Liane.'

Liane hesitated, then sat in a chair on the other side of the room, keeping her knees pressed together.

'So,' Biedermann went on, 'if I give you some information about your family, you can give me some information on other matters.'

'What other matters? I have not left this flat for more than an hour at a time for the past month. I am sure you know that, Herr Captain.'

'I do, but that is not to say you do not have information. You are, or were, a friend of the prefect of Chartres, were you not?'

'Monsieur Moulin is a friend of my family, yes.'

'So much of a friend that he was willing to sacrifice himself for the sake of your reputation.'

Liane frowned. 'I do not understand you.'

'Well, you see, we approached him a week ago, and invited his cooperation. In view of the absurd accusations made by you and your American friend, we felt it would be best for all concerned if he were to issue a statement, made as an old friend of you and your family, that you, and she, were two mentally unstable young women whose claims could hardly be taken seriously. Do you know, he refused to do this.'

'Of course he would. He is an honourable man.'

'He is a very stupid man.'

'What have you done to him?'

'Well, we felt that he could be persuaded to change his mind, so we took him into custody.'

'You are a bastard. You are all bastards.'

Biedermann smiled. 'Do you know, he used that word as well. Only he screamed it as we crushed his testicles.' Liane gasped. 'Unfortunately,' Biedermann continued, 'when locked in his cell he was stupidly given a sharp knife with his evening meal, and this he used to cut his throat.'

'Jean is dead?' Liane's voice was high.

'Oh, we got to him in time. But he had to be placed in hospital to be stitched up. And do you know, he managed to escape.' Liane clapped her hands. 'I am glad you are pleased, mademoiselle. I would like you to remain pleased. So tell me, where is he now?'

'You expect me to know this?'

'For the moment he has disappeared. As all of this, all of the torment he has suffered, is on account of you, it seems obvious that he would come to you for help, or at least contact you.'

'Well he has not.'

'Again it is obvious that you would say that. Would you like me to take you down to headquarters? I, and my men, would find that most enjoyable. Of course I understand that you have no testicles to crush, but I am sure we will find many interesting bits of you to, shall I say, handle.' Liane felt her chest constricting even as her heart pounded violently. Her emotion was less fear than an almost convulsive anger at what this thug had done to Jean Moulin and was now threatening to do to her, all with the complete blessing of the law . . . Nazi law. 'Perhaps your sister has told you what it is like to be interrogated by the Gestapo,' Biedermann suggested.

Liane's head jerked. 'You have arrested my sister?'

'Did you not know? Oh, yes, she spent a couple of days in our custody. What a pretty child.'

'You . . .' Liane felt as if she was going to choke, but kept her voice under control with an effort. 'I have two sisters,' she said in a low tone.

'Of course you do. This was the younger one. The would-be Jewess. Did you not know of it?'

'You arrested Amalie? What crime can she possibly have committed?'

'A very serious crime. She struck a Gestapo officer on the head, so hard as to put him in hospital.'

'Amalie did that?' Liane had a strong temptation to clap again. 'What has happened to her?'

'She should have been executed. But your other sister appears to have some influence, and she was released without charge. It was very regrettable. Still, we left our mark upon her. I do not think she will ever be the same.'

'You are unspeakable,' Liane said, even as her brain went off into another spin. He had said that Madeleine had influence? How could Madeleine have any influence, except possibly with Jean, and if Jean was a fugitive, how could *he* have helped? But Amalie, sweet, innocent Amalie, in the hands of these brutes . . . Even her sometimes lurid imagination could take her no further.

'We have an eye for a pretty face,' Biedermann agreed. 'And even more, a handsome figure.' He allowed his gaze, slowly and deliberately, to roam up and down Liane's body; she hugged the dressing gown tighter. 'And in the case of someone who has aided and abetted the escape of a wanted enemy of the Reich, I do not think even a Wehrmacht officer would dare interfere.'

A Wehrmacht officer had helped Amalie, because of Madeleine? Madeleine knew no German officers. And in any event, she was in love with James Barron. But that was a question for the future. She had first to survive the present. 'I have told you that I have not seen or helped Monsieur Moulin in any way. I did not even know he had been arrested until you told me just now.'

'But how do we know what you have claimed is true? How can we know until we have investigated further, investigated you more closely?'

Liane stood up. 'I wish to telephone my lawyer.'

'We do not deal through lawyers, mademoiselle. However, it may be possible for *me* to assist *you*. If you were to cooperate with me, fully and in every way, I could perhaps consider allowing you to remain here, in your flat, under house arrest, while I, by conversation, you understand, endeavour to ascertain the truth of the matter.' Liane stared at him, now scarcely breathing. 'I see that you understand. So, take off your dressing gown.'

Liane drew a deep breath and let the dressing gown slip from her shoulders. She remembered that in Auchamps she had reflected that women only triumphed over men by a combination of beauty, charm and mystery. Never force, because they could not compete in terms of physical force. But for her,

131

only physical force was left, whatever the consequences. Force, combined with beauty and charm.

'Exquisite,' Biedermann said. 'To have you strapped to a frame while I applied electric charges to the most, shall I say, succulent parts of your body would be an unforgettable experience. But I am sure you are capable of providing some other unforgettable experiences first. Come here.'

'I would be better in bed,' Liane said in a low voice.

'Ha ha. I like that. Yes, it would be better in bed. I am sure you have a magnificent bed.' He stood up, followed her into the bedroom, undressing as he did so. He left his jacket on the chair, exposing his shoulder holster, which he now removed and draped over it. But she could not use the gun here; everyone in the building would hear the sound of the shot.

She went to the bedside table, her back to him, and expertly palmed the little bottle of sleeping tablets. Then she felt him behind her, his hands coming round her waist and then up to hold her breasts while his mouth nuzzled her neck, actually sucking her hair. 'Would you not like another glass of cognac?' she asked.

'If you will join me.'

'Get into bed.' She went into the lounge, looked around herself. She was, after all, abandoning her treasures. She sighed, filled two goblets and dissolved four of the tablets in one of them; a single tablet was sufficient to put her out for the night. Then she returned to the bedroom and sat beside him. 'Here is to an interesting future.'

They touched glasses and he drank deeply, as did she. 'This is excellent brandy,' he commented. 'Such a distinctive taste.'

'It is made in our own vats,' she said. 'Would you like me to order some for you?'

'I would like that, yes.'

Liane finished her drink, and he did the same, then he lay back, arms outstretched. She climbed on to the bed beside him.

My last ever fuck, she thought. What a shame it is that he has to die happy.

Six

The Fugitive

'Pierre?' Madeleine stared at her brother. 'Oh, Pierre.' She ran down the steps of the huge, rambling Gruchy mansion, situated on the banks of the Gironde several miles west of Paulliac, and threw her arms round the neck of the man who had just emerged from the trees that bordered the river. She was followed by three Alsatian dogs, all barking delightedly. 'But . . . what has happened to you? Where have you been?'

He kissed her again. 'Nothing has happened to me, save that I have lost weight. As to where I have been, that is a long story.'

'But those clothes . . . They look as if they have come off a scarecrow.'

'Who knows. Perhaps they did.'

'You poor boy. Let me take your rucksack.'

'I can manage. It would be too heavy for you anyway.'

It was certainly very large. Madeleine held his hand as they went up the steps. 'Mama!' she shouted. 'Pierre is home.'

Barbara de Gruchy came out of the doorway. 'Pierre. Oh, my God, Pierre.' She hugged her son while tears streamed down her cheeks. 'Jules!' she shouted at a gardener who had appeared. 'Get on your bicycle and ride to the combine. Tell Monsieur Albert that Pierre is home. Come inside, come inside. You look as if you could do with a square meal.'

'And a hot bath,' Madeleine said, wrinkling her nose. 'Amalie! Amalie! Look who's here.'

They were in the entry hall, and Amalie was standing on the grand staircase. 'Where is Henri?' she asked.

'Henri? I do not know where he is.'
'You were with him in the battle. Was he killed?'
'He was not killed in the battle. We were together after-wards. But then we became separated. I imagine he went to Dieppe, just as I have been making my way here.'
'You abandoned him.' Amalie went back up the stairs.
'Well, there's a welcome,' Pierre remarked.
'She's had a difficult time,' Madeleine said.

'I give you a toast, on this happiest of Bastille Days.' Albert de Gruchy stood at the head of the table and raised his glass. 'The family! Reunited.' His eyes gleamed with tears.
'Except for Liane,' Madeleine said.
'Where is Liane?' Pierre asked.
Madeleine could tell that he was happier than anyone to be home, wearing his own clothes, eating good food and drinking good wine, dining with his own family. As to where he had spent the last two months, how he had survived, he would no doubt tell them in his own time. But she also wished that Liane could have been here with them tonight.
'Liane is in Paris,' Barbara said, somewhat sharply. 'And appears to wish to stay there.'
'But she's all right? She's been in touch?'
'We have not heard a word from her since she drove off with you, and Henri, and those Americans, and that English officer, on the day the invasion started.'
'But . . . my God! Something must have happened to her.'
'Nothing has happened to her. We know she is all right because Brissard has seen her. She called at the office. And she has been drawing money regularly from her account. She just does not seem to wish to be in touch.'
'Haven't you tried to contact her?'
'We tried while we were in Chartres. But the phones were down. Now we cannot get permission to telephone from here.'
'We have written,' Albert said. 'But we do not know if she received our letters; there has never been a reply.'

'She is enjoying herself,' Amalie said, bitterly. 'Liane is always enjoying herself.'

'I think someone should go to Paris and see her,' Madeleine said, and looked at her parents. 'But they won't let me.'

'It is far too dangerous for a young woman to travel about the country, even if we could get permission,' Barbara said. 'When we think of what happened . . . well . . .' She flushed.

Pierre looked from face to face.

'Mama is referring to me,' Amalie said. 'I was arrested by the Gestapo.'

'Arrested? My God! But why?'

'I hit one of their people on the head.' Pierre stared at his sister with his mouth open. 'It was when they arrested Monsieur and Madame Burstein. Just for being Jews. I lost my temper.'

'But . . . you are here.'

'Madeleine's boyfriend got me out,' Amalie said, contemptuously.

Pierre looked at Madeleine. 'He is a friend,' she said, cheeks pink. 'Not a boyfriend.'

'A German?'

'He had to be German, or he could not have helped me.'

Pierre scratched his head.

'You know they arrested Jean Moulin?' Albert asked.

'What did *he* do?'

'I don't know. They just took him off, and he disappeared.'

'Well,' Pierre said, 'when I go to Paris, I will find out what happened to him. And I will visit Liane and give her a lecture.'

'You are going to Paris?' Barbara asked, concerned.

'Papa is sending me to take over the office there.'

Everyone looked at Albert. 'It is what he wants to do,' Albert mumbled, not meeting any of their eyes.

'So Papa's toast was an empty one,' Pierre remarked. He and Madeleine walked by the river, with the dogs. The morning mist was just starting to clear, but there was little traffic to be seen, save for a German patrol launch slowly making its way upstream.

'Five of us are here,' Madeleine protested.

'But there is no unity. Amalie is traumatized and miserable, desperate for news of Henri. It may be years before she gets over what has happened to her, if she ever does.'

'Do you think that Henri is dead?'

'It is very likely that he is. And if he is not dead, he is an outlaw, simply because he is a Jew. Liane has cut herself off from us. I suppose she is having a great time entertaining German officers. Mama is on the verge of a breakdown. And you . . .'

'I did what I had to do to save Amalie's life.'

'She does not seem to see it that way.'

'As you said, she is traumatized. And what right have you to criticize any of us? You are going to Paris to sell wine. Who are you going to sell it to, if not German officers? So you are doing it to save the business, keep us all from penury. I do not see how you can claim to be any different from any of us.'

He looked at her in a fashion she had never known before; she felt quite uneasy. Then he said, 'I must get back. The bus for Bordeaux leaves in an hour.'

She caught his hand. 'Pierre! Take me with you.'

'Why do you want to go to Paris?'

'I want to find out for myself what Liane is doing.'

'You mean you are afraid that if I find her sleeping with German officers I will beat her up?'

'Won't you?'

Another strange look. 'I can't take you with me. My travel permit is for me alone. I will let you know what I find, and we will discuss what to do.'

'Papa,' Madeleine said, entering the office. 'Did Pierre tell you what he was doing for those eight weeks?'

'It is his business. What matters is that he is here now.'

'But he is not here now. He is in Paris now. Or he will be tomorrow.'

'Well, he must have something to do. And Brissard is getting on.'

'But Pierre knows nothing about the business. He has been in the army since he left school.'

'He will learn quickly. Brissard will teach him.'

Madeleine knew he was lying. Her own father, lying? 'Don't you think he has changed?' she asked. 'He seems different. He does not smile anymore.'

'War, battle, does that to a man. I remember, from 1914.'

'You smile.'

'That is because my experience was a long time ago. I have got over it. So will Pierre, in time.'

'Will he be in trouble?'

Albert frowned. 'Why should he be in trouble?'

'Well . . . he's a deserter, isn't he?'

'A deserter?'

'If he had stayed with his regiment he would have been taken prisoner by the Germans. Those of our people who were taken prisoner are only now being released.'

'I do not know about that. And I do not care. Neither should you. Pierre is my son and your brother. That he is alive and well and back with us is all that matters, or should matter.'

'Yes, Papa.' Madeleine left the office and went on to the porch. It was a lovely summer's day, and never had she felt so discontented, so uneasy. Her life seemed to have escaped her. There was so much happening in the world, and she was doing nothing. She had no idea what she should do, or could do. Worse, she had no idea what she *wanted* to do. Whom she wanted to be with. She had found James Barron most attractive, because of his innocence, the wonder he had revealed at her surroundings, her aura, his so carefully practised manners – while understanding from their first meeting that had it not been for the sudden egalitarianism induced by the war she would never even have considered speaking with him. Now she did not even know if he was alive. She did know that, alive

137

or not, there was no likelihood of any British soldier setting foot on French soil again for the duration of the Reich, and according to Hitler that was going to last a thousand years.

But James Barron, if he was alive, was still fighting against the Nazis. Every true Frenchman, or Frenchwoman, had to respond to that, at least emotionally, even if the people in Vichy were denouncing this man de Gaulle as a traitor for refusing to accept his country's surrender. The point was, where did that leave Frederick? Supposing he ever did wish to see her again? Frederick was handsome, attractive, beautifully mannered, clearly in her own social class . . . but he was a Nazi, an enemy of her people and her country. Of herself.

Well, she supposed, like James, she was very unlikely ever to see him again either. And then stiffened as she watched a command car coming down the drive.

Her instincts told her that it was Frederick before he was close enough to be recognized. Then she nearly ran into the house. But she stood her ground, smoothing her dress as the car came to a halt, because now her instincts were warning her that this was not a social visit. Frederick was accompanied by a man, tall and thin and with a hatchet face, and not wearing uniform. Both got out, ignoring the barking, frisking dogs, and Frederick led the way up the steps. His greeting was warm enough. 'Madeleine! How good it is to see you again.' But his eyes were watchful. 'I would like you to meet Colonel Kluck of the Gestapo.'

Madeleine swallowed, but held out her hand. Kluck ignored it. 'Is your father at home?'

'Yes.'

'And your sisters?'

'My sister Amalie is here.'

'Summon them. And your mother.' Kluck walked into the hall.

Madeleine looked at Frederick, and received a quick nod. Alphonse the butler had now arrived, and she told him to call the family. 'If you will come into the drawing room, gentlemen,' she invited, and led the way. Her knees felt weak with apprehension, even if the presence of Frederick was reassuring. But it had to be something to do with Pierre. 'Would you like anything to drink?'

'No.' Kluck stood in front of the fireplace, and turned to face the room, drawing off his gloves.

'Later, perhaps,' Frederick said, gazing at her. She could read nothing in his expression, but at least one eyebrow twitched.

Albert hurried into the room, followed by Barbara. 'Gentlemen?'

'I wish to see your daughters,' Kluck said.

'This is my daughter,' Albert said.

'I wish to see the others.'

Albert turned to Alphonse, who had followed him into the room. 'Madame Burstein refuses to come down, monsieur,' Alphonse explained.

'Oh.' He turned back to the two officers. 'She is having a difficult time. Her husband died in the war.'

'I know of this woman,' Kluck said. 'I will speak with her later. I am looking for your other daughter.'

'Liane is in Paris,' Madeleine explained.

'We do not think she is any longer in Paris,' Kluck declared. 'We think she has come here. Or will shortly do so.'

'I wish she had come here,' Barbara said. 'We have not seen her or heard of her since May.'

'Why should she have left Paris?' Madeleine asked.

'I shall tell you, mademoiselle.'

Helsingen spoke sharply in German, and Kluck responded, equally sharply. Helsingen glared at him, then addressed Barbara. 'I think you should sit down, madame. You too, monsieur. And you, Madeleine.' The Gruchys sank into chairs.

'Your daughter has committed murder,' Kluck announced.

'What?!!' Albert shouted.

'Oh, my God!' Barbara moaned. Madeleine's brain went blank.

'She killed an associate of mine, a Captain Werner Biedermann, in the most cold-blooded manner.'

Madeleine looked at Helsingen. 'I'm afraid it appears to be true,' he said.

'Where did this happen?' Albert asked.

'In her Paris apartment, five days ago,' Kluck said. 'But her crime was only discovered two days ago, when Captain Biedermann's whereabouts were traced. As I have said, it was a most cold-blooded and premeditated crime. Your daughter lured Captain Biedermann to her apartment, plied him with drink, in which she had dissolved some sleeping tablets, had sexual relations with him' – Barbara gasped – 'and then, when he had fallen asleep, cut his throat. Following which she simply walked away, leaving him to rot. Quite literally.'

Barbara burst into tears. 'You cannot know this,' Madeleine cried. 'You were not there. He must have forced himself on her and she was defending herself.'

'Our forensic people have been able to reconstruct the crime almost completely, Fräulein. Captain Biedermann's clothes were found in the apartment lounge, undamaged and unstained by blood. This indicates that he undressed himself at leisure. Your daughter's dressing gown was also found in the lounge, undamaged and unstained. This indicates that she undressed of her own free will. There are no scratch marks or contusions on the captain's body to suggest that any resistance was offered to his advances. A post-mortem examination has revealed that he had a sexual discharge immediately before his death, and also found traces of a barbiturate substance in his bowels. The knife which cut his throat was a kitchen carver, and was wielded from behind by a right-handed person. This indicates that the captain offered no resistance to his murderer, which means that he was unconscious when he was killed.'

Barbara fanned herself vigorously. 'But the blood,' Albert said. 'There would have been blood everywhere.'

'There was indeed blood everywhere. Which further indicates your daughter's cold-blooded guilt. It would appear that when she had finished, she bathed herself in a large, hot tub. This is not the act of a panic-stricken or emotionally disturbed woman. However, she did not bother to clean the bath afterwards, and there are traces of blood around the plug hole and on the sides, sufficiently high to indicate, as I have said, that the tub was well filled when she sat in it.'

Madeleine clasped both hands to her neck. The vision of Liane, sitting in a tub full of bloody water, calmly washing herself clean minutes after killing a man, was mind-numbing. She did not dare look at Helsingen. 'Mademoiselle de Gruchy's acts on leaving the bath,' Kluck went on, 'are the most sinister of all. Captain Biedermann's pistol, his spare magazine, his papers, which included several blank travel documents and rail passes, as well as a considerable amount of German currency, are missing. And finally the concierge has told us that Mademoiselle de Gruchy left her apartment at seven o'clock in the evening Captain Biedermann died, carrying a valise. Since then she has vanished. However, one of the passes has been used, to indicate that she travelled south, openly, as far as Tours, before choosing to disappear. They are also not the actions of a distraught or frightened woman. So now she is on the loose, armed and dangerous, waiting to kill again. She must be found and brought to justice.'

'I can't believe Liane would do anything like that,' Barbara muttered.

'And you think she will come here?' Albert asked.

'I would say almost certainly. This is her home. You are her family. Here is security. I may tell you, Herr de Gruchy, that my first instinct was to place you, and all of your family, under arrest. However, Major von Helsingen has persuaded me not to do this, at this time. There are two reasons for this. One is that were you to be arrested, your daughter would never come here. The second is that Major von Helsingen assures me that you, and your family, will be willing to assist us in every way possible. I am making that assumption now. I would like you to understand that should your daughter come here, or should she contact you in any way, and you do not immediately inform us, you will be regarded as guilty of aiding and abetting an enemy of the state. And will suffer the same penalties.'

'Oh, my God. My God,' Barbara moaned.

'You do not wish to search the house?' Albert asked.

'I will not waste the time. I have no doubt that if she is here she will be adequately concealed. However, now that I have, shall I say, put you in the picture, I expect you to hand her over immediately.'

'She is not here,' Albert said.

'Then I look forward to hearing from you the moment she turns up. She will. Herr Major.'

Helsingen looked at Madeleine, eyebrows arched. Madeleine gave a hasty nod. 'I think I will stay here for a while, Herr Colonel,' Helsingen said. 'Perhaps you will send the car back for me this afternoon.'

Kluck shrugged. 'As you wish.' He left the room.

Albert and Barbara stared at the German officer. 'Is there something else?' Albert asked.

'Oh, Papa,' Madeleine said. 'This is Major von Helsingen. I told you, he is the man who made the Gestapo drop the charges against Amalie.'

'Then we are grateful to you, monsieur. But this business . . .' He paused, hopefully.

Helsingen sighed. 'I'm afraid I cannot hold out any hope in this case. There seems to be no possible doubt of Mademoiselle de Gruchy's guilt. But I can tell you the background to this tragedy. Your daughter is not a cold-blooded killer. At least she had a motive for what she did.'

'Because this man Biedermann *did* force himself on her,' Madeleine said.

'As the colonel said, there is no evidence of that. However, she underwent a most unfortunate experience in the early days of the war. She and an American friend were well north of Paris when French resistance collapsed. But surely you knew this?'

'We knew they had gone up there,' Albert said. 'But we understood that they had got back to Paris safely.'

'Unfortunately, while they did get back to Paris eventually, before then they fell into the hands of some deserters from our army, and were quite savagely mistreated. I am sorry to say, if you will excuse me, Madame de Gruchy, they were both raped, several times.'

'Oh, my poor girl,' Barbara cried.

'You mean Joanna Jonsson was raped?' Madeleine asked. Her imagination found it as difficult to cope with that as it had done at the thought of Liane cutting a man's throat. 'But . . . her brother was with them.'

'According to the statement they gave after they were rescued, Aubrey Brent was killed during an air attack on the refugee column they were with.'

Madeleine's shoulders hunched. 'But you say they eventually got back to Paris,' Albert said.

Helsingen nodded. 'They went in with our forces when we occupied the city.'

'You mean they were held prisoner for several weeks?'

'They were held in hospital for that time, monsieur. They needed extensive recuperative treatment, both mentally and physically.'

'So that's why Liane never attempted to contact us,' Barbara said. 'She must have been so terribly ashamed. The poor child. And now . . .'

Madeleine was still trying to decipher what Frederick was saying. 'Where is Mademoiselle Jonsson now? Is she still in Paris?'

'No. She left the country, presumably to return to the States.'

'And what happened has never been made public?' Albert asked.

'Regrettably, it was felt important to hush it up, for propaganda purposes. However, the men involved have been hanged, for desertion. The end result was the same.'

'Not for Liane,' Madeleine muttered.

'Yes,' Helsingen agreed. 'And you see, Captain Biedermann was one of the Gestapo officers who interviewed her after her rescue, and who pooh-poohed her story. Well, it was his business to do so. But she must have formed a severe dislike for him. And when he visited her in her flat, and appears to have made advances to her, and, I suspect, told her what had happened to her sister, well, she must have lost her head. That is my interpretation of what happened, anyway.'

'But what you have told us,' Albert said, 'surely that provides mitigation for what Liane has done?'

'Sadly, monsieur, there is no factor that can mitigate the murder of a German officer. I am most terribly sorry, but I wanted you to know the facts. Now, if you wish, I shall leave. I can wait outside until the car comes back for me.'

'Of course you must not leave,' Madeleine cried. 'You have so tried to help us. Papa . . .'

'A drink,' Albert said. 'You must have a drink. Ring the bell, Madeleine.'

'And you'll stay to lunch,' Madeleine said. 'Mama?'

'Oh. Yes. I must tell cook.'

'I feel I am imposing,' Helsingen said.

'You could never impose on us,' Madeleine told him.

'You have a very compact family,' Helsingen remarked.

They sat together on the back porch, watching the sun decline over the not very distant Bay of Biscay. Lunch had been a bit stiff, mainly because of the presence of Amalie, but now they were alone. 'It was, once,' Madeleine said. 'Now, Liane is on the run. Amalie . . . well, you know about Amalie. Pierre . . .'

'You have had news of him?'

'He has been here.'

'When?'

'Three days ago.'

'You told me you had not heard of him since the first day of the invasion.'

'We hadn't, then. And we didn't, until he suddenly turned up.'

'After two months? Where had he been all that time? In one of our prison camps?'

'I don't think so. He wouldn't tell us, or at least he wouldn't tell me, where he had been, but I think he would have if he had been a prisoner. The fact is, I think he deserted to avoid being taken prisoner. Oh . . .' Her mouth formed the letter. 'Will you have to report that?'

'I am not concerned with discipline in the French army. But where is your brother now?'

'In Paris. Papa sent him there to take over the office.'

'How long ago?'

'He left yesterday. He only spent a couple of days here.'

'Is that not very odd? To have been away for two months, and considered dead, then to come home, but only for two days?'

'I suppose it is odd. But he was desperate to get on with his life.'

'Do you think he will have visited Liane?'

'I know he meant to. But according to the colonel she won't be there.'

'I meant, during the two months when you did not hear from him.'

Madeleine frowned as she considered. 'I don't think so. I'm sure he would have mentioned it. He seemed as surprised, and bewildered, as any of us that we had not heard from her. If he had seen her himself, he would have known what happened, and I am sure he would have told us. Is it important?'

'It could be very important.' He held her hand. 'I did not wish to upset your parents, but they are in a very dangerous situation. One of their children has committed an act of war against the Reich, after the surrender of your country. In most circumstances what Liane did would be considered the responsibility of the entire family, and as Kluck said, you would all have been arrested.' Madeleine stared at him in horror. 'Now, I managed to talk him out of doing that, firstly by vouching for you personally, and secondly by pointing out that his best chance of capturing Liane is to leave her a sanctuary to which she could flee. I don't think the first interested him very greatly, but the second did. However, if Liane does not come here, and if she is not captured elsewhere, or even if she is, I suspect that he will soon enough decide that you have outlived your usefulness and should be arrested anyway.'

'But why? We have done nothing.'

'The main reason will be because Biedermann was Kluck's personal aide, and he is determined to avenge his death.'

'My God! What are we to do?'

'There is nothing you *can* do. However, I think I can protect you. In certain circumstances.'

'But you may not be here.'

'That is exactly it. You must always be with me.'

Her eyes were enormous. 'You want me to be . . . ?'

'My wife.' Madeleine gasped. Now he held her other hand as well. 'This is something I have wanted to say to you almost from the moment we met. It has nothing to do with what has happened since. I fell in love with you from the very first moment, Madeleine.' Madeleine could not speak, but neither could she take her eyes from his, and she made no effort to free her hands. 'I had planned a proper courtship, letters, flowers, the opera . . . but now there is no time for that. I am to leave Chartres. I have been promoted to colonel, and am to join the Führer's staff in Berlin. I shall be hundreds of miles away from Bordeaux, from you. I cannot take the risk of something happening to you before I could intercede.'

Madeleine could only clutch at straws. 'But if you marry me, a Frenchwoman, will it not harm your career? The Führer—'

'Will be delighted. He is anxious for integration, where it is suitable. It is his goal to bring about a general Aryanization of Europe, providing the blood is pure on both sides. Anyone can see that you are of Aryan stock. You will have to become a naturalized German, but that will not be difficult.'

'But my sister is guilty of murder. You say.'

'Every family has at least one skeleton in its closet. Believe me, the Führer will be pleased. My father was one of his first associates. He helped to finance the Party from the beginning, long before it came to power. Hitler will want to help my wife, in any way he can.'

'You mean, if I married you, you would be able to help Liane?'

Helsingen sighed. 'No. There is no one on earth that can help Liane now. You simply have to accept the fact that to all intents and purposes she is already dead, and try to forget her. Mourn her, by all means, but you cannot resurrect her, any more than you could resurrect a corpse. But if you are my wife, and we can swear that neither you nor your family had anything to do with Liane's crime, I can protect all of you.' Madeleine had been clutching his hands tightly. Now her fingers slowly relaxed. 'But I do not want you to marry me simply to protect your family. I love you, Madeleine. Can you not love me?'

Yes, I could love you, she thought. I have been steadily falling in love with you, or at least your memory, for the past month. But you are an enemy of my people. Yet you are offering to save my family from a ghastly fate. If I entirely turn my back on my sister. The odd thing was that were all things equal, Liane was the one to whom she would have turned for advice. But was he not right to say that Liane was gone from her life, all of their lives, had to be gone for ever? Had there been no war, and she had committed murder, she would still have been executed, by her own people. But had there been no war, there would have been no multiple rape, no necessity for a moment of madness. Liane was gone. It was the remainder of the family who now needed protection. And only she could provide that. By marrying an enemy? But also by marrying about the most charming, generous, honest man she had ever met.

'Have you nothing to say?' he asked.

Madeleine stood up, still holding his hand. 'I think we should tell Mama and Papa.'

James turned the pages of his diary. 'Three weeks,' he said. 'Long enough.' He looked at his watch. 'We call at five our time.'

'I feel quite excited,' Rachel confessed.

Living virtually in each other's pockets, as they had done for the four weeks they had been together, they had settled into an easy camaraderie, while still preserving certain essential barriers. At least he considered them essential. He could not be sure of her feelings on the subject.

He supposed that he had made a mistake, on the day he had both sent Joanna to the academy and Pierre on his way to France, by becoming so emotional he had wanted to lose himself in an alcoholic haze. He and Rachel had sat together, refilling each other's glass, looking at each other, not talking much. She had released her bun and her hair had come tumbling down in black profusion, turning her from a woman who had suggested she could be attractive into one who very definitely was attractive, especially when she had taken off her glasses and laid them on the desk. 'How badly do you need those?' he had asked.

'I can see well enough, close up,' she had replied provocatively.

In their mutual inebriation things had very nearly got out of hand. Already sexually stimulated by two days of resisting the temptation of Joanna, he had found himself stroking her hair and then the line of her chin before his hand had dropped, almost inadvertently, on to her shirt-front. As she had made no effort to restrain him, had merely sought to kiss him, he had realized that she was his for the taking . . . and realized at the same time that he was on the verge of creating an impossible situation. Not only was he, an officer, using his rank to seduce an enlisted soldier, but he did not love her, nor could he ever, not in the way he had fallen for Liane. It would be an act of pure sex. Did that matter if they both wanted it? But the wanting was a matter of the moment. It was what came after that mattered. He had to be in total control of their relationship, the man who gave the orders, made the decisions, however unpalatable those might be for both of them, the man whom she had always to respect and obey without question. Those requirements could not possibly endure with an in-house mistress.

If she had been disappointed at his sudden change of mood she had not revealed it, and the next morning had been as trimly polite and eager as always, and since then there had been no more bottle sessions. He actually felt that he might have accomplished something by his indication that he was not the totally cold-blooded controller of other people's destinies that she had supposed him to be in the beginning. But she still looked for insights into his character, his strength of mind.

'What happens,' she asked, 'if a German answers?'

'We close down immediately.'

'Just like that. What about Pierre?'

'If the Germans have got hold of his radio, he is either dead or in the hands of the Gestapo.'

Rachel shivered. 'Can people really live with something like that hanging over them?'

'It's not a lot different to being in a campaign. The secret is never to accept that it can happen to you. It's time.' She switched on the set, selected the correct wavelength. James sat at the table, adjusted the earphones. 'Sterling,' he said. 'Sterling.'

There was no reply. He waited for five minutes then said again, 'Sterling.'

'Sterling,' said the voice. Rachel gave a thumbs-up sign.

'Thank you,' James said. 'Out.'

'Wait!'

'We do not wait.'

'This is urgent. Liane.'

James drew a sharp breath. 'Liane is with you?'

'Liane is on the run. She has killed a Gestapo officer.' For a moment James could not speak. His heart seemed to have stopped beating. 'Did you hear me?' Pierre asked.

James still could only stare at the set. Rachel took the mike from his hand. 'We hear you. Does this affect your position?'

'It does not appear so. I have been questioned as to when I last saw her, but that was months ago.'

'Then nothing has changed. Carry on. Out.'

'Wait!' James snatched the mike back. 'You say she is on the run. Does that mean . . . ?'

'She has not yet been captured. But they are confident of doing so.'

'And then?'

'There is no defence. They will cut off her head.'

'Are you all right?'

'Yes. I am all right.'

'I am so terribly sorry. Out.'

The set switched off. Rachel looked at him. 'That was a long chat. Have we compromised him?'

'Hopefully not, as it was our first call.' James left the radio table and sat behind his desk. He felt suspended in mid air, one half of his mind saying there must be some mistake, that conversation never happened, the other half screaming, Liane, Liane, in the hands of the Gestapo. And there was no limit to what they could do to her before sending her to the block. While he sat here . . .

Rachel stood beside him. 'This person, Liane, is she very important?'

'She is Pierre's sister.'

'Oh, dear. I can see that he would be upset. But is her situation dangerous for our set-up? He wouldn't have told her about it, would he?'

'I shouldn't think so.'

'Then she can't hurt us, can she? I mean, even if they catch her, and, well . . .'

'Torture her?'

'I know it sounds grim, sir. But seen against the overall picture . . .'

'She is also the woman with whom I am in love,' James said.

'Oh! Oh, my God! I am most terribly sorry, sir. I didn't know . . . well . . .'

'It was not your business. It was nobody's business, except Liane's and mine. She was not supposed to get involved.'

Rachel rested her hand on his shoulder. 'If there is anything I can do . . .'

'You can go home. It's past five. Call it a day.'

'While you stay here, all by yourself?'

'If you stay here, Rachel, I am liable to hurt you.'

'I think it is my business to prevent you from hurting yourself.' She took off her glasses. 'What are you going to do to me?'

She was still standing beside him, and when he turned his head he was looking at her stomach. Do to you? he wondered. Do to you? What would the Gestapo do to Liane? He remembered reading various booklets, propaganda handouts circulated through the troops to keep them informed as to just what they were fighting for. Or against. The Gestapo favoured whipping women. There was a thought to make his blood boil.

'Sir?' Rachel asked. He raised his head, and the telephone jangled. 'Shit,' Rachel muttered, and picked it up. 'Sterling.'

'Sterling,' said the voice on the other end. 'Let me speak to Sterling.'

'It's the brigadier,' she whispered.

James took the receiver, and she placed the mouthpiece in front of him. 'Sterling.'

'Has your man been installed?'

'Yes, sir. I confirmed not ten minutes ago.'

'Very good. I am afraid you will have to contact him again.'

'Sir?'

'There has been a cock-up, for which you will have to take responsibility.'

'Sir?'

'Your American protégée has done a runner.'

'Sir?'

'For God's sake, stop saying "sir". I have just received a telephone call from Ashley Manor, from Colonel Marsham herself. It seems that your friend has not been amenable to discipline, and when her behaviour became so outrageous as to require disciplinary action, she simply left.'

Part Three

Resistance

'What reinforcement we may gain from hope
If not what resolution from despair.'

John Milton

Seven

Outlaws

'But . . . where is she?' James asked. 'She was staying at the Dorchester.'

'We checked that out. She hasn't been there.'

'The embassy . . .'

'We've checked that as well. They don't know, and we gained the impression that they don't want to know. Seems she was rude to the ambassador.'

'That sounds about right. But with respect, sir, people do not just disappear, certainly in wartime, with all the restrictions . . .'

'They can if they have the right connections and sufficient time. Jonsson has had three days.'

'Three *days*?'

'It appears that she has done this sort of thing before, just taken off. But the last time she came back after two days, and was disciplined. So this time Colonel Marsham waited for her to turn up again. It was only yesterday that she began to worry and decided to call me. Jonsson has both an American and a Swedish passport, as you know, as well as apparently unlimited funds. And we do know that a Swedish ship left Harwich last night. We're trying to get hold of a passenger list now. But with her connections it is quite possible that they accepted a false name even if it didn't gel with her passport. I'm afraid it looks like water under the bridge. We can't involve the police: we don't want anyone even to suspect the existence of places like Ashley Manor. If, as I suspect, this bitch had you along just so she could get into it and have an exclusive for her paper,

155

we are going to have shit all over our faces. While if she's a double . . .'

'I can't believe that, sir. After what happened to her, and the death of her brother, she hates the Nazis.'

'What proof have you got that *anything* happened to her? Or her brother? So she told you a story, which, conveniently, cannot be confirmed or denied by anybody. And you went for it.'

'There were two of them . . .'

'That is your only hope, and perhaps ours as well. Tell de Gruchy to get in touch with his sister as rapidly as possible, and have her confirm or deny Jonsson's story.'

James drew a deep breath. 'I'm afraid that won't be possible, sir.'

'Don't give me any twaddle about endangering them. War is a dangerous business.'

'Yes, sir. But Mademoiselle de Gruchy is on the run from the Gestapo.'

'Already? Why?'

'She appears to have killed one of them.'

'Well, that's a step in the right direction. But that doesn't mean her brother can't reach her. If she's in trouble she'll be relying on her family for support. Now listen very carefully, James. You set this thing up; thus you are going to have to carry the can. By all means confirm Jonsson's story, if you can. But that will not alter the fact that she has defected after having been thoroughly trained in the methods we intend to use for the movement and security of our agents. Now we're in the same position as Jerry. We can't touch her legally because she's a high-powered neutral. But we can't leave her roaming loose, either. I'm putting our people in Sweden on to it, but our agents in France also need alerting, and especially de Gruchy. If she returns to France, as she is a friend of his, it is pretty certain she'll contact him. When she does, he will have to handle it.'

'Ah . . . what exactly did you have in mind, sir?'

'I am talking about executive action, James. Just remember

two things: one, we are fighting a war for our very existence, and two, it is your neck that is ultimately on the line. If you require any additional support, let me know. Good evening.'

Slowly James replaced the phone, and looked at Rachel, who had been listening at her extension. Her mouth was open.

'Don't say a word,' he recommended.

'I was just going to ask if I should call Pierre now?'

'No. To make two calls in one evening would be highly dangerous for Pierre. And if Joanna left England last night for Sweden, there is no way she can get back to France, supposing that is what she means to do, for another week at the least. There's even a chance her ship might be torpedoed, even if Sweden is on good terms with the Nazis. Anyway, I need to think what I am going to say to him. She is a close friend of his family, and of him. And I have just been instructed to order him to kill her on sight. I'm not sure he would be able to do that.'

'Would you?'

'At this moment, probably yes. Unfortunately, I am not likely ever to see her again.'

'What if she is playing her own game, with your friend Liane as a partner?' James glared at her. 'I know that's hard to accept, sir. But we have to consider every possibility. And if they are up to something of their own, and maybe working for the Germans, well, the whole family could be involved. Including Pierre.'

'That idea is obscene. And impossible. Why should Liane kill a Gestapo agent if she was working for them?'

'With respect, sir, do we *know* that Mademoiselle de Gruchy has killed anybody? We only know what Pierre has told us.'

'Oh, Jesus! What a fucking awful mess. If only we had someone on the ground we could trust.'

'Yes, sir.'

He raised his head. 'Believe me, I'd happily go myself, if the brigadier would wear it. But with my French I'd be done in a minute.'

'I speak perfect French,' Rachel remarked. 'I spent a year

there as an exchange student, in 1936. I lived in Bordeaux,' she added.

Amalie de Gruchy walked by the river. It was early in the morning, and the mist was thick; although the water was only a few feet away, and she could hear it, she couldn't see it. And as all traffic invariably waited for visibility to clear, the whisper of the rushing water was the only sound.

Amalie walked by the river every morning at this time. The sensation of being the only person left in the world suited her mood. Because she *was* the only person left in the world, her world. Henri was dead; she had to accept that now. Dead without ever having shared her bed. She did not know if, after what the Gestapo had done to her, she would ever be able to accept sex from any man, even her husband. But it would have been so nice to have lain in his arms. Mama and Papa were strangers, their lives so shattered that they could only go through the motions of living. Madeleine did not bear thinking about. She might claim she was doing it to protect them, and she could claim that von Helsingen had secured *her* freedom, but that could not excuse her marrying one of the hated Boche. Pierre had also changed. She could not be sure how, or why, but she did know that he had gone to Paris to sell wine to the Germans, make them into friends and customers.

Only Liane had preserved her honour, and Liane was either dead or soon to die. Therefore should she not do the same? The river, whispering by, so softly and so enticingly . . . No one would even suspect what had happened for several hours, and they would probably never find her body as it was swept into the bay. They would be so unhappy. But did they not deserve to be unhappy?

She stopped walking, stared into the white wall before her, and heard a sound. She turned, sharply: there should be no one else about at this hour. Then she drew a sharp breath. 'Oh, my God!'

'Is that all you can say?' Liane asked.

'Oh, my *God*!' Amalie said again, and was in her arms. 'Everyone thinks you're dead.'

'Let's keep it that way, at least for now,' Liane suggested.

Amalie stepped back to look at her. 'But . . .' Never had she seen Liane, the most elegant, perfectly groomed of women, looking so like a scarecrow, her shirt and slacks torn and earth-stained, her hair tied up in a filthy bandanna, her lace-up boots cracked and muddy, her face gaunt and entirely lacking make-up.

'It hasn't been fun,' Liane agreed. 'But thank God I bumped into you. Are there any Germans at the house?'

'No. But . . .'

'Thank God for that, too. Do you know what I have dreamed of for the past week? A hot, scented bath and a glass of Gruchy 1914.'

'You can't go to the house.' Amalie brought her up to date as succinctly as she could.

Liane rubbed her nose. 'You really think they would turn me in to the Gestapo? Mama and Papa?'

'Mama and Papa, no. But if they saw you they'd have such hysterics the whole Gironde would know of it. And Madeleine . . . she's gone over completely.'

Liane's knees gave way and she sat on the ground. 'Shit! You mean I've wasted all this time getting here? And you say Pierre is in Paris?'

'I wouldn't trust him too much, either.'

'What's happened to us, Amalie?'

'I guess we just weren't brought up to handle crises. What will you do?'

'What can I do? Disappear. One of the people who helped me on my way down said there are some refugees in the Massif Central, people, like me, who won't accept the Nazis. If I can get there . . .'

'Can you?'

'I got here, didn't I? There are always people willing to help, even if they won't do it openly.'

'But your hot bath? Your wine?'

Liane gave a sad smile. 'They'll have to wait.'

'Not the food and wine. You stay here. Can you manage until this evening?'

'I have a bit of stale bread left.'

'Right. Leave it to me.'

'And some clean clothes?'

'Of course. And you know what? I'll come with you.'

'No, you mustn't. It's too dangerous.'

'I'm not staying here. Do you know what I was going to do if you hadn't turned up?' She snapped her fingers. 'Of course. I'll do it anyway. That way they'll never know.'

'How are they?' Frederick had driven down from Chartres the moment he had heard of the tragedy.

'They are quite shattered,' Madeleine said. 'I think we all are.'

'And there is no doubt?'

'The police do not have any. Her clothes were found on the bank. And then, her behaviour, ever since . . . well . . .'

He squeezed her hand. 'That memory haunts me. Now, listen. This changes things. We will be married immediately, quietly, and you will come to Berlin with me, now.'

'I cannot abandon Mama and Papa.'

'Pierre will look after them.'

'Pierre is in Paris.'

'As soon as I heard what happened, I went to Paris myself, and saw him.'

Madeleine's eyes were enormous. 'You have seen Pierre?'

'I saw him the day before yesterday. He was a little stiff, until he heard what I had to say. I have secured him permission to do as he thinks best. He has a permanent travel permit, enabling him to move from Paris to Bordeaux and back again as he chooses, and also permission for him to take his parents to Paris to be with him, if he thinks that is necessary.'

'Oh, Freddie! The things you are doing for us.'

'I am doing them for you. But I cannot escape my own feelings of guilt, that this should have happened at all in the

name of Germany. Now, Pierre is on his way here. He just
had some loose ends to tie up. Once he is here, he will take
charge, and do as he thinks best. He is happy to assume this
responsibility. But you, me, *we*, have our own lives to live.
Tell me that you understand this.'

'I do, but . . . I am so miserable about it all.'

'About marrying me?'

'Well, of course not. But that I should be looking forward
to so much happiness, while Amalie is dead, and Mama and
Papa are so unhappy, and Liane is gone, almost certainly
dead . . .'

Frederick held her close and stroked her hair.

Hans Kluck studied the report on his desk. 'They would appear
to be a most unfortunate family,' Captain Roess remarked. He
had replaced Biedermann.

'Or a most devious one. Have you seen this?' Kluck indicated another report.

Roess picked it up and scanned it. 'Did you follow this
up, sir?'

'Of course I did. It led nowhere, and frankly, I have received
so many reports of a strikingly handsome blonde woman being
spotted in various parts of France that it is hard to take them
very seriously any longer. However, I am still convinced she
will eventually turn up in Paulliac. That is the only place she
can hope to find shelter.'

'But it has been more than three weeks since Biedermann
was murdered. How has she survived?'

'Oh, she will have had help. These peasants may bow and
scrape when we pass by, but they hate us. And she had a
considerable amount of money with her. But here, you see, the
last supposed sighting was four days ago, there. Twenty-five
miles north of Blaine. That is on the Gironde. And the sister
is supposed to have drowned herself two days later. Do you
not think that is a coincidence?'

'Would not our surveillance team have reported it?'

Kluck snorted. 'We are not allowed to keep the house under

close surveillance. That bastard Helsingen would not permit it. Harassment, he says. If he wasn't so well connected I'd have his balls for breakfast.'

'You know he has been recalled to Berlin? To the Führer's personal staff?'

'Yes, I know it. And is going to marry that bitch, with the Führer's blessing. Have you seen the telegram I have received from Heydrich? Lay off these people, he says. Personal feelings must not be allowed to influence our behaviour. If the woman is not already dead, she will eventually turn up.'

'But if she *has* turned up,' Roess said, 'are we not entitled to act?'

'Only if we can prove that she is there. Or has been there.'

'Or been there and run away with her sister. The point I am making is that Colonel von Helsingen, and his bride, are leaving in a week's time. If after they have gone we were to pay the Gruchys a visit . . .'

'Don't you suppose the fair Madeleine will be keeping in close touch with her parents?'

'We will be acting on information received, which we are entitled to do.'

'And you seriously think that after more than a week you will be able to turn something up? Without frightening the Gruchys into a complaint?'

Roess grinned. 'Leave it with me, sir.'

'Thank God for that,' James said into the mike. 'We have been calling every day for the past week. Where the devil have you been?'

'I have been in Paulliac,' Pierre said, stiffly.

'For a week?'

'We have had a tragedy. My sister is dead.'

James stared at the radio in consternation. 'Liane?'

'Oh, I imagine she is also dead. Nothing has been heard of her since she fled Paris. I am talking about Amalie.'

'Amalie? How did she die?'

'She drowned herself.'

'Oh, my God! I am most terribly sorry, old man. How are the family taking it?'

'My mother and father are in despair.'

'And Madeleine?'

'Madeleine has married a German officer and gone to live in Berlin.'

'*What* did you say?'

'She has abandoned us for the good life.'

'I cannot believe that.'

'Because you found her attractive? You did not know her well enough. Neither did I. My own sister!'

'Shit!' James muttered. 'Does she know what you are doing?'

'Of course not. I am not that much of a fool. No one knows except my father. There is someone at the door. Over and out.'

James remained staring at the set for several seconds.

'You didn't warn him about Jonsson,' Rachel remarked.

'How the hell was I to tell him to murder an old friend when this has happened? My God, that lovely little girl, dead. Madeleine, defecting . . .'

Rachel took off her glasses and wiped them with a handkerchief, then placed them on the table. 'I thought Liane was the one you were interested in.'

'Liane . . . but Madeleine . . . shit!'

'You, sir, are a man of hidden depths,' Rachel said. 'Do you wish me to log that call?' James raised his head. 'Well, sir, if the call is logged, the brigadier may wonder why the executive instructions were not given. Or does he know how close your involvement with this family is?'

'No, he does not,' James said. 'But if it is not logged and he ever finds out it was made, you could lose your job. You could even wind up in the glasshouse.'

'Yes, sir. But if it is not logged, how is he ever going to find out, unless you or I tell him?'

They gazed at each other. 'Your depths are also considerable,' James observed. 'Aren't you afraid of disgracing your family? Your boyfriend?'

'I don't have a boyfriend, sir. At the moment. I think you need a drink. There is half of that bottle of scotch left. Would you like some?'

James realized that he did need a drink. It was dawning on him that he was totally unfitted for this job. The brigadier had asked him if he could make difficult decisions, and he had blithely said yes, not imagining for a moment that the decisions could possibly involve someone like Liane or Madeleine, even after he had been warned of their possible danger. He had supposed he would be able to protect them, and even more, Amalie, that so tragic figure. He had still not come to terms with the possibility that Liane might be dead, or about to die if she were to be captured. Now Amalie was gone as well. And Madeleine . . . the thought of her in the arms of a Nazi made his skin crawl.

As for Joanna, she would have to go. The very next time he spoke with Pierre. No more weakness. No more sympathy. No more humanity. The concept of the job he had been given as a great romantic game had become obscene. Rachel placed a glass in his hand. 'I didn't bother with water.' She had poured one for herself. 'So, here's to . . .' She raised her glass. 'What, exactly?'

'You tell me.'

'Well . . . what about us? Seems to me that we either progress together, or we fall together.'

'Rachel, if you stay here tonight, in my present mood, I'm likely to do you an injury.'

'You keep promising that.' She drank. 'I'm protecting my rear. Well, up to a point.'

'And Mrs Hotchkin will know about it.'

'Mrs Hotchkin has assumed we have been sleeping together ever since my first day.' She reached behind herself to unbutton her dress.

'You weren't by any chance educated at Benenden?'

'Good God, no, sir.' Her tone was contemptuous. 'I went to Roedean.'

*   *   *

'Liane,' Amalie whispered. 'There are people. All around us.'

'I know,' Liane said.

They had been climbing for some time, and were now several hundred feet above the valley where they had sheltered during the day. This was their usual pattern, the pattern adopted by Liane since fleeing Paris: hide by day, move by night. This meant very slow progress, but also meant safety. Nor had she varied it since entering Vichy territory, which in fact had been reached only a few kilometres east of Bordeaux. They had crept across the frontier in the dead of night, and immediately gone into hiding; Liane had no doubt that she was a wanted woman throughout the whole of France, whether occupied or not.

When they sought civilization, it had invariably been at dusk, entering a village to knock on the door of the bakery or the charcuterie to buy food. They were never refused, nor had they yet been betrayed, although the appearance of two very handsome but bedraggled young women must have been a fruitful source of speculation after they had disappeared into the night.

But their situation remained hazardous. The general feeling of the people they had spoken with was that Petain, or certainly Laval, who seemed to be actually running the rump of the country, was utterly in Hitler's pocket. If that were true, she did not suppose they could look for any official help in escaping the Gestapo.

Thus the future looked very grim, certainly now that they had just about run out of money. When she thought of the luxury of her Paris apartment, or of any of the family houses, she felt quite sick. But when she thought of all the other things that had happened to her, and to Amalie, since the invasion had started, she felt nothing but anger. Certainly she felt no guilt, or even remorse, at what she had done, even if she did have a continuing sense of disbelief that she had actually done it, had actually knelt, naked, above the unconscious man and drawn that knife across his throat, so decisively that it had been accomplished with a single stroke. She remembered that she had been thinking less of what his like had done to Amalie, or even the soldiers to her and Joanna, than of the dead bodies scattered across the road after the strafing of the refugee column.

Then she had thought of nothing at all, had gone through the motions as if she had been a zombie, but an ice-cold zombie, who had known exactly what needed doing and had done it. She had even hummed a little tune as she had sat in her bath and watched the water turning red. Then the future had been unfathomable, but nonetheless exhilarating.

The exhilaration had steadily worn off in the exhaustion, mental and physical, of being a fugitive. She had found herself thinking the most absurd thoughts, as of having James Barron beside her. Why him? Because he had been the last man to hold her in his arms with real longing, a real anxiety to please . . . who had no doubt already forgotten all about her. At least, according to what Pierre had told Amalie, James had been evacuated from Dunkirk, and was safely back in England.

She had frowned when she heard that. It did not tie in with the other things Amalie had said Pierre had told his family, none of which had apparently been questioned by any of them. If Pierre had known that James had been evacuated, he must have been in Dunkirk himself. And if he had been in Dunkirk, and had not been himself evacuated, he would have been taken prisoner by the Germans: according to what she had heard during her weeks in hospital, everyone left in and around the seaport had been killed or captured. And then, his story of working his way back to Paulliac . . . for two months? It had taken her less than a month to get there with every Gestapo officer in the country looking for her. Dunkirk could only possibly add another week to that. Therefore, if Pierre had been in Dunkirk with James, he must have been evacuated too. And remained in England for two months before mysteriously reappearing, telling lies about where he had been and what he had done, but yet persuading Papa to give him the managership of the Paris office. That had raised possibilities that she found difficult to envisage, but which had slowly been crystallizing in her mind over the past few days. But which now had to be put out of her mind in order to face this immediate crisis.

'What are we going to do?' Amalie asked. 'If they were to attack us . . .'

'We will defend ourselves.'

'But how? Two women . . .'

Liane felt in her knapsack and took out the Luger.

Amalie gasped. 'Where did you get that?'

'It belonged to the German officer I killed.'

'Do you know how to use it?'

'I do not think it will be difficult. But these are Frenchmen. We do not want to shoot them unless we have to. Just keep walking.'

Amalie hunched her shoulders, but obeyed, while Liane cast a surreptitious glance to left and right. The darkness and the trees made all images indistinct, but she reckoned that there could be about eight men, some on either side, and for all her brave words to Amalie, she had never actually fired the gun, while for all her hatred, the memory of Biedermann's body giving a little jerk as the knife cut into his flesh, the blood suddenly gushing as she cut through his carotid artery, haunted her. But she also knew that she was not going to submit to rape; she did not actually want to have sex again, with any man, for as long as she lived – and she suspected that Amalie felt the same way.

And it was going to come to that: a man suddenly appeared on the track in front of them. Liane took a deep breath, and drew the pistol. There were nine bullets in the magazine, and a further nine in the spare. More than enough to take care of these people, if she aimed carefully and kept them at a distance, which meant a pre-emptive strike. In the gloom the man had not seen the gun. 'Stop,' he said. 'Where are you going, women?'

Liane left the pistol hanging at the end of her fingers, but she stopped walking, as did Amalie. 'Up the hill.'

'Why?'

'To get to the other side.'

'What do you think is on the other side?'

'I have no idea.' Movement, behind her now. Liane presented the pistol at the man's chest. 'Move aside, or I will kill you.' The movement behind her stopped.

'Where did you get that?' the man asked.

Liane made a quick decision. These men were not in uniform to suggest that they might be policemen. 'I took it from a German officer,' she said.

'Did he not object?'

'Not after I had killed him. I am Liane de Gruchy. Have you not heard of me?'

'Liane de Gruchy! There is a reward offered for your head.'

'How much?'

'Ten thousand francs.'

Amalie gasped.

'And do you wish to collect it?' Liane asked.

'You are a fugitive.'

'And are you not fugitives?'

The man laughed. 'Will you walk with us, mademoiselle? And your friend.'

'Why should we do that?'

'Because you have no alternative. Do you not know that you are climbing into the mountains? Winter is coming. You cannot survive in the mountains. We can give you food and shelter.'

'In return for what?'

'That is for our leader to say. It is not far.'

'Who is this leader?'

'He will tell you himself, if he wishes you to know.'

'Are these men really going to help us?' Amalie asked as they continued to climb.

'We must believe so,' Liane said.

'But are they not brigands?'

'What are we?'

Amalie hunched her shoulders.

'We camp here,' the man decided.

'It is too early. There are several hours of darkness left.'

'We cannot go on in the dark. The way is too difficult. We will camp, and rest, and go on at daybreak.'

'Won't the police see us in daylight?'

He gave one of his brief laughs. 'There are no police up here.'

Liane and Amalie were so exhausted they fell down. The men sat around them and gave them bread and sausage, and some rough wine. Nothing had ever tasted so good. 'Do you know how to fire that gun?' the man asked.

'Of course.'

'And do you not realize that we also have guns? If you had shot me, my men would have killed you.'

'But you would have been dead first.'

He stared at her, and she stared back. He was not much older than herself, she estimated, for all his growth of beard. His face was purposeful rather than handsome, and if his accent was that of a peasant, his voice was clear and resonant. 'You have blankets?' he asked.

'No.'

'You must have a blanket, or you will freeze. It gets very cold up here at night.' It was already very cold. 'Use this.' He gave her his own.

'What will you use?'

'I will share. You must share also, with your friend.'

'She is my sister.'

'And your name is de Gruchy. Your father is the wine merchant. Does he know you are here?'

'No.'

'And two pretty women like you have no husbands?'

'No,' Liane said before Amalie could speak. 'What is your name?'

'My name is Etienne. Drink, and then sleep.' Liane and Amalie each drank, from the neck, and he took the bottle away.

Huddled against each other, and tired as they were, they both

169

slept heavily, arms round each other, cheeks pressed together. The blanket was quite large, and when it grew very cold in the hours before dawn, they pulled it over their heads as well. 'Are we going to live?' Amalie asked.

'Until we die,' Liane promised her.

Etienne was already up, as were his men. Breakfast was the same as dinner, but the wine was even more palatable. The men were absolutely courteous, looking the other way when the two women went behind some bushes. 'Now we go,' Etienne said when they returned.

'How much farther?' Liane asked.

'We will get there today. But it will be hard.'

She soon determined that was an understatement. The way was all up, save for the occasional, and brief, little plateau. Often enough they were following a path on the hillside, with sheer drops of more than a hundred feet beside them. Liane understood that they could not indeed have done this in the dark. Nor did she suppose they could have survived, had they not encountered these men. 'Are you fugitives from the law, or the Germans?' she asked.

'As the Germans are making the laws, you could say we are both.'

'Are you going to fight them?'

Etienne snorted. 'The whole army could not fight them. How can we?'

'Then what do you hope for?'

'Survival. We hope for survival.'

'Until when?'

He shrugged. 'Until something happens. Something must happen, eventually.'

It was the middle of the afternoon when they were challenged. 'Who comes?'

'Etienne's patrol. With prisoners.'

'We are not your prisoners,' Liane snapped.

'You are, until the commandant says otherwise.'

'Prisoners?' A man emerged from the trees, and Liane saw

several more to either side. 'You are not supposed to take prisoners. And to bring them here . . .' He peered at them. Liane did not like the look of him at all. He was big, bearded, with heavy shoulders and a lumbering walk. 'Women! You know the rules.'

'They are not just women, Jules,' Etienne said. 'This one is Mademoiselle de Gruchy, for whom the Gestapo have offered a reward. The other one is her sister. I think the commandant will be pleased to speak with them.'

Liane gave a sigh of relief: she had feared that this uncouth man *was* the commandant.

'Well,' Jules said. 'Bring them along.' They went through the trees, now surrounded by quite a few men, and came out on another brief plateau. In front of them the hill rose almost straight, and in the hillside there was a cave, outside of which were some more men. Seated in the cave doorway, but now rising to his feet, was Jean Moulin.

If it could possibly be him. The handsome features were those of an old man, the hair lank and uncut, and he moved hesitantly. But he certainly recognized them. 'Liane?' he asked. 'Amalie?' Liane stared at him, because she did not recognize the voice. Jean had always spoken in soft, well-modulated tones; this was a hoarse croak. 'I know,' he said. 'I cut deep, but not deep enough. As I thought then.' His throat was concealed by a neckerchief. 'But you, my dear girl, and Amalie . . . we had supposed you dead.'

'It's a long story,' Liane said. 'But not as long as yours, I would say.'

'Then let us exchange stories. Jules, wine and food for our guests. Who brought you in?'

'Etienne.'

'Etienne! Come here and let me shake your hand.'

'She is a dangerous woman, monsieur,' Etienne said. 'She carries a pistol, and threatened to shoot me.'

Moulin looked at Liane. 'Only if he attempted to molest us,' Liane said. 'I did not know he worked for you.'

171

'He does not work for me. We are a gathering of like-minded men. And now women.'

'There are no other women?'

'We considered it wisest not to allow them. Women breed discord. But you . . . There is not one of us here who has yet killed a German.'

'But you intend to?'

Moulin sighed. 'One day, perhaps. When it is possible. Come and sit down and drink, and tell me. Amalie, I was so distressed when I heard . . .'

'I am all right,' Amalie said. 'Only I have not yet killed a German, either.'

'We heard how you escaped the Gestapo,' Liane said. 'But how did you get here?'

'Much as you did, I imagine. I walked. People helped me. And eventually some, these good fellows, came with me. Have some wine.' Jules passed around the cups. 'Not exactly Gruchy Grand Cru, eh?' Moulin asked.

'It is excellent wine,' Liane said. 'Tell me what we are going to do.'

'We are going to try to survive.'

'That is what Etienne said. Survive for what?'

'Until things get better. They always do. That is the lesson of history.'

'You are talking of centuries. We will not be alive to see these changes. Are we going to live the rest of our lives as fugitives? In that case, we might as well die now.'

He held her hand. 'Liane, there is nothing we can do. France has been conquered. That is an inescapable fact. Now we have no army – except what is permitted us by the Germans – no air force, and only a fraction of our fleet. We have no friends . . .'

'What about the British?'

'The British? They abandoned us in June. It is the British who destroyed the main part of our fleet.'

'Because it would not join them. They are supporting de Gaulle.'

'De Gaulle.' His tone was contemptuous. 'That is pure propaganda. Who has ever heard of de Gaulle?'

'We have. And we are fugitives. That means a great many people have.'

'De Gaulle, like the British, ran away.'

'You are starting to sound like a Nazi yourself. De Gaulle, like the British, ran away to fight another day. We have just run away to die on an empty mountainside.'

He looked at her for several seconds. Then looked at Amalie, whose face was expressionless, but whose eyes were glowing. He refilled their cups. 'You are very convincing, Liane. Believe me, I would like to fight them as much as you, but with what? A handful of pistols, a couple of shotguns, a couple of dozen men . . .'

'Once you start fighting, the men will come. And the women, too.'

'To take on the panzers with pitchforks?'

'To strike them from behind in the dark. To make every German in France feel he is living on borrowed time.'

'That is a rhetorical ambition. Because you managed to get away after killing a German does not mean that anyone else will be able to. Nine times out of ten they will be caught, and hanged or shot.'

'Then they will have died for France.'

Another long look. 'You would be prepared to do that?'

'Of course. Wouldn't you? And your people?'

'I do not know. I have not asked them to sacrifice themselves to so little purpose. You say we must kill Germans. What do you recommend? One German a week? There are over a million German soldiers in France. That is a lot of weeks.'

'The propaganda value of a succession of murders of Germans will be immense.'

'It will not exist. The Germans are not going to publicize anything like that, and if we seek to do so, as we will not be able to prove what we say, people will only laugh at us . . . where they do not betray us.'

'Well, then, we must do something at which they cannot

173

laugh, and which the Germans cannot keep secret. We must blow something up. Something very big and important.'

'That is a brilliant idea. Supposing we had any explosives.'

'Can we not steal some?' Amalie asked.

'From where? The Germans do not leave their arsenals unguarded. And an attempted raid on one of them would put them on the alert.'

'Then we shall have to obtain them from somewhere else,' Liane said.

'So what did you discover?' Kluck inquired.

'The answers to all of our questions, Herr Colonel.'

Kluck frowned. 'You have not arrested the Gruchys?'

'No, no. I was most respectful, and they were most cooperative. But I have sufficient evidence *to* arrest them, whenever we choose.'

'Give me this evidence.'

Roess laid his briefcase on the table, opened it, and took out a sheaf of papers. 'I interviewed each of the servants separately, with Albert de Gruchy's permission, and I discovered a succession of facts which, taken by themselves, apparently meant very little to the Bordeaux police, but which, when added together, give a clear picture of what happened the day that Amalie de Gruchy is supposed to have drowned herself.'

'Supposed?'

'Oh, indeed. Item number one: the day after her disappearance, a large cured ham and several other preserved items of food were found to have disappeared from the larder.'

'They could have been stolen by the staff.'

'Of course. These things are always happening in large family houses. This, as I have said, taken by itself, it was not worth reporting. Item number two: the upstairs maid delivered clean laundry to every room the day before Amalie's disappearance. Included in the clothes delivered to Fräulein Amalie's room were two pairs of women's trousers, known as slacks, two blouses, and two jumpers.'

'Aren't those the clothes found on the river bank?'

'Indeed, Herr Colonel. One jumper, one blouse, and one pair of slacks were found. But the other complete set was also missing from the room.' Kluck stroked his chin. 'Item number three: two days after Fräulein Amalie's disappearance, the housekeeper made a routine check of all the bedrooms, and in Fräulein Liane's room, which contains many of her things even when she is not living there, she found several articles of clothing which had been removed from her wardrobe and drawers and laid on the bed. She could not say if any had been taken, but she did say that the only person to have entered that room over the past several months was herself; she makes these tours of inspection every week. This must mean that at some time over the preceding week someone else entered that room and went through Liane's things. That several items were laid on the bed indicates that whoever it was was sorting through her clothes, choosing some of them to take, while the fact that the items not chosen were left lying on the bed would indicate that the person was both in a hurry and in a state of some agitation.'

'And the French police did not investigate this?'

'The French police found the clothes of a missing girl, known to have been suffering from depression, on the banks of the river, and drew the obvious conclusion. Besides, as I say, taken separately these three disclosures mean nothing. But taken together, they delineate a clear pattern. The night before she drowns herself, Amalie de Gruchy takes several substantial and long-lasting items of food from her parents' pantry, takes two complete sets of clothing from her own room, obviously takes some items from her sister's room, and disappears. Those are not the actions of someone determined to commit suicide. Those are the actions of a woman who has met up with her sister, and determined not only to help her but to accompany her, wherever she was going.'

'That is a brilliant piece of work, Roess. I shall commend you. And you think the parents knew all of this?'

'No, sir, I do not. If they did, Amalie would not have had to act so clandestinely and in such haste. But with the written evidence I have we can certainly implicate them if you wish to do so.'

'Hm. Do you have any idea where the two women have gone?'

'No, sir. They have not been sighted since.'

'But you think the parents may know?'

'No, sir. As I have said, I do not believe they were implicated.'

'What about the brother?'

'I think that is also unlikely. Pierre de Gruchy only went down to Paulliac after he learned of his sister's death. There is no evidence of either sister having contacted him before then. In fact, according to the servants, he and his sister were estranged.'

'Therefore we will not gain anything by arresting the senior Gruchys.'

'Well . . . there is the matter of satisfaction. And there is also the point that if they are arrested and the fact is published, it may well bring the sisters out of the woodwork, as it were.'

'It will also bring Helsingen breathing down our necks. I think we will leave things as they are for the time being, Roess. I would say that these women will eventually wish to get in touch with either their parents or their brother. As long as we keep them under surveillance we will get them in time, and with irrefutable evidence that the family is trying to protect enemies of the Reich. Who knows, we may even be able to involve the other sister, and her bastard of a husband.'

'Pierre?' Jean Moulin frowned. 'He was reported missing back in May.'

'He has since returned,' Liane said. 'And is manager of the Paris office of Gruchy and Son.'

'That must be a great relief to your parents. And to you. But I do not see why he should wish to place himself, and the rest of the family, in danger by attempting to arm us. Equally, I do not see where he can obtain such arms. Certainly sufficient high explosive to blow up anything of importance.'

'Where do you think Pierre spent the two months before going missing and reappearing in Paulliac?' Moulin frowned. 'Let me tell you what I think he was doing.'

She did so, and both Moulin and Amalie listened with growing interest. 'If that could be true,' Moulin said.

'Oh, Pierre!' Amalie cried, and clapped her hands. 'And I thought he had defected, like Madeleine.'

'Madeleine has defected?'

More explanations. 'But she is irrelevant now,' Liane said. 'It is Pierre who matters. If he has really been sent back to France by the British, for whatever purpose, he must have some means of keeping in contact with them. And if he tells them he is also in contact with a group of patriots who are prepared to take the fight to the Germans, providing they can be given the necessary weapons, they will surely cooperate.'

Moulin stroked his chin. 'He would be taking a terrible risk.'

'By coming back at all, if he is working for the British, he was taking a risk.'

'Hm. I take your point. But the difficulties . . . Pierre is in Paris. We are here. How do we contact him?'

'I will go to Paris to see him.'

'You? That is impossible.'

'Why? I still have several blank travel documents, taken from Biedermann, stamped by the Gestapo. They are undated, so that is not a problem.'

'The problems are two. One is that you are a wanted woman; just about every German policeman knows your face. And even if they don't, your identity card will give you away.'

'Can you people not steal an identity card for me? Or forge one?'

'It would still be too risky for you.'

'But not for me,' Amalie said.

'You?' Moulin and Liane spoke together.

'No one is looking for me. I am supposed to be dead. If you can get me an identity card, with Liane's travel vouchers I will have no trouble at all.'

Moulin and Liane looked at each other. 'I could not permit it,' Liane said.

'You talk about fighting for France. Am I not entitled to fight for France? My husband was killed fighting for France. My mother- and father-in-law have been put in prison. This is something I must do, and something I *can* do.'

Again Moulin looked at Liane. Who stared at her sister for several seconds, then nodded. 'It will take a great deal of organizing,' she said.

Eight

The Agent

'Well, my darling? What do you think of it?'
Madeleine von Helsingen looked from the café table
up the length of the Unter den Linden towards the Brandenburg
Gate. As so often in the past month, she had a sense of
unreality. It was partly that she should be here at all, sitting on
a sunlit street, beneath the huge limes, surrounded by laughing,
carefree people basking in the sense of euphoria induced by
their Führer's sensational victory over the democracies.

Equally unreal was that she should be sitting next to this
handsome, confident man, so romantic in his uniform . . . with
whom she had sex every night. She had wanted to explore the
joys of sex since she had been a teenager, without ever having
the courage to go out and get it, as Liane had done. She could
not stop herself from wondering if what had happened to Liane
had not been some kind of divine judgement for the life of
unashamed hedonism she had adopted. But for her it had
been worth the wait, because Frederick was so very gentle,
and yet so very knowledgeable, able to give her as much
pleasure as he was clearly experiencing himself, whispering
sweet compliments and words of love into her ear, making her
happy. She could never do otherwise than wish to make him
happy in return. So she said, 'I think it is stupendous.' Almost
as stupendous as the Arche de Triomphe, she thought.

'But you are not happy.'

Madeleine reached across the table to squeeze his hand.
'I am happy when I am with you. I just wish the war
would end.'

'So that you could go home? This is your home now.'

'It would be nice to be able to visit.'

'And you shall, soon. Until then, you must not worry. Pierre says your parents are as well as can be expected.'

'But they will not write me, personally.'

'They will get over it.'

'When, Frederick? When? You said the war would be over by now.'

Helsingen sighed. 'I know. The British are proving difficult. They have to be the most irrational people on earth. They must know that there is no way we can be defeated, yet they go on fighting. You know that we have been flooding them with leaflets, pointing out the hopelessness of their position, asking them— no, begging them to get rid of warmongers like Churchill and make a sensible and dignified peace. We are not asking them for anything more than the return of the colonies taken from us in 1918, and for them not to interfere in European affairs.'

'And they won't accept those terms?'

'It seems not as long as Churchill remains in power. Sadly, the Führer's patience is running out. So far we have only been nibbling at them to remind them there is a war on, bombing their Channel traffic and the odd port or industrial site. But I can tell you that the orders have been given. Britain's capacity to defend herself will now be destroyed.'

'Can you do that?'

'Of course. It will be a carefully planned campaign. Starting now, all the airfields in the south of England will be bombed out of existence. This will effectively ground the RAF. This should not take more than a couple of weeks. Once that is done, we shall obliterate her seaports. Then, next month, when we have control of both the air and the sea, our army will cross the Channel and complete the job. We are realists. We know the British will not easily accept invasion; we expect there to be hard fighting and we anticipate that there are elements who will wish to continue resisting us in the mountains of Wales or Scotland, but their elimination will only be a matter of time.

Once we control London and the great industrial centres, the war will effectively be over. This will be before Christmas.'

'Oh, Frederick, when the army crosses, will you have to go?'

'I do not *have* to go. I am on the Führer's personal staff. But I have applied for a field posting.'

'Frederick!' She could not, she dared not, envisage life without him at her side.

'That is the way to high command. Don't you want your husband to be a general? And it has to be done now, before the war ends. Once peace is restored, promotion will become a matter of dead men's shoes, and that can take a very long time. Now stop looking so gloomy and finish your champagne. We have an appointment at Gebhardt's.'

'What is that?'

'Berlin's leading boutique. We are going to buy you a dress.'

'But I have lots of dresses.'

'There is always room for one more. And this is for a very special occasion. A grand ball, at the Chancellery.'

'And we are invited? You never told me.'

'It is a surprise. But you must look your best: the Führer will be there.'

Madeleine was more nervous than ever before in her life, this despite the fact that her deep red gown with its black sash – Nazi colours – was the most outstanding outfit in the room, if one overlooked the dazzling uniforms of the men, which ranged from several different shades of blue through to the sinister but so dashing black of the SS officers. But none of them had the exposed beauty of her face, as she wore her hair upswept with just a pearl necklace to break up the flawless sweep from her forehead to the first swell of her breasts. Yet her dress no less than her face contributed to her feeling of being an outsider, and of everyone knowing that she was an outsider, accentuated by the fact that her German was still far from perfect. They were polite, but cold.

Hitler was not cold. He greeted her warmly, but was clearly preoccupied – indeed, he only visited the ball for half an hour before hurrying off – while she reflected that he was a somewhat disappointing little man. Not so Hermann Goering, a towering and dominating figure, with a booming voice, who enveloped her in a bear hug and slid his hands up and down her back. 'I know he is a pain,' Frederick said. 'But he is the man who is going to conquer England.'

Poor England, Madeleine thought, and as usual when she thought of England, found herself thinking of James. But she simply had to stop thinking of that, and a moment later did so as she was introduced to another German officer, and his partner of the moment, and found herself staring at Joanna Jonsson.

It was difficult to decide which of them was the more surprised. 'Joanna?' Madeleine asked.

'Madeleine?' Joanna spoke English. 'Say, you're looking swell. But . . . here?' She looked at Frederick.

'You mean you know this lady?' Frederick asked.

Joanna switched to German. 'Sure we do. I don't get it.'

'Frederick and I are married,' Madeleine explained.

'Holy sh— . . . Married?'

'That is what people do when they are in love,' Frederick said, somewhat coldly.

'Oh, sure. Forgive me for being surprised.'

'And you are . . . ?'

'Joanna Jonsson,' Madeleine said. 'She's American, and an old friend of my family. But—'

'I remember,' Frederick said. 'You were involved—'

'Water under the bridge,' Joanna interrupted. 'I got a bit uptight when the invasion started, I guess.'

Madeleine stared at her. A bit uptight! She wondered if she knew about Liane?

'We were told you had returned to America,' Frederick said.

'That was the idea, but my editor talked me out of it. So here I am, reporting on the war for our readers, from a German point of view.'

'Well, I am sure that is very gratifying,' Frederick said. 'Both for your readers and for Germany. You'll excuse us.'

'It's been great seeing you again,' Joanna said. 'We must get together, and you can bring me up to date on the family news.'

'Yes,' Madeleine said. 'I'd like that. Perhaps . . .' She felt Frederick's hand on her elbow, tightly, as she was guided away.

'How well do you know her?' he asked in a low voice.

'Not all that well. She was at school with Liane. They're both older than me.'

'But you know the allegations she made during the invasion.'

'I only know what you told me.'

'She fled France, leaving Liane to face the music. With such a terrible result.'

'I'm sure they decided what to do jointly. They were very close.'

'And now she's back. Here in Berlin.'

'I'm surprised your people let her in.'

'Our people, Madeleine. Our people. As for letting her in, her ambassador wangled that after she had made a full apology, confessed that she and Liane had made the whole thing up.'

Madeleine stopped walking to gaze at him. 'But you said what happened was the cause of Liane—'

'Shhh!' He smiled at another officer and his lady. 'May I present my wife, Madeleine.' It was some minutes before they were again able to speak. 'I'm sorry,' Frederick said. 'But only my superiors know anything about your background, and they wish it kept private.'

'Did you mean what you said that day?' Madeleine asked.

'Yes, I did.'

'So you don't trust her apology.'

'I don't trust anything about her. And now that she is here in Berlin, pretending to be a journalist—'

'She is a journalist. I would like to be able to have a talk with her,' Madeleine said. 'I could have her to tea.'

'I'm not sure that would be a good idea.'

'I might be able to find out what she really feels, what she really is doing. If I tell her about Liane, she might open up. Or would you rather leave that to the Gestapo?'

Frederick frowned at her, then smiled. 'I would rather leave it to you, my darling. But be careful. And remember—'

'That I am a German now. It's not something I'm ever likely to forget.'

'Nice,' Joanna remarked, strolling around the living room of the Helsingen flat, picking up ornaments and putting them down again. 'But then, your husband seems pretty nice.'

'He is,' Madeleine said, pouring tea. 'Oh, I am being thoughtless. You'd rather have a drink.'

'Tea will be fine. I have given up alcohol.'

'Oh. Well, I must say, you're looking very well. Very fit. You've lost weight.'

Joanna sat beside her. 'Every woman needs to lose weight from time to time. Tell me why your husband doesn't like me. Is that because I'm an echo from your past?'

'Perhaps. One lump or two?'

'Oh, two. You mean you're not yet fully accepted in this society.'

'I am, at the moment. But of course, he doesn't want the Liane business to become known in Berlin.'

'Don't tell me she's still making waves. I must have a serious chat with her. I'm going on to Paris in a couple of weeks. She still in the same flat?'

'No, she's not in her flat.'

'Don't tell me she's gone down to Paulliac? Shit! That's a long way out of town.'

'She's not in Paulliac either. We think she's dead.'

Joanna stared at her in utter horror. 'Dead?!! Liane? She can't be dead. What do you mean, you *think* she's dead?' Her voice was almost harsh. Madeleine outlined what had happened, watched the tears rolling down Joanna's cheeks as she finished. 'Oh, Liane! My poor, poor Liane.' She produced a handkerchief and mopped herself up. 'I suppose you condemn her, now that you're a Nazi and all.'

'I am not a Nazi,' Madeleine said fiercely. 'I am married to the nicest man I have ever met.'

'Who happens to be a Nazi. Don't you know what they do?'

'They rule Germany. In time they will rule all Europe.'

'And you reckon you're on the winning side. I'm talking about what they *do*, to people they don't like.'

Madeleine thought of poor, tragic Amalie. But she was not going to concede anything to this woman. 'Do you know what your police forces in America do to people *they* don't like?'

'The people our cops don't like are usually known criminals. What about the Jews? The concentration camps?'

'It is necessary to lock up people like the Jews because they are known to be opposed to the state, and in time of war they could be dangerous. As soon as England makes peace they will all be released.'

'Frederick told you all this, right?'

'He tells me what is going on. We have no secrets from one another.'

'So has he ever taken you to a concentration camp?'

'I have no wish to go to a concentration camp.'

'Try forcing yourself some time. Madeleine, don't you have any sympathy for Liane? Your own sister?'

'Of course I have sympathy for her. But I cannot condone her crime.'

'Jesus! And have you any idea what the Gestapo will do to her when they catch her? Or maybe they've already done it, before they murdered her.'

'I think,' Madeleine said, 'that you had better leave.'

Joanna hesitated, then stood up. 'I'm sorry. I didn't mean to upset you. But you need to think of this: when you guys lose this war, there's going to be the devil to pay.'

'How can we lose the war? We've beaten everybody. We rule Europe.'

'You haven't beaten England yet. Nor, come to think of it, Russia.'

Madeleine felt thoroughly shaken, less by what Joanna had actually said, or even implied, than by the deep-seated feelings she had aroused. These were mainly guilt. She *had* married an enemy of her country, even if France and Germany were no longer at war. And if Frederick was indeed the nicest man she had ever met, he was still a supporter of a regime which had savagely mistreated both of her sisters.

She knew that Frederick, like most Germans, he had assured her, hated and feared the Gestapo and their fearsome controllers, the SS. But they accepted they were a necessary evil. Why? Because they felt they could only carry out their enormous programme of restoring Germany, and through Germany, all of Europe, to its former glory by repressing all opposition? Or because they knew that their own regime was essentially evil, and could only be sustained by suppressing or eliminating all opposition?

She could not let herself believe that. And besides, she only had Joanna's suggestion that concentration camps were anything more, or worse, than large prisons. But there was also a sudden fear lurking at the edges of her consciousness, stoked by her guilt. What Joanna had insinuated had to be nonsense. But suppose Germany, somehow, did lose the war? She did not believe the fatherland could be defeated by England. But Russia . . . Russia was Germany's ally, or at least, her business partner in controlling Europe. But everyone knew that two such opposing ideologies as Communism and Fascism could not exist very long in partnership. And if Germany were to lose such a conflict, when they had made themselves the most hated people on the continent . . .

When Frederick came home that evening, she could not help asking him, 'What will happen when England stops fighting?'

'We will have peace. I have told you this.'

'What about Russia?'

'We are friends with Russia.'

'I know. But . . . well . . . the Führer did not always wish that.' As a good German housewife her first duty had been to read *Mein Kampf.*

Frederick grinned, and handed her a glass of wine. 'Who's a clever girl? You're right. The Führer regards the East, the Ukraine, and the Crimea and Caucasus certainly, as essential to the future of the Reich. So the Russians will have to give them up.'

'Will they?'

'We may have to twist their arms a little.'

'Can we beat Russia?'

'Easily. Russia is like a house of cards. One push, and it will collapse. Have we not beaten France, and now England? They were both much stronger than Russia.'

'Ah . . .' But she decided against reminding him that they had not yet actually beaten England. So she asked, 'Have you ever visited a concentration camp?'

'Good Lord, no. I am a soldier, not a policeman.'

'But you could, if you wanted to?'

'I could obtain permission, if I wanted to.'

'I should like to. We could go together.'

'What an absurd idea. Concentration camps are not for sightseeing tours. I would just put them out of your mind, my dearest girl.' It was the first time he had ever refused her anything.

'Good morning, sir.' Rachel hung her hat behind the door, smoothed her dress, and stood in front of James's desk. Her refusal to allow their relationship to impinge on their professional code of conduct was one of her most endearing characteristics, he thought. But she had a great many more.

Over the past few weeks he had found himself wondering more than once what she really felt about the situation, just how important or even relevant it was to her. They had no existence, as a pair, outside of these rooms. Inside, they lived almost as man and wife, but they never even lunched together unless he sent her out for sandwiches; one of them always had to be on standby. But once she departed for the night he had no idea what she did, whether she went straight back to her hostel and stayed there, or whether she sometimes visited her parents' home – he did not even know if the Cartwrights had a London home, but he supposed they did – and if when she did so she encountered other bright young things, members of her social set, who would undoubtedly want to know how she was spending her war.

He was totally confident that she would never betray the work she was doing or the people she was working with; he could not be certain that she would not reveal at least the existence of her love life. So, did she have a love life, or was she merely indulging in war-induced lowering of the barriers, both social and moral? Her lovemaking was certainly enthusiastic. She might not be voluptuous, but she had splendid legs, which she seemed able to wrap around his as if her hips were double-jointed, and whether he had anything to do with it or not, she seemed able to climax both quickly and repeatedly. All without ever raising the question of 'after the shooting stops', or any of the other questions that had haunted him when he had initially rejected her advances.

In many ways she reminded him of the Gruchy sisters. Madeleine certainly had been affected by the war. He could not be sure of Liane, who he felt had pursued her own course long before things like war had interrupted their lives. But neither Madeleine nor Liane could be thought of anymore. The one had become an enemy; the other had crashed to an unthinkable fate. The only saving aspect of the situation was that he had been responsible for neither of their fates – and he could so easily have been responsible for Liane's. But dreaming of the past, of what might have been, was a dangerous distraction to someone in his position. He should just be grateful that he had found someone who, whether she was doing it as a duty or not, had been able to channel his emotions into his work – as his secretary, that is.

He waited as she came round the desk, carefully removed

her glasses, and lowered her head for a kiss on the mouth.
'All well?'

He put his arm round her thighs to hug her against him.
'So far. But you'd better wind it up.' Despite his gaffe over
Joanna, he had been given three more agents to monitor, and
they made a radio check every morning just in case there was
an emergency. As for Joanna herself, she had been traced to
Sweden, but as she had apparently decided to remain there,
living with her father, and as no revealing articles had appeared
in either Swedish or American newspapers, the brigadier had
dropped his call for immediate executive action, although his
agents kept her under surveillance.

Rachel seated herself before the radio, donned the earphones,
switched on the set to their frequency, and waited, tapping her
fingers on the desk.

'Something?' James asked.

'Yes, sir. Stockholm. In Morse.'

'Oh, no. Tell me.'

Rachel was scribbling on her pad. 'Joanna Jonsson left
Stockholm ten days ago. Destination believed to be Berlin.
Delay in information due to clandestine nature of departure.
Advise requirements. Sterling.' She looked up.

'Shit,' James said. 'Shit, shit, shit. Ten *days*.'

'Can we do something about it?'

James sighed. 'I'll have to speak with the brigadier. Ten
days. Whatever she's intending to do, she's probably done it.
Oh, well. Get the old buzzard for me, will you.'

'Yes, sir. Hold on, there's something else coming through.'

'Let's pray it's Stockholm saying she's actually gone to
the States.'

'It's Paris.'

'What?' James left his desk to hurry to her side and pick
up the spare headphones.

'Sterling,' Pierre's voice said. 'Sterling.'

James took the mike from Rachel's hand. 'Sterling. Have
you seen Jonsson?'

'Eh?'

'For God's sake. She's loose, and very probably coming your way.'

'I know what to do.'

'If you have not seen her, why are you calling?'

'I have the most tremendous news. You will not believe who is standing beside me.'

'I hope this is not a social call.'

'It is my youngest sister.'

'Am –' James bit off the word. 'She is dead.'

'She is alive, and here in my flat. And do you know who else is alive? My eldest sister.'

James stared at the mike in consternation. 'Say again?'

'She is alive and living with friends. One of them is the prefect. You remember the prefect? We thought he was dead too, but he is alive, and wishes to fight, eh? Take down this list of their requirements.' As James was still incapable of speech, Rachel took down the list. 'Let me know as soon as these will be available, and how they can be delivered. I will tell you where they can be dropped,' Pierre said. 'Out.'

Rachel closed down the set. 'Are you all right, sir?'

James took off the earphones and returned behind his desk, sitting rather heavily. He did not know what to think. He did not know what he wanted to think. Liane was alive, alive, alive! And certainly kicking. Or anxious to start.

Rachel stood on the other side of the desk. 'I'm afraid we're all out of scotch. And besides—'

'One does not drink scotch at half past eight in the morning. But we'll open a bottle of champagne this evening.'

'Yes, sir. Would you care to look at this list?' She placed the sheet of paper on the desk before him. 'It would appear that this, ah, woman intends to start a private war on her own.'

James scanned the list. 'She always was inclined to go over the top.'

'Are we going to respond?'

'Well, we have to. You were going to get the brigadier.'

'Yes, sir.' Rachel did not move. 'Would I be right in assuming that this woman is Liane de Gruchy?'

'Yes. The one we thought was dead.'

'I can see that you are very pleased about that, sir. And you knew her before the war?'

'I met her the day before the war exploded. I knew her for precisely two days.'

'And in that time . . .'

'Oh, for God's sake! I fell for her. I'm sorry, I didn't mean to snap. You are quite entitled to know. I can only say that these things happen in times of extreme stress.' Except that Liane had happened before there had been any stress at all.

'I am only trying to discover where I stand in all this, sir.'

'You saved my life. Or at least my reason.'

'Thank you, sir. But now I would say that you have no more need for me.'

'Rachel, I need you now more than ever. Don't abandon me now.'

Rachel regarded him for several seconds. Then she said, 'I'll get the brigadier.'

The brigadier actually came to the apartment, accompanied by an RAF group captain named Patton; both wore civilian clothes. 'Our technical expert,' he explained, looking around the somewhat untidy office with a sceptical expression, then sat behind the desk, which James had vacated to greet him. Rachel hastily provided her chair for the other officer. As there was no other chair, she and James stood together before the desk, rather like two delinquent schoolchildren in the headmaster's study.

'What are you doing about Jonsson?' the brigadier asked.

'You instructed me never to take executive action without reference to you, sir.'

'I gave you the requisite instructions several weeks ago.'

'I was under the impression that had been rescinded, sir.'

'Hm. And now she is in Berlin. Who have we got there?'

'I do not think it would be a sound idea to have her taken out in Berlin, sir. I think it could compromise our people there. At the moment she isn't doing us any harm. If she were to return to

Paris now, and contact de Gruchy, well, he has his instructions, and knows what he has to do.'

'Hm. Well, I suppose you could be right. Now, what is this nonsense about arming some group of bandits?'

'With respect, sir, these are not bandits. They are led by Jean Moulin, who was the prefect of Chartres, a most prominent man before the war. He will be able to command considerable support, and if he is willing to undertake subversive action, I think we should support him, if only for propaganda purposes.'

The brigadier looked at Patton. 'I think Barron-ah, Sterling may well be right, sir. I just wonder if we shouldn't bring de Gaulle in on this. These are his people.'

'I don't think we want to involve de Gaulle at this stage. Next thing he'll be telling us how to handle it. Can you deliver these arms?'

'If the proper arrangements are made, yes.' He turned to James. 'This will be your responsibility.'

'When I confirm that it's on, we'll be given a dropping area—'

'There is no way we can drop a load of gelignite without blowing something up. What we have to have is a landing strip, where we can be met by these people, and the aircraft unloaded.'

'You think you can put an aircraft down in France without the Germans spotting it?' the brigadier asked.

'This will be a small, light plane, a Lysander. It has the range, but I'm afraid its load capacity is strictly limited. So we won't be able to supply all these people want in one trip. They must give us a list of priorities.'

'Yes, sir,' James said. 'But what about German radar?'

'As far as we know, they don't yet have radar to any large extent. Certainly they don't have any stations in the south of France. Anyway, that is our problem. Your responsibility is to have your people on the ground to meet us. We will need the exact location of the landing field, and we will need the assistance of flares, or some sort of lights.' James nodded, and glanced at Rachel, who was making notes. 'The plane will have a crew of just one: the pilot,' Patton said, and looked at the brigadier. 'But we will need the assistance of one of your people, both to fill the place of a crew and to handle the people there. I'm sure we do not want our armaments to fall into the wrong hands.'

'Oh, quite,' the brigadier agreed. 'We'll find someone. It'll have to be a French-speaking volunteer.'

'That's me, sir,' James said.

'Good God! I didn't know you can speak French.'

'I've been taking lessons, sir. From Sergeant Cartwright. She is fluent in the language, and, well, so am I, now.' Rachel opened her mouth and then closed it again.

'Well, I suppose it's your baby. And you know these people. I'll leave you to set it up. Group Captain?'

Patton stood up. 'You can reach me through the brigadier. My arrangements will be completed within a week.'

'Mine will take longer, sir, as my agent on the ground is at present in Paris and will have to regain her principals.'

'Understood. Did you say her?'

'It takes all sorts, sir.'

'Apparently. Well, I look forward to hearing from you.'

Rachel closed the door behind them. 'Well, I suppose it's your baby. You unutterable bastard,' she remarked. James raised his eyebrows. 'You don't speak enough French to order a glass of beer,' she pointed out. 'And now you want to go swanning off on some suicide mission . . .'

'What's suicidal about it? Patton seems confident enough.'

'He's not actually going, is he? Has it occurred to you that this may all be a trap?'

'Don't be absurd. I'd trust the de Gruchys with my life.'

'That is exactly what you are doing.'

'Anyway, who would possibly be interested in trapping me? There is no German that knows I exist. I have never even met one, other than the odd prisoner of war.'

'Ha! Will you admit you are only going in order to see your lady love?'

'I told you, I only met her for two days.'

'But she made a big impression.'

'Yes, she did. But we were ships that passed in the night. Okay, I was shattered when I heard she might be dead. And okay, I do want to see her again, make sure she is all right. But I'll be coming back.'

'Mind that you do,' she said, and came round the desk.

'Let's get on the blower to Pierre, first.'

'That is splendid news,' Pierre said. 'Priority should be given to the explosives. Anything else that can be managed will be a bonus. Let me give you the map coordinates for the delivery.'

'How can you possibly know that already?' James asked.

'Because it is an area where I used to hike as a boy. My sister has told me where her friends are situated. You cannot put down there, because it is in the mountains. But I know where there is level ground, sufficient to land a light plane.'

'And take off again?'

'Oh, yes. It would have to be turned, but there will be sufficient people for that.'

'How close will the Germans be?'

'They will not be close at all. This is inside Vichy.'

'That's tremendous. Give me the coordinates.'

'It is section three, subsection D.'

Rachel made a note. 'Check,' James said.

'Do you wish me to leave Paris?'

'I do not think you should become involved. I take it your sisters will be there?'

'Of course. When will the delivery be made?'

'You tell me. How long will it take your sister to regain her friends?'

There was a brief hesitation. 'She says ten days.'

'Then shall we say a fortnight today? Give her my love and best wishes. Out.'

Rachel shut down the key. 'You did not tell him you would be accompanying the delivery.'

'I did not think it was necessary for him to know it.'

194

'And Liane?'

'Let's hope she will be pleasantly surprised.'

Rachel blew a raspberry.

'This is not very satisfactory,' Colonel Kluck remarked, scanning the map on his desk. 'This is a huge area.'

'These calls are very difficult to pin down, Herr Colonel,' explained Lieutenant Bliquet. 'Especially in a city like Paris, where there are so many people crammed into so little space, so many apartments one on top of the other. And I am afraid that this man is not the only one using an illicit radio. We will find him, sooner or later.'

'I would like you to make it sooner,' Kluck suggested. 'This intercept is very disturbing. It is a pity you were not able to get on to it sooner.'

'I appreciate that, Herr Colonel. But these things take time after the signal has first been identified . . .'

'Oh, go and listen some more. And bring me something worthwhile.'

'Yes, Herr Colonel. Heil Hitler.' The lieutenant left the room.

'Well?' Kluck asked Roess.

'I agree, Herr Colonel. Disturbing.'

'I want an idea, Roess. Or at least a speculation. According to this very brief intercept, which is clearly the very end of the conversation, this French traitor is arranging for the British to make a delivery of some sort of goods in a fortnight's time. What sort of goods? And where will this delivery take place? *How* can it take place, under our very noses?'

'France is a very big nose, Herr Colonel. But I think if we find the traitor, we will have all of our answers.'

'Sooner or later,' Kluck reminded him, disparagingly. 'The delivery is to be made in a fortnight. Less than that, now.'

'Perhaps sooner. As soon as Bliquet showed us the map, I recognized something.' Roess bent over his superior's shoulder. 'There, right in the middle of the area marked as the source of the signal, Gruchy and Son's Paris office.

195

And here, only three blocks away, is the apartment of Pierre de Gruchy.'

'Really, Roess. You are becoming obsessed with this man.'

'Would you not like to catch him out, Herr Colonel?'

'It is his sister I wanted to get hold of,' Kluck said. 'And she is dead. What possible reason have you for supposing Pierre de Gruchy is our mysterious radio operator?'

'Simply because his sister is dead, for which we are responsible, at least as he will see it. He will also consider us responsible for his other sister's suicide.'

'And you think that would drive him to committing suicide himself? Not very logical.'

'I think that might encourage him to attempt to harm the Reich in any way he can. At least let me search his flat.'

'Do you think he will leave his radio equipment lying about the place?'

'I am confident that I could find it.'

'By tearing the whole place apart. And if you do not find it, and word gets to Berlin that you have destroyed the apartment of Colonel von Helsingen's brother-in-law without adequate reason, do you know whose head is going to roll? Oh, yours, certainly. But mine as well.'

Roess suppressed a sigh of frustration. 'There is another line of approach. Gruchy has a mistress.'

'All Frenchmen have mistresses, Roess.'

'This one is living in. She was observed by my people, four days ago, entering his apartment.'

'So?'

'She has not come out save to go shopping in the morning, and then she goes straight back to the apartment. She has a key. Gruchy goes to his office every morning, leaving her alone in the apartment.'

'She is obviously someone he trusts.'

'That is an important point, certainly. But more important, we know she was there when he made that call.'

Kluck held up a finger. 'If he made that call.'

This time Roess did sigh. 'Yes, Herr Colonel. However, *if*

he made that call, she will know about it. If she were to be brought in for questioning, on a quite separate matter . . .'

'You would be putting our careers at risk.'

'I am sure we could frighten her into keeping quiet.'

Kluck stroked his chin. 'It could be done. But just in case it *is* a mistake, we must not be involved. Have you someone you can trust?'

'Several.'

'Choose one. A sergeant. Have him keep a watch on Gruchy's apartment. The next time this woman leaves, he can arrest her, place her in a van, and question her. She must not be brought to headquarters. If he finds out something worthwhile, then he can bring her in. If he does not, he will let her go and drive away. If Gruchy brings charges against us, and this woman can identify the man who arrested her, then he will have to suffer the consequences.'

'You are telling me to ask him to put *his* career on the line.'

'Whose career concerns you more, Captain? Yours or his? Heil Hitler.'

'I hate the thought of you travelling the length of France on your own,' Pierre said.

'There is no danger,' Amalie said. 'I travelled the length of France to come here, didn't I?'

'You were fortunate.'

'Fortune had nothing to do with it.'

'Amalie, you are a lovely girl. Are you saying that no man made advances to you?'

'Oh, yes. Several did.'

'What did you do?'

'I giggled and said that I would love to go with them, but that I had a confession to make first.'

'You told them you were a nun.'

'That is not always a protection. I told them I had the clap.'

'You . . .' He regarded her with amazement. This was his baby sister? 'How do you know about such things?'

197

'Liane told me. She told me exactly what to do, and say. She knows everything about, well . . . naughty things.'

'Yes,' Pierre said grimly. 'Well, take care, little sister.'

'Of course.' She kissed him, hung her satchel on her shoulder, and closed the door behind herself. She was filled with a tremendous sense of exhilaration as she went down the stairs, smiled at the concierge, and stepped on to the street. Not only was she excited at the prospect of the return journey, which, however exhausting she knew it was going to be, was also going to be an adventure, but also because she at last felt she was doing something, for France, for the memory of Henri, and most of all, for herself. Liane had told her she was helping to bring down the Boche, and she always believed everything that Liane told her. Liane was always right.

She turned the corner, down a side street, meaning to rejoin the boulevard a few blocks along, and half turned her head as a van passed her and stopped immediately in front of her. She continued on her way, swinging her satchel, and the back doors of the van opened. Two men got out and, while she looked at them in amazement, seized her arms and threw her into the interior. She was so astonished she didn't even cry out. She needed both her hands to stop her face from hitting the floor, and before she could catch her breath, hands grasped her thigh and turned her over so that she was looking up at four male faces. They were not wearing uniforms, but she knew they were not French. That meant they were Gestapo. Again! She had an urgent desire to scream, even as she felt sick. This could not be happening to her.

'Who's a pretty girl then?' one of the men asked, in good French.

Amalie wanted to shout at him, but then remembered Liane's instructions. 'If you run into trouble,' Liane had told her, 'say as little as possible. Nearly all criminals give themselves away by talking too much.' She had kissed her. 'And the Germans will regard you as a criminal.'

'Lost your tongue?' the man asked. He grasped her jaw before she knew what he intended, squeezing so hard that her mouth opened. She brought up her hands to strike at him, and had her arms seized by the men behind her. 'What a pretty tongue,' the man said. 'Shall I cut it out for you?' He released her. 'Speak.'

Amalie swallowed. 'What do you want?'

'We want to know about your boyfriend, eh?'

'I have no boyfriend.'

'No boyfriend? A smasher like you.' He said something in German, and the men holding her pulled her backwards so that she was lying on the floor. The spokesman knelt beside her. She tried to kick, but that was a mistake; her skirt rode up to expose her legs and her knickers. 'I'd be your boyfriend,' he said, and pulled the cotton down.

Oh, God! Amalie thought. When she remembered those questing fingers in Dieppe . . . But she was stronger now. She had to be. 'I have no boyfriend,' she panted 'Who would have me?'

'I can think of hundreds.' He grasped her groin, again moving with such speed that she could not anticipate it, and squeezed so hard that she could not suppress a shriek. 'What of that Gruchy, eh? You have been with him for the past week. What did you do in that time? Play cards?'

Think, Amalie told herself. Keep calm. Follow Liane's instructions. 'I was Monsieur de Gruchy's woman,' she gasped.

'Well, then, you can tell us.'

'But this morning he threw me out.'

'Tell me another.'

'He threw me out,' Amalie shouted, 'because he discovered I have the clap. I have syphilis.' Liane had not told her to claim that, but she might as well go the whole hog. The man had still been grasping her pubes, his fingers between her legs. Now he released her, jerking his hand away. 'He had me tested yesterday,' Amalie panted. 'The results came through this morning, then he threw me out. He thought something was wrong, so he had me tested. Then he threw me out. Now I can only go back to my village.'

199

The man jerked his head, and shouted in German. The van stopped. 'Get out,' he commanded. The doors were opened, and the men holding Amalie threw her through the door. Her satchel was thrown behind her. They hadn't even looked inside.

Pierre stared at the closed door for several minutes. He felt a curious mixture of pride that his sisters should be doing so much and apprehension that they were both living on borrowed time, overlaid by the persistent feeling of disbelief that they should both be alive, that Amalie had actually shared his life for the past five days. Now he had to put them out of his mind, concentrate on the business.

He went into the bedroom, contemplating the secret compartment – it used to hold a wall safe – in which his radio equipment was situated. He had the strongest temptation to call London, hear James's voice, be reassured that everything was going ahead as they had agreed. But that would be dangerous. Over the past week he had used the set far too often, and once or twice for several minutes at a time. If the Germans had not traced the signal yet, they would be close to doing so. The set could not be used again for at least a month. By which time the proposed action would be over. How he wished he could be part of it. But, he reminded himself, he *was* part of it. He had set it up.

He went into the lounge, to the sideboard, poured himself a Pernod, and swung round when the doorbell rang. Oh, God, he thought. They are here! But surely the Gestapo would have broken the door down in preference to merely ringing the bell. It had to be Amalie, returning because she had forgotten something.

He hurried to the door, opened it, and gazed at Joanna Jonsson.

Nine

The Railway

'I'm not a ghost,' Joanna said. 'Aren't you going to ask me in?' Pierre stepped back, then closed the door behind him. 'Nice place,' Joanna commented. 'You must be having a good war.'

Pierre licked his lips. How to handle it? How to do it? How to get rid of the body afterwards? But . . . to do it! Although he had fired at people from inside his tank, he had never personally killed anyone in his life. And Joanna, on whom he had had a tremendous crush as a teenager? How simple it had seemed when James had given him the command over the radio. The odds on her ever turning up had seemed so remote as to be not worth considering.

Joanna had turned round to look at him. 'You expecting someone?'

'Ah . . . no.' Had she seen Amalie leaving? But surely she would have said so. 'Would you like a drink?'

'Sure. But no alcohol.'

'*You* do not wish alcohol? I have champagne.'

'I've given it up. I'll have a soda.'

'Oh. Right.' He bustled at the sideboard, took a cognac for himself; he suspected he was going to need it. 'What brings you to Paris?'

Joanna accepted her glass, sat down and crossed her knees. 'Liane.'

Pierre all but dropped his glass. 'Liane?'

'I was in Berlin last week. I saw Madeleine. She told me Liane is on the run, for killing a German officer. Is that true?'

201

Pierre stood in front of her. She was such a big, strong woman. It would have to be a knife. But then, the blood! And actually to cut into that pulsing white flesh . . .

'You okay?' Joanna asked. 'Liane, remember?'

Pierre swallowed his cognac. 'Yes. She killed a German officer. A member of the SS. Name of Biedermann.' He was talking at random, trying to give himself time to think.

'Biedermann? That bastard!'

'You knew him?'

'Oh, sure. One of those guys who strip you naked with their eyes. I guess Li is in line for a medal. You know where she is?'

'Ah . . . nobody knows where she is.'

Joanna regarded him for some seconds. 'You're lying.'

'If I did know where she is, I would not tell you.'

'For Christ's sake, she's my best friend. I can help her.'

'Are you her best friend?'

'Look, what the fuck has happened to you people? Madeleine married to a Kraut and kow-towing to the Nazis, Amalie bumping herself off, you acting like I'm some kind of female Dracula . . . Well, if that's how you want to play it.' She drained her glass and stood up.

'Ah . . . don't go,' Pierre said. 'Why don't you stay to supper?'

Joanna turned back to look at him. 'Are you nuts?'

'In wishing you to stay for a meal? Are we not old friends?'

'We were, once. Before you started acting like a weirdo.'

'I am sorry. I was confused. Seeing you again . . .'

'I'll stay if you'll tell me about Liane.'

What difference does it make, he wondered? If I am to kill her anyway. 'Yes, I'll tell you. Liane is in Vichy. In the mountains. She is with a group of refugees.'

Joanna sat down again. 'Well, that's a relief. Where exactly is she? We must get her out of the country.'

'I'll just put something in the oven.' Pierre went into the kitchen, opened the cutlery drawer, and selected the largest sharp knife he owned. This was how Liane had dealt with her problem; he could do no less. 'I don't think she wants to be taken out of the country,' he said, coming back into the room and gazing at the back of Joanna's head. 'She wants to fight the Germans. She's organizing the people she's with into a guerilla group.'

'Good for her. I'd still like to get in touch. I bet I could be a lot of help.'

He stood immediately behind her. Now he reached forward, to grasp her chin and pull her head back for the cut on her throat, and she turned her head to look up at him. She did not immediately see the knife, but she saw the expression on his face, and reacted instantly – and in a way he had not envisaged.

Without getting up she twisted, grasped both of his wrists, jerked him forward, and then rose, crashing her shoulder into his stomach while still exerting her forward pressure so that he shot over her to land on the floor beyond with a resounding crash. For a moment he was utterly winded and only half-conscious, and in that moment she had risen, kicked him in the side of the head, kicked the knife away from where it had fallen, rolled him on his face and was sitting astride his back, skirt pulled up to her thighs, holding his head in both hands. 'Move, and I'll break your fucking neck,' she warned.

He panted. 'Where did you learn to fight like that?'

'I've been to school. You tried to kill me. You! So who's controlling you? The Gestapo?'

'For God's sake, no. I work for James Barron.'

Joanna gazed at the back of his head. 'Repeat that?'

'James Barron. He's the one who sent you to school, isn't he? He was your control. He's mine too. But when you ran off, the British named you as a traitor. All British agents on the continent are under orders to execute you if you approach them.'

Joanna released his head, and slowly swung her leg over to get up. Just to be sure, she picked up the knife. 'James Barron,' she said. 'I put him down as some kind of glorified gutless office boy.'

'You were wrong. He's as cold, and as ruthless, as a shark.'

'Yeah.' Joanna sat down, still holding the knife. 'And he ordered my execution. Well, well. Time to break the rules. You got any Gruchy?'

'Of course.'

''14?'

'There are a couple of bottles left.'

'Open two. We'll drink one raw and let the other air.'

Slowly Pierre pushed himself to his feet. 'What are you going to do?'

'You mean apart from getting drunk? We are going to have a nice long chat, and you are going to tell me everything you know about that bastard and his set-up.'

Pierre pulled the first cork. 'I can't do that. Then he'd send an assassin after *me*.'

'That's very likely. But look at it this way. James is in London. I am here in Paris, and in your flat. I have first shot.' She took the little Walther automatic pistol from her handbag.

Pierre spilled the wine he was pouring. 'You wouldn't dare. You'd be arrested. You'd be executed.'

'Do you really think so? I'm busy proving myself a Nazi sympathizer. So I'm in Paris, and I pay my old friend Pierre de Gruchy a visit, and guess what? He proudly boasts to me that he is actually a British agent, and shows me his equipment. Because you do have equipment in this flat, don't you?' Pierre swallowed. 'I thought you would. So, having done all this, you then realize that I can betray you, and so you try to kill me. So I had to shoot you. When I've done that, I'll call the Gestapo myself. Let's have that drink.'

He gave her the glass. 'What are you really going to do?'

'That depends on what you have to tell me. Come and sit here. And do remember that I can take you apart, if I have to. Bring the bottle.' Pierre obeyed. 'Now talk. I want to hear everything you have done, or been told, since you waved goodbye on 10 May.'

Pierre did as he was told. He tried to think while he was doing so, but it was difficult while she was staring at him, very much as he imagined a hungry lioness might do.

'Great stuff,' she said when he had finished. 'Sterling, eh? Now you can start cooking, and we'll start on that second bottle. Maybe you'd better open a third. Then you could offer me a bed for tonight. I don't mind sharing yours.'

Pierre opened the third bottle, and went into the kitchen. For the moment, at least, his ability to think had been entirely taken over.

Joanna followed him. 'By the way, you do realize that if, after I leave tomorrow, you get on to James and tell him what's happened, he will certainly send a hit man after you.'

'You want to destroy him yourself, do you? And his whole organization.'

'Why should I want to do that? I really would like England to win this war. But I sure do mean to get even with that bastard.'

The RAF sergeant saluted. 'Sterling, sir. The car is waiting.'

'Right.' James put on his cap.

'I still think it's crazy for you to be wearing uniform,' Rachel said.

'It's absolutely essential that I wear uniform. That way, if I'm captured, the Jerries will have to lock me up as a POW rather than shoot me as a spy.'

'Your faith in their ethics is touching.' She handed him the valise. 'There's everything you need. You'll be back tomorrow morning. Right?'

'That's the idea.'

'Well, then . . . Oh, fuck it.' She took off her glasses and tears dribbled down her cheeks.

'I'll take your valise down, sir,' the sergeant said, picking up the case and leaving the room.

'I'm sorry,' Rachel said. 'I just wish I was coming with you.'

'I'll be here when you come in tomorrow.'

'I'm not coming in tomorrow. I'm spending the night right here. Well, someone has to mind the shop. Right?'

'Right.' He held her close, kissed her mouth. 'I wouldn't have you anywhere else.'

'And you'll give Liane my love. I feel I've known her all my life.'

'Maybe I'll bring her back to meet you.' A last kiss, and he was hurrying down the stairs.

It was a long drive from the East End to Northolt, and it was seven when they arrived; the early September evening was just drawing in. The sergeant spoke little on the journey, which suited James very well. He had to concentrate, to forget what he was leaving behind and be concerned only with what lay ahead. And who. After four months. And she was again about to endanger her life. But from what he had been told, her life had been in danger just about every day of those four months. Well, he was determined to change that.

Group Captain Patton was waiting for him, together with his pilot, a fair-haired young man who also sported an outsize moustache. 'Flying Officer Brune, sir. Glad to have you aboard. You've flown before, I take it?'

'No, I haven't.'

'Piece of cake, really.'

'You mean it's not dangerous.'

'Well, sir, driving a motor car is dangerous, if the wrong person is behind the wheel.'

Patton had been listening with quiet amusement. 'He'll take care of you. Now, you're loaded with everything you can safely carry. You understand that because of the extra fuel tanks we have only been able to fill half the order.'

'Which means we'll come back a hell of a sight faster than on the way out,' Brune grinned.

'So we could have room for a passenger.'

'If you want to bring a Froggie back, that's okay by me. But just one. The fuel situation is going to be pretty tight even with our reserve tank.'

'Your flying gear is in that hut,' Patton said. 'So I'll wish you good luck. I look forward to hearing how it went.'

Brune showed James how to put on the gear, and his mae west. 'You ever had to use one of these?' James asked.

'No, sir. It was a hard landing where I was concerned.'

'You mean you've been shot down?'

'The old Gladiator just wasn't fast enough for a 109. If I'd had a Spit, now . . . But they were saving those, even back in the winter.'

'You were hit in France?'

'That's right, sir.'

'But you survived.'

'Well, in a manner of speaking. When I came out of hospital they told me I was down to this lot. Reaction's shot, you see.' He gestured at the rather flimsy-looking upper-wing monoplane they were approaching across the tarmac. 'Still, it's better than nothing, and as the used car salesmen say, it'll get you there and back.'

An orderly was holding the door for them, and they climbed into the fuselage, having to crawl over the various bags and boxes that coated the floor. There was no way of telling which were the explosives, but James didn't suppose it really mattered until they got there. Supposing they got there. 'Will it fly with this load?' he asked as they reached the flight deck and strapped themselves in.

'She'll fly, all right, if we can get her off the deck.'

'What happens if you can't get her up?'

'Be positive, sir.'

A ground crew spun the propeller, just as James remembered from films like *The Dawn Patrol*. The engine spluttered but did not fire.

'Hear the one about the lady pilot who backed into her aircraft propeller?' Brune asked.

James managed to unclench his teeth. 'No.'

'Dis-ast-er. Haw, haw, haw. Get it?'

The propeller had been swung again, and the engine spluttered into life. The ground crew jumped aside, Brune gave the thumbs-up sign, and the aircraft taxied across the parking apron to the end of the runway. Brune put on his earphones and engaged a distant voice in some incomprehensible exchanges regarding wind speed and direction, and a moment later they were rolling down the runway, slowly gathering speed. Brune watched his air speed indicator, then brought his yoke back. For a moment nothing happened. 'Come on, you silly cow,' he muttered.

James watched what appeared to be a perimeter fence rushing at them. What a way to go, he thought. Then the nose lifted, and they cleared the fence by a few feet.

'Gotcha!' Brune said. 'Well, sir, that's the hard part over.'

James waited for his stomach to drop back into place. 'What about coming back down?'

'Piece of cake, if it's reasonably flat.'

'And the bit in between?'

'You can sleep if you like.'

'Thank you. What the hell is that?' It was dark now, and away to their right there were flashing lights.

'Jerry's early tonight. We'll have some overhead in a few minutes.'

'Dropping bombs?'

'That's what they do best.'

'We're underneath them. What happens—'

'You do think about the oddest things, sir. That is one question to which we are never going to have the answer. So why ask it?'

'What time is it?' Amalie asked.

Liane peered at her watch. 'Ten past one.'

'Shouldn't we light the flares?'

'They said one forty-five. Are you all right?'

'Of course I'm all right.' But her voice was trembling. As they were sitting against each other, Liane knew that her entire body was trembling. She supposed it was tension more than actual fear, and after what Amalie had been through she could not be blamed for being perpetually tense.

Jules crawled towards her. As Moulin could no longer move very quickly, he was in nominal command of the reception party. 'You think they are coming?'

'I have no doubt of it.'

'You know them?'

'Yes. I know them.' Him, she thought. How can one know a man after two days, even if those days had included a fuck? She had not intended to know him at all. He had been different, and amusing, and she had been excited at the thought of Amalie getting married. Even a little dejected that it had not been her? She would never admit that, even to herself. But James had definitely been no more than an episode. She had been genuine in her invitation for him to look her up next time he was in Paris, but she had never expected it to happen, even had the French army not collapsed so dramatically. But now he was sending weapons to help her! Amalie had listened to the wireless conversation, and had told her he had sounded quite overcome at the news that she was alive. Well, she thought, it was nice to know that she had made an impression. She looked at her watch. 'Time.'

Jules crawled away to where Etienne and the other six men were waiting. These now hurried from torch to torch, setting them alight; the flames flared in the breeze drifting through the shallow valley. Liane peered into the gloom; the lights would only burn for half an hour. 'I see it,' Amalie said.

A moment later the aircraft could clearly be seen, slotted between the mountains to either side, sinking slowly to the ground. Liane found she was holding her breath. The approach was accurate enough, but the pilot would have only his altimeter to tell him how far above the ground he was. Yet there was no hesitation. The Lysander dropped to the ground, bounced once or twice, and then rolled to a halt not fifty feet from where she stood.

Instantly the Frenchmen ran forward. The two women followed more slowly, and Liane stopped when she saw the big man climbing down from the aircraft. Even in the darkness there could be no doubt who he was, but he was the

209

last person she had expected to see. 'That's Captain Barron,' Amalie said. 'I told you. He's Pierre's contact in England.'

'I remember Captain Barron.' Liane went forward.

'Parlez-vous Anglais?' James was asking, and then saw her. 'Thank God! Liane . . .'

'James!' She embraced him, kissed him on both cheeks. 'We did not expect you to come in person.'

'Did you really expect me to stay away, once I knew . . . well . . .'

She stared at him. My God, she thought. He is still carrying a torch. But there was no time for that. 'Tell us what we must do.'

He returned her gaze for several seconds before replying. 'Get the plane unloaded. Then we'd appreciate a hand in turning it.'

Brune had now also climbed down. 'You know this lady, sir?'

'Yes,' James said. 'I know her. Liane de Gruchy, Flying Officer Brune.'

Brune shook hands. 'My pleasure, mademoiselle. But could we make it a quick job? We need to be out in the bay by dawn.'

'Of course. But would it not be safer to remain here for the day?'

'Here?' Brune looked from left to right.

'My people will camouflage your machine with branches, and stand guard over it. We intend to leave the munitions here anyway. There is no point in carrying them up the mountain just to have to bring them down again.'

'Well . . .' Brune looked at James.

'I think that is an excellent idea,' James said.

'You're the boss, sir. But let's get her unloaded.'

The Frenchmen were already passing boxes down from the aircraft, unable to resist the temptation to open them and look inside; they exclaimed in delight as they uncovered the hand grenades and automatic pistols, and even four tommy-guns.

'Chicago comes to France,' Amalie remarked.

James had not noticed her before. Now he embraced her. 'Amalie, my dear girl. Are you all right?'

'Yes,' Amalie said.

James didn't know what to make of her tone, and looked at Liane, but as she didn't comment, he asked, 'Do you people know how to use this stuff?'

'They're anxious to have a go.'

'And what about the gelignite?'

'That too.'

'But they haven't used it before?'

'Well, no. Blowing things up is not a usual peacetime activity.'

'But you have an explosives expert?'

'Of course. At our headquarters.'

'He and I need to have a talk. But for God's sake tell them to be careful, or we are all going to be just a hole in the ground.'

Liane gave instructions, and the boxes of explosives were carefully removed from the plane and carried into the shade of the trees bordering the improvised runway. 'Now where do we go?' James asked.

'We stay here until daybreak. There is coffee. Not good, but drinkable, and it should still be quite hot.'

'But . . . daybreak?'

'We cannot climb the mountain in the dark. Daylight is perfectly safe. Nobody dares interfere with us.' She led the way into the trees, where they had been camped while waiting for the plane. Here was food and thermoses of coffee. Brune and Amalie joined them.

James sat beside Liane. There was so much he wished to ask her, say to her, do to her, but she was clearly preoccupied. Nor could he glean any inkling as to whether or not she wished to invoke the past. So he asked, 'Why do we have to go up the mountain? Your explosives man should be down here.'

'I wish you to meet our leader.'

'Moulin?'

'That is right. Do you remember him?'

'Very well. What exactly are your plans?'

'We are going to blow up the Paris–Bordeaux railway.'

'With what objective?'

'Why, to destroy it. It is a major link.'

'But the Germans will simply repair it.'

'Of course. But it will let them know, let the world know, that there are Frenchmen, and women, who are prepared to fight, no matter how they have been betrayed by their government.'

'And to die?'

'If necessary. But there is no need for us to die.'

'You'll be very lucky if none of you do. And you understand that there will be reprisals?'

'That has to be accepted.'

'Innocent men, maybe.'

'You brought us the goods. Are you now telling me we must not use them?'

He held her hand. 'I just want to be sure you have considered every aspect of what you are planning.'

'We have. Now get some sleep. We have a long climb ahead of us.'

Sleep was impossible, with Liane in touching distance. But he dared not do so. She had changed from his memory of her. Presumably any woman would change after undergoing what had happened to her. His problem was that he did not know if the memory he had, of such an utter hedonist, careless of either yesterday or tomorrow, was in the least accurate. She had revealed, briefly, a serious side of her character during the drive north. Yet even without make-up or nail varnish, wearing pants and blouse which had seen better days, her hair almost invisible beneath a bandanna, she remained the most exciting woman he had ever known. Would she agree to come out with him? But he knew she would never leave Amalie. Then would Brune feel able to take them both and still get back to England?

He was glad to have a full day to work on it. Brune elected to remain in the valley with his aircraft and two of the Frenchmen, and the store of weapons and explosives. There was little time for conversation on the climb, which took them until noon, while James reflected that he would almost immediately have to begin the return journey. 'You understand,' Liane warned, 'that Jean is not the man you will remember. He was most savagely tortured by the Gestapo.'

A cue. 'Are any of us the people we remember from that dinner party?' She glanced at him, then resumed climbing.

But Moulin was certainly pleased to see him; he clasped his hands and embraced him. 'It is good to be all working together,' he croaked.

'Absolutely,' James agreed. 'Now, sir, what I really need to do is have a chat with your explosives expert.'

Moulin looked at Liane. 'I will handle the explosives,' she said.

'You said you knew nothing about them.'

'So tell me what I need to know. We have an hour.'

'An hour? Good God! You can't learn how to handle explosives in an hour. Have you ever used a detonator or a trip line or a remote control?'

'I do not know what you are speaking of. I intend to place the explosive on the track and wait for the train to run over it.'

'And hope that it will explode. Besides hoping that it will not have already been found. The Germans will certainly maintain patrols along the tracks of all major lines.'

'You are determined to raise difficulties. You have brought us what we need. We are grateful. Now you must let us get on with our business.'

They gazed at each other. He knew she was as uncertain of her emotions as himself. But the idea already half formed in his mind was slowly taking shape. She would never agree to come with him, not at this moment, but afterwards . . . Supposing she survived. It was his business to make sure of that. Or go out with her in a blaze of glory.

'It happens to be my business too,' he said quietly. 'I am responsible for the success, as I will be held responsible for

213

the failure, of this mission. And without an explosives expert it is bound to fail. Therefore I will carry out the business for you. And with you.'

'You are such an expert?'

'I have been trained in the use of explosives, yes.' Amalie clapped her hands.

Liane looked at him for several seconds. Then she looked at Moulin. 'If that is the major's decision,' Moulin said, 'we should be grateful for his assistance.'

'Do you intend to take command?' Liane asked.

'Yes. With deference to your command of your men, and your local knowledge.'

'Well, then,' she said. 'We had better get started.'

Brune rubbed his nose. 'That's a turn-up for the book. How long do you reckon, sir?'

James looked at Liane. 'Three days to the line, three days back.'

'So if you were to return one week tonight,' James suggested.

'With respect, sir, I can't guarantee that I'll be able to. The brass hadn't anticipated this development. I'm not sure they'll go along with it.'

'You mean they'd write me off.'

'Well, sir . . . but if I don't go back . . .'

'They'll write you off as well.'

'If we don't turn up tomorrow they'll decide we've been nobbled. So when we do turn up, in a week's time, they'll be relieved. Mind you, I'm not saying they'll be pleased. Unless . . .'

'We have had a whopping success. All right, Flying Officer. I will give you a command to remain here with your aircraft until this operation has been completed, whether successfully or not. Give me your log book, and I'll put that in writing. That way, only one of us can be cashiered.'

He wondered how Rachel would take the news that he had gone missing.

*　　*　　*

214

'You are taking a great risk,' Liane said as the little band walked into the night; there were four Frenchmen, commanded by Jules, and including Etienne, James and herself – she had refused to allow Amalie to accompany them. Now that they were leaving the shelter of the mountains they had to reverse their tactics; in a day's time they would have crossed the border into German-occupied territory.

'No more than you or your people.'

'We are all risking our lives. But you are risking your career.'

'I'm not really. If we succeed, I think they'll be happy enough. If we fail, I'll be dead.'

She gave a little shiver. 'You can speak of it so calmly.'

'Aren't you speaking calmly?'

'I have nothing to live for. Only vengeance.'

'You have everything to live for, Liane. Your family . . .'

'My family? My family is destroyed. My parents are shattered wrecks. Oh, my brother is playing his part, but it can only be a matter of time before he is found out. Then he will be hanged. Amalie, she is a shell, containing only misery. Madeleine . . . you know about Madeleine?'

'No.'

'She's married a German officer.'

'Madeleine did that?'

'Amalie says she claims it is because she wanted to protect the family. I don't know what she thought she could do. Anyway, she's now living in Berlin, moving in high society. Nazi society.'

James found it difficult to believe. Madeleine, if so rapidly overtaken, in his estimation, by her sister's compulsive charm and vivacity, remained the most perfect woman he had ever met. 'She must have had a reason.'

'Of course. She accepted defeat. She is a traitor. When the time comes for settling up, or before then if she ever dares return to Paulliac, she will have to be executed. I will do it myself.'

*　　*　　*

They halted just before dawn. 'Tonight we cross the frontier,' Liane said.

'Will that be a problem?'

'Not going in. No one suspects that we exist. Coming back out, now, that may be more difficult. But we will make it.'

As they dared not light a fire, they ate cold meat and bread, and then settled down in a copse. From their position they overlooked a road, but there was very little traffic. 'The border is four kilometres further,' Liane said, sitting beside James. 'These are marvellous weapons.' She was carrying one of the tommy-guns.

'Let's hope you don't have to use it.'

'But I want to use it, one day.' She settled down, her head on her arm.

James watched her for several minutes. But he too was exhausted, and soon slept, surprisingly deeply. There was so much he wanted to think about, but more than ever now the time for thinking was past. Only the task ahead mattered. Yet when he awoke, about noon, it was with a start of alarm as he realized that she was not there. Then he saw her, talking with her fellow guerillas.

She saw that he was awake, and brought him food and a cup of wine. 'I have sent Etienne into the village to buy some more food.'

'Is that safe?'

'Oh, yes. He is from this neighbourhood. No one will interfere with him.' She sat beside him as they ate. 'Did you sleep?'

'Indeed I did. Liane—'

'You are about to be serious.'

'Yes. I am. Listen to me. When this is over, and we get back to the valley, I would like to take you out with me.'

'Why? I am more useful here than I could ever be in England. Besides, these are my friends. My comrades. I could not desert them.'

'And do you think I can desert you, having found you again?'

She regarded him for a few moments. 'You are talking like a lover.'

'Yes. I am a lover. Your lover.'

She lay down with her hands beneath her head. 'You do not know me.'

'I think I know enough about you to know you are the woman with whom I wish to spend the rest of my life.'

She made a moue, very reminiscent of Madeleine. 'Because you once held me naked in your arms?'

'Because I have held you naked in my arms in my dreams ever since.'

'That is lust, not love.'

'I have also dreamed of your face, your smile, your voice, your scent, of *you*, for all that time. Why else do you think I am here at all? I could have sent someone else. But the thought of regaining you . . .'

She sighed. 'Do you know what has happened to me?'

'Yes.'

'How could you know?'

'Joanna told me.'

Liane frowned, and rose on her elbow. 'You have seen Joanna?'

'We met in London. She told me about Auchamps.'

Liane stared at him for several seconds, then lay down again. 'And you still want me?'

'I want you more than ever. I want to make you forget what happened. I want you to laugh again.'

'I will laugh again, when the war is over. When we have driven the Boche from France. But if you really came all this way, and risked all this much, to see me again, then I will be happy to make you happy once again.'

Beggars, James reflected, cannot be choosers. There was no way he was going to refuse her invitation, however grudgingly given, any more than he could have resisted her invitation in that bedroom at Chartres. There were enormous differences. Chartres had been a business of a soft mattress and pristine

217

white sheets, not the hard ground and an unwashed blanket. Chartres had been a place of sweet scents and glowingly clean bodies, not sweat and earth. In Chartres they had been, for that hour, the only two people in the world; here, although they removed themselves further into the little wood, they could still hear the chatter of their companions, nor could there be any doubt that the men knew exactly what they were doing. But in Chartres, he at least had had too much to drink, the alcoholic haze shrouding both what had been happening at the time and his memory of it; here they were both absolutely sober. Perhaps that was why he now said, 'There is something I have always wanted to ask you.'

'Then ask it.'

'Why were you expelled from Lucerne?'

'Did Joanna not tell you that also?'

'No.'

'Did you sleep with her?'

'No.'

'Yet you seem to have exchanged a lot of confidences. We were expelled because we were discovered in bed together. Oh, we were guilty. What else did they expect? We were two good-looking girls. We were both passionate. And there were no men. The nuns did not see it that way. Does that shock you?'

'No,' he said, by no means certain he was telling the truth. 'Are you still lovers?'

'We have been, from time to time. But nowadays we only ever see each other from time to time. I don't know that we shall ever see each other again. You say you met each other in England. Do you know where she went from there?'

Time for one of those decisions. To lie to Liane was almost unthinkable. But to tell Liane the truth about Joanna could only make her more unhappy and confused than she already was, and besides, it would be betraying his job. He stuck carefully to the truth. 'I know she left England, but she did not tell me where she was going.'

*   *   *

They made love again before the evening, Liane with a desperation which revealed how nervous she was. 'Listen,' she said. 'Should anything happen to me, you must take Amalie with you.'

'If anything happens to you, it is going to happen to me as well.'

'Promise me.'

It could do no harm. 'I promise.'

They crossed the border, as Liane had assured him, without difficulty. They heard a German patrol, but the soldiers were bored and disinterested, and while their dogs barked, they were on leashes and their masters apparently did not take them seriously.

Once across, the guerillas made good time; both Liane and Jules clearly knew the country very well. By dawn they were in another little wood on a hillside overlooking the track, watching a train rumbling by beneath them. 'That is a local,' Jules said. 'A milk train, eh?'

Liane translated while James studied the position through his binoculars. To the left the track bifurcated, and there was a large signal box. That could well be the key to their survival, he reckoned. 'When does the express come through?'

'It has been. It gets to Bordeaux Central at four.'

'So, another lazy day.'

But they did not make love. The tension was too great. James had to admit, at least to himself, that the tension was probably greater for him than anyone else because this was a new experience for him, while all of his companions, and certainly Liane, knew what it was like to be on the run, with death a daily hazard.

He had not supposed he would sleep, but he did, deeply, waking with a start when Liane squeezed his arm. 'Is it time?' The day was still bright.

'It is time for you to tell us exactly what you wish of us. Look there.' Coming slowly down the track was a motorized trolley manned by three soldiers. As with the border patrol, they were showing no great urgency or interest in their work, although they were obviously inspecting the track.

'There have been four of those during the day,' Jules said.

Liane translated, and James asked, 'And at night?'

'I do not know.'

James levelled his binoculars again. Obviously the trolley could not be used if there was an express or any other train approaching. But the fact that it was being used at all meant that the line was almost certainly patrolled during the night. Their great advantage was that as this would be the first such attack, after several months of peaceful occupation, the Germans would not be anticipating one; their relaxed attitude was obvious.

The trolley had reached the signal box, the lines had been switched, and it was moving down a siding. 'That's our target,' James said. 'Take out that box, and we cripple both the main line and the subsidiary. We also knock out their local communication centre. That box is linked to the telephone system.'

As always, Liane acted as interpreter. 'You mean we must attack the box?' Jules was aghast.

'That's what your weapons are for.'

'But . . . those men will not surrender.'

'Certainly they will not surrender. They will have to be killed. What is more, they will have to be killed before they can send a message.'

'We can cut the telephone wires,' Liane said, her eyes gleaming.

'Agreed. But they may have a radio. The whole lot has to go.'

'I have never killed a man,' Jules muttered.

'If you intend to hurt the Germans, they have to be killed.'

Liane stroked Jules' head. 'I have killed a German. It is not so difficult.'

Jules swallowed, and made the sign of the cross.

'You say the express gets into Bordeaux at four,' James said. 'Is it punctual?'

'As a rule,' Liane said.

'That means it will pass this junction at a quarter to. Does it blow?'

She asked Jules. 'He says yes. As it approaches the box.'

'Excellent. Now, I cannot be in two places at once. Jules will have to carry out the assault on the box. First we need to synchronize our watches. Ask him what time he has.'

Liane inquired. 'He has no time. He does not have a watch.'

Little details which had not occurred to him. 'But you have a watch,' he reminded Liane. 'Is it accurate?'

'Of course. It is Cartier.'

'Okay. Then we'll use yours. Synchronize.'

'Seventeen minutes to six.'

'Right.' He unstrapped his watch and handed it to Jules, who gazed at it with wide eyes. 'Now, Liane, repeat to him exactly what I am going to say to you, and make sure he understands it.'

'That will not work. He is not the brightest of men. Tell me what you wish, and I will see that it is done.'

'I don't want you to be involved in the attack on the box. I want you with me.'

'Do you need me?'

'I need you. I will keep my instructions as simple as possible.'

She gazed at him for several seconds, then said, 'What must I tell them?'

'They go in at twenty to four, or when they hear the whistle, whichever comes first; there is always the chance that the train might be ahead of schedule. They will approach the box five minutes before that, positioning themselves but taking care to remain concealed. They go in behind their grenades. They should hurl the grenades through the windows. They should use every one of them. Then they must carry out the assault with their tommy-guns and pistols. The box must be destroyed.'

'And the people inside?'

'Them too. I'm sorry.'

She nodded. 'And after?'

'As soon as they are satisfied that the box is completely out of action, they must withdraw and get back to the border as quickly as they can. They should have a start of several hours, owing to the confusion that will follow the destruction of the train.'

'And us?'

'We will join them, but they must not wait for us.'

'Suppose some of them are hit?'

'If they can move freely, they must be brought out. If they cannot—'

'You are sorry. Does this go for us as well?' He did not reply, and she gave a little smile.

'What's so funny?'

'We all thought you were such a nice, innocent, well-mannered boy. We never guessed what lay beneath.'

'I'm a soldier. But Liane . . . please don't get wounded.'

She kissed him.

James spent the last hour of daylight explaining exactly what they were going to do while the men fidgeted and fingered their weapons. None of them had ever fired a tommy-gun or thrown a grenade before. With Liane translating, he showed them how to handle their weapons, how to change their magazines, how to pull the pin on their grenades and count to four before hurling. But he did not suppose a less well-trained force had ever gone into battle.

Then it was a matter of waiting while night fell and the valley became shrouded in darkness. 'What do you think about before a battle?' Liane asked.

'I've never been in a battle.'

'You were at Dunkirk. And before then, in Flanders.'

'Those weren't battles in the old Great War sense that you knew in one hour's time you would be encountering the enemy face to face.'

'But the enemy was all around you. Were you afraid?'

'I was too anxious to survive, to be afraid. Fear comes

afterwards, when you realize that you *have* survived, where so many others, people you knew quite well, have not.'

'Will we survive?'

'If we don't believe we will, we won't.'

'That is a simple philosophy,' she remarked. 'A soldier's philosophy.' Then she appeared to sleep.

But she was awake at three. A last check of the watches, and they moved down the hill, separating when they were about a hundred yards from the line. To their left the signal box glowed with light. James studied it through his binoculars; there were two men inside. This information he passed on to Jules via Liane. 'Frenchmen?' Jules asked.

'They are wearing German uniforms. We shall see you back in the mountains.' They shook hands, and James and Liane crawled away from them and made their way up the line for a quarter of a mile.

'There will be Frenchmen on the train,' Liane said. 'Maybe women and children too.'

'I thought movement is strictly controlled by the Germans?'

'That is true. But there are some people who get permission to travel.'

'If they do, shouldn't we assume they are collaborationists?'

'Not all. Pierre has permission to travel from Paris to Bordeaux to see Mama and Papa whenever he wishes. My God, he could be on this train.'

'He won't be. I gave him instructions not to leave Paris until this business is over.'

'And you are the boss.'

He squeezed her hand. 'Does that bother you so much? Somebody has to be the boss.'

'I am glad it is you.'

They reached the position he had chosen, where there was a slow bend in the track. The drivers of the express would not see the signal box until they came round this bend, and it was here they would sound the whistle.

James crawled up to the track, Liane immediately behind him, and they sat together as they unpacked the explosive from Liane's knapsack. 'What else do you have in there?' James asked. 'There seems an awful lot.'

'Just about everything I still possess,' she said. 'It is not a lot.'

'Keep down,' he warned, studying the ground in front of them. Then he crawled forward with the gelignite, and carefully placed it between the sleepers on both sides of the track. The wires were inserted, and he crawled back to where Liane waited, with the box, slowly laying the wires out behind him.

'That looked simple enough,' she said. 'How far back do we go?'

'It'll be a big bang. Another thirty yards will take us into the trees. We should just about stretch that far.'

James started to unwind the wire, when they suddenly heard a noise. They both turned to look back at the track, and saw two German soldiers walking down the line. 'Shit!' James muttered.

Liane drew her Luger from her knapsack, and he caught her wrist. 'We don't know where the rest are,' he whispered.

'Suppose there are no others. Look, they have seen the explosive.' The two men had certainly noticed something beside the track. 'What do we do?'

'Listen.' Suddenly the roar of the express filled the night. The soldiers stood up. One blew a shrill blast on his whistle, the other took a flashlight from his belt, switched it on, and ran to the bend, obviously intending to stop the train. 'That's done it,' James said. He took the Luger from Liane's hand, held it in both of his to aim, and squeezed the trigger. He had always been an excellent shot; the German soldier went down without a sound, the flashlight flying from his hand. His companion swung round, unslinging his rifle as he did so, while from out of the gloom behind him there now came four more men, shouting as they ran. 'The tommy,' James snapped. Liane had already unslung it. Now she gave it to him. He levelled it and sprayed the track, carefully aiming above the lines. Two of the Germans fell. The rest went down voluntarily, returning fire. Bullets sang through the air over their heads. 'Keep *down.*'

Liane pressed her cheek into the earth as she had done when sheltering from the air attack in May. 'Are we done?'

'Not until we fire the train.' He sent another burst over the tracks to prevent the Germans from investigating the suspicious objects. Now he heard a series of cracks and explosions from further down the track as Jules' people went into action. But now too the roar of the train was very close. A moment later it came into sight, rushing round the bend, a long glittering sequence of light. James heard shots and saw flashlights being waved, but it was too late. The engine was just coming up to the explosive. 'Are we too close?' Liane asked.

'Yes,' James said, and pressed the plunger.

Ten

The Spy Who Came Home

'My darling! I did not expect you to wait up.' Frederick von Helsingen entered his bedroom.

Madeleine was sitting up in bed, a book on her lap. 'Did you not hear the raid?'

'We were down in the bunker.'

'So was I, for over an hour. It was terrifying. I thought Goering said it could never happen?'

'Another of his mistakes. I'm afraid we may have to put up with them for a while longer.'

Madeleine peered at him. She could see that he was in a state of some exhilaration. 'You mean until after the invasion.'

Frederick kissed her, then got up and took off his tunic. 'There is not going to be an invasion.'

'What did you say?'

'This is top secret.' He continued to undress. 'The fact is that we have not succeeded in defeating the RAF. No one must know that we have reached this decision, and we will keep up the pressure on them, on Britain, throughout the winter, certainly. But we have more important fish to fry.'

'I don't understand.'

'The Führer has made a decision that the time has come to deal with Russia.'

'To do *what*?'

'I told you it must come to this.'

'You mean we are actually going to war with her?'

'Stop looking so terrified.' He got into bed beside her. 'Don't you remember what I told you? Russia is a house

226

of cards. Her people basically hate the Stalinist regime. Her
army is a shambles; they couldn't even beat the Finns. Stalin
has executed all his best generals. One big push and it will
all come tumbling down. And we have a very big push:
the Führer has authorized the formation of ten new panzer
divisions, double the existing number.'
    'Will you have to go?'
    'Well, as you know, I have put myself down for a field
command.'
    She rolled over to put her arms round him. 'Oh, Freddie, if
something were to happen to you . . .'
    'Nothing is going to happen to me. It is going to be the
quickest and most complete campaign in military history. Just
remember that what I have told you is a deadly secret. The
Russians may not be worth a damn, but there are an awful
lot of them, and if they knew we were coming it could be
tricky. Did you know that they have several armies, they call
them fronts, all stationed quite close to the old Polish border?
OKW has the plan to bypass these fronts, encircle them, and
force them to surrender. That will virtually eliminate the Red
Army in one short campaign. That is why it is so important that
the plan is kept absolutely secret. If the Reds were to learn of
it, the whole thing would collapse.'
    'Yes,' Madeleine said absently, her mind still totally con-
sumed by the thought of Frederick going off to war, and being
killed, and leaving her alone. She had burned every boat she
had. She could never go back to France. And she had never
really been accepted in Germany. She was Frederick von
Helsingen's wife. Without him she was nothing.
    He kissed her again, switched off the light, rolled over
to take her in his arms preparatory to mounting her, and
the telephone jangled. 'Oh, goddamn it!' He rolled back
again, switched on the light, sat up, and took the receiver
off the hook. 'Helsingen!' He listened. 'Who? Good God!
Yes, of course put him on. Franz? How good to hear from
you. You are in Berlin? Bordeaux? What has happened?'
Again he listened, while Madeleine also sat up. She knew

that Frederick's friend Franz Hoepner, who had been best man at their wedding, had been transferred from Dieppe to Bordeaux. If he was calling in the middle of the night it could only be because something had happened to Mama and Papa.

'My God!' Frederick was saying. 'They did that? Who are these people?' He listened, and Madeleine watched the colour draining from his cheeks. 'Are you serious? Yes. Yes, I see. Well, of course she cannot be involved. She has been here, in Berlin, for the past two months. She does not correspond with her family at all. Yes. Yes. I see. Yes, I will handle it at this end. Thanks for letting me know so promptly.' Slowly he replaced the phone.

'What has happened?' Madeleine asked.

Frederick did not look at her. 'Last night, or I suppose one should say before dawn this morning, the Paris–Bordeaux express was blown up, only a few miles short of Bordeaux.'

'Oh, my God! Were many people hurt?'

'There were very many people hurt. There were very many people killed. The train was full, mainly with German personnel.'

'How terrible. Do they know who was responsible?'

'Yes. It was a group of French criminals, of course. And do you know who was with them? Indeed, she may have been their leader.'

'Oh, my God! Liane? They've captured her?'

'She got away. At least for the moment. But they found some of her belongings on the ground close to the position from where the explosive charge was detonated. One was a purse with her name engraved on it. Did you know that Liane was an expert in explosives?'

'Of course she is not. Liane?'

'Well, she has either been trained or she had an expert with her. The charge was apparently placed and fired with the utmost precision, and at the same time a raid was made on the signal station a few hundred metres down the track. At least a couple of those assassins were killed. But the station is

228

destroyed. Franz estimates that the line and the box will take several weeks to repair.'

'But if Liane has been identified . . . Mama and Papa!' She leapt out of bed.

'What are you doing?' Frederick demanded.

'I must go to Bordeaux. They may be in trouble.'

'They are in trouble. They have been arrested.'

Slowly Madeleine turned to face him.

'I imagine Pierre is involved as well, although Franz did not know about that.'

'We must do something. *You* must do something.'

'Do something. I will tell you what I have done. I have ruined myself by my association with your family.'

She sank on to the bed beside him. 'Oh, Frederick.'

He squeezed her hand. 'So now it is a case of looking out for number one. I will undoubtedly have to accept a reprimand for having prevented Kluck from arresting them back in July. But I can survive that. The important thing is for everyone to understand that you were not involved, could not be involved. That you abhor what was done and will cheer when Liane is finally apprehended and hanged. You must make that perfectly clear to everyone you meet. Please obey me in this. It could be a matter of life and death.'

'But Mama and Papa. We must do something about them.'

'Madeleine, try to understand. There is nothing we *can* do about them. There is no court that will believe they did not know what was going on. We can only harm ourselves by attempting to defend them.'

Madeleine stared at him in horror. 'What will happen to them?'

'If they are not executed, well . . . they will have to go to prison.'

'Prison? You mean a camp. A concentration camp.'

He sighed. 'I'm afraid so.'

'Oh, my God! My God! My *God*!'

'I do not think even He can help them now.'

*   *   *

Madeleine did not sleep. Her brain was a torment of conflicting images. Her mother and father, so rich and prosperous until a few months ago, in a concentration camp, being beaten and humiliated, if anything Joanna had said was true.

But of course it couldn't be true. Nothing Joanna ever said was true. She made things up to cause the maximum effect. But even if it wasn't true, Mama and Papa would still be going to prison. They, who had never lifted a finger to do anything, who had had servants waiting on their every whim, locked up, having to make their own beds, empty their own slops . . . while she lay in a comfortable bed.

But even more, Liane, so brave, so determined, so loyal to the ideal that was France, now even more than ever a fugitive, who would be hunted from one end of the country to the other. While she lay in a comfortable bed.

And Pierre! Frederick had said he might be implicated. Would that explain his odd behaviour when he had so strangely returned? Then he also was a hero of France, while she lay in a comfortable bed.

But, she thought wryly, she had made that bed, and could not now get out of it. There was absolutely nothing she could do. Nothing. How she wished she could strike against Germany as her siblings were doing. They had not accepted the suggestion that the Reich would last, and would occupy France, for the next thousand years. But what could she do? To help France, or at least the Allies, and yet not harm Frederick.

And he was going off to war with Russia, leaving her behind to face the suspicion of the Gestapo. If they were to arrest her once he was safely out of the way, they might well force her to tell them that he had confided that immense secret, and the equally immense secret that Britain no longer has to worry about an invasion – she knew she would never be able to withstand the sort of pain and humiliation that had been inflicted on Amalie.

She discovered it was daylight. She had slept after all. And Frederick was dressing to go out. He saw that her eyes were

open, and bent over her to kiss her mouth. 'I must dash off,'
he said. 'I have people to see.'

'Who?'

'Well, Heydrich, for a start. And I must get an audience
with the Führer. I must take the initiative. Don't worry. I shall
see that you are not involved.' He kissed her again, and left
the room.

I must not be involved, she thought. But I am involved. I am
their flesh and blood. I need to act, now. If the Russians could
be warned . . . Frederick had said it was absolutely essential
that they should not know what was going to happen, so that
their armies could be destroyed before they could react. But if
they knew, and let the Germans know that they knew, then the
attack would probably never take place at all. Frederick would
not be in danger, and the mighty Reich would have suffered an
embarrassing slap in the face, perhaps even more embarrassing
than the destruction of the express train.

But that was a dream. There was no way it could be done
without sending both Frederick and herself to the gallows.

She got out of bed, bathed and dressed. The maid had come
in by now and had her breakfast waiting, but she did not feel
like eating. Instead she drank several cups of coffee, then
curled up on the settee in the lounge, a book on her lap.
But she did not feel like reading, either. Her mind felt utterly
adrift. There was so much to think about, so much she dared
not think about.

The doorbell rang. Madeleine jerked upright, heart pounding, and looked at her watch. Ten o'clock. It could not possibly
be Frederick home so soon. Then . . . The Gestapo! She rose
to her feet as the door opened. 'There is a lady to see you,
madame.' Hannah spoke excellent French; she indeed had
been chosen by Frederick for that reason.

'A lady?' Somehow she expected it to be Liane.

'A Fräulein Jonsson, madame. She says she is an old
friend.'

Rachel watched the door opening, and slowly rose to her

feet. 'James? Oh, my God! James! I mean Sterling.' She raced across the room to hug him. 'We thought you were dead! But . . .' She pulled her head back. 'What happened to you? All those little cuts. And your clothes . . .' These were certainly in rags.

'I got too close to an explosion.'

'I'll call a doctor.'

'I have nothing a few days won't cure.'

'Well, the brigadier . . .'

'He can wait. Get Paris. Tell Pierre to destroy his equipment and get out. Tell him to join his sister, if he can. But he must leave his Paris flat. Now.'

'His sister . . .'

'Later. Send that now.'

He went into the bathroom, washed his face. It still felt sore, and was indeed badly cut up. But it would all heal. As would Liane's cuts. Oh, Liane . . .

He stripped off his tattered uniform, sat on the bed. He had slept most of the way home, but he still felt exhausted. Vaguely he listened to a wailing sound.

Rachel appeared in the doorway. 'All done. I think he was expecting it.'

'That figures. Why is there a siren going off in the middle of the day?'

'That's been happening for the last couple of days. Seems they've decided to obliterate London. Didn't you notice the damage on your way in?'

'I'm afraid I had other things on my mind. Well, I suppose you'd better get the boss on the phone.'

'Aren't you going to tell me what happened first?'

'Briefly, I discovered that none of the guerillas knew anything about explosives, so I decided I should stay and do it for them.'

'Just like that? Was it a success?'

'Oh, yes. But there was a downside. Two of our people were killed. And as I said, I didn't get as far from the explosion as I should have.'

'And Liane?'

'Her too.'

'But she's alive.'

'She's alive. And like me, she'll soon recover.'

'You said something about bringing her out.'

'Did I? Look, get the brigadier on the phone, will you.'

Oh, Liane, he thought. Liane, Liane, Liane. He had actually thought he'd lost her, as the blast had sent her tumbling through the trees, her knapsack ripped from her shoulders, its contents scattered far and wide, her headscarf also blown away, her shirt reduced to ribbons. But like him, she had been essentially unhurt.

The return to the Massif had been an unforgettable experience. As he had promised, the sheer unexpectedness of the attack, added to its magnitude, had left the Germans shell-shocked for several hours, and the destruction of the signal box, with its radio and telephone communications, had left them unable to coordinate their response for even longer. Even so, the manhunt had been massive. Nor had it stopped at the border. The Vichy police had been called into action, and while they had responded enthusiastically, it had been with deliberate incompetence. It was not possible for them not to have discovered the trail of the retreating guerillas, or to estimate where they had to be heading, but they had claimed to be unable to do either.

For those three days he and Liane had lived as one, achieving an intimacy he would never have supposed possible, and if he had realized that she would never again be the utterly irresponsible pleasure-seeker he had first met and fallen for, he had loved the new edition more. Certainly he had never doubted that from then they were a pair, and would work as a pair. Thus her decision not to fly out with him had been a great shock.

'What would I do in England?' she had asked.

'Well . . . what I would like you to do would be to marry me.'

'And sit at home and make tea while you got on with winning the war.'

'Don't you think you've contributed enough to winning the war?'

'No one can contribute enough until France is free.' She had laid her hand on his. 'Please do not misunderstand me. I am flattered and honoured by your proposal. There is no man I would rather marry, and there is no other man I could love. But . . .'

'You love France more.'

'Is that so unforgivable?'

'Of course it is not. But if I leave you here now, I may never seen you again.'

'You will see me again. It is our fate. And besides, now you have brought us a radio, I can speak to you. Is that not so?'

'It must be used very sparingly. It can be traced.'

'I will be careful. And you will take care of Amalie?'

But Amalie had also refused to leave. 'It is also my business to stay and fight for France. My husband died fighting for France. Do you expect me to run away?'

James had looked at Liane. Who had shrugged. 'Do you know, ten days ago she was twenty-one?'

Now Rachel stood in front of him. 'The brigadier is out of town for a few days. But his secretary says he will want to see you the moment he returns. She will call us. But until then we are to do nothing about anything. Do you think it's the chop?'

'It sounds like it.'

'Oh, James.' She burst into tears. 'But at least we have a few days.'

'We have him,' Roess declared. 'There can be no doubt of it. We know our mystery radio caller was arranging for the British to deliver something. That something can only have been the explosive used by those thugs outside Bordeaux. There is no other way they could have got hold of it. Now we know that one of the gang was Liane de Gruchy. Therefore she must have used her brother to arrange the delivery.'

'That is entirely circumstantial,' Kluck objected.

'I regard it as irrefutable.'

'So what do you propose to do?'

'I have already done it. The moment I heard from Bordeaux, with the evidence of Liane de Gruchy's participation in the outrage, I ordered our people there to place the senior Gruchys under arrest.'

'You did *what*? Without reference to me?'

'I considered it essential to prevent them escaping to join their daughter.'

'And what do you think Helsingen will do when he learns that?'

'I imagine he already knows. His friend Hoepner is now commanding the Bordeaux district. But there is nothing he can do. He has to watch his step very carefully due to his close association with that family. Now is our opportunity to round them all up. All we can lay hands on, anyway. I would like your permission to raid Pierre de Gruchy's flat and place him under arrest.' Kluck stroked his chin. 'It has to be now, Herr Colonel, before he has time either to destroy any evidence against him, or to make his escape.'

Kluck sighed. 'Very good, Captain. Just remember that I am granting this permission on the basis of the evidence you have presented to me. Should that evidence turn out to be incorrect, you will have to take the responsibility.'

'Of course, Herr Colonel. But if it turns out to be correct, I assume I will also be allowed the credit.'

'Monsieur de Gruchy?' the concierge commented. 'Well, his rooms are on the third floor. But he is not there.'

'Not there?' Roess looked at his watch. 'Where would he be, at four o'clock on a Sunday afternoon?'

'I do not know, monsieur. He left at dawn this morning. Said he was going for a holiday in the country.'

'Shit,' Roess commented. 'Shit, shit, shit.'

'Monsieur,' the concierge protested. 'I do not permit such language in my house.'

'You will be lucky if I do not burn your house down,' Roess told her.

'He will not get far, Herr Captain,' Sergeant Klein said soothingly.

'You think so? Thanks to that swine Helsingen he has travel documents allowing him unlimited access to anywhere in the south of France, including Vichy. And he has a twelve-hour start. He could be halfway to the border by now. Ah well, put out a general alarm and a description of him. And at least we will have the pleasure of tearing his apartment to pieces.'

'Well?' Rachel demanded. 'You're still in uniform, here?'

'I am wearing uniform, here,' James said, 'because here is no longer an intelligence headquarters, but simply a love nest which is about to go out of existence.'

'Oh, good Lord!' She sat down with a thump. 'But that's not fair.'

'Life isn't always, or even often, a very fair business. But from the brigadier's point of view, it is entirely fair. I was allowed the use of an aircraft for one night; I kept it for ten. I was sent to deliver some goods to a guerilla band; I had no orders to take command of the band, thus endangering the lives of myself and my pilot, and the aircraft of course, not to mention, far more importantly, the risk of my being captured and revealing under torture the very existence of Special Operations, which, so far as we are aware, is unknown to the enemy.'

'Fiddlesticks! You'd never give away any classified information, even under torture.'

'According to the brigadier, everyone does, and he probably knows more about it than we do.'

'*I* think you deserve a medal. That was a tremendous thing you did.'

'You know, I think the old buzzard agrees with you. He actually shook my hand. But the fact is, as he sees it, as a Special Operations officer I'm a bust. He's never forgiven me for that Jonsson foul-up, or for the fact that we've lost all track of her. And now this business . . . As he put it, spying, and even more, spy-mastering, is a business of secrecy, caution, and behind-the-scenes activity, not dashing into action with all guns blazing, as it were.'

'But from what you've told me, if you hadn't taken command the business would have been a disaster.'

'I think he accepts that. But it would have been their disaster, not ours. The fact that we actually had a triumph he regards as a stroke of luck that will hardly be repeated. So he doesn't want to risk a repeat. So . . . it's back to the regiment for me, and back to the ATS pool for you.'

'Shit! Bugger it! I was so enjoying it. And just as we had something going. Will we be able to see each other?'

'Perhaps. From time to time. You'll soon forget me.'

'Like hell. Oh . . .' She swung round when there was a knock on the door.

'Excuse me, Mr Sterling,' Mrs Hotchkin said. 'There's a lady to see you. She has the password.'

'How in the name of God . . . a lady?'

'Only in a manner of speaking,' Joanna said.

'Are you out of your mind?' James asked. 'Coming here?'

'I thought you'd be glad to see me.'

'Do we know this person, sir?' Rachel asked.

'Her name is Jonsson.'

'Oh, my God!' Rachel dashed to the desk, opened a drawer, and took out her Webley service revolver.

'Oh, my!' Mrs Hotchkin cried.

'There's nothing to worry about, Mrs Hotchkin,' James said. 'I'll explain it later. Thank you.'

Mrs Hotchkin obviously wanted to stay, but she reluctantly closed the door behind herself.

'And please don't shoot her immediately, Sergeant,' James suggested. 'I'm sure she has a lot to tell us first.'

'That little girl is a sergeant?' Joanna asked.

'And a trained markswoman,' James said. 'But she won't shoot until I tell her to. Now, sit down.'

Joanna sat in the straight chair by the radio desk. 'Why all this hostility? I thought we were on the same side.'

'We were, until you absconded from a top secret establishment.'

'Oh, sure. And then you put out a shoot-on-sight order to all your people. Pierre told me all about it.'

'You have seen Pierre de Gruchy?'

'We spent a night together. It wasn't a lot of fun, although the wine helped. How else do you think I got your password? Or this address?'

'He gave you my password? And made no attempt to . . . ah . . . deal with you?'

'Well, he tried. But I talked him out of it.' She grinned. 'That Captain Lennox sure knows her stuff when it comes to knocking people about.'

'My God! Well, I'm sorry to say that I am going to have to place you under arrest. And kindly do not attempt any strong-arm tactics here. I have received the same training, and I am bigger than you. Besides, as you may have noticed, Sergeant Cartwright is just itching to shoot you.'

'Look, I didn't come here to fight you guys. I came to help you win the war.'

'I imagine we can do that without your assistance.'

'Yeah? Tell me this: when do you reckon Hitler is going to come across the Channel?'

'He's welcome to try.'

'But would it make you happy to know that he's not coming? I mean, at all. He's issued orders for what he calls an "indefinite postponement". But it's off for good.'

'I assume you didn't notice the bomb damage on your way in.'

'Oh, he means to keep up the pressure, for the next six months or so, but he's no longer that interested. He believes you guys are beat, but just won't lie down. Now he reckons it's time to settle up with Russia.'

'What did you say?'

'The first week of May next year, the Wehrmacht is going to march on Moscow.'

'Hitler told you this personally, did he?'

'I've never met the guy. But he sure told his staff to draw up the plans, just over a week ago. And one of his staff officers is a guy called von Helsingen. You heard of him?'

James frowned. 'He's not the fellow who married Madeleine de Gruchy?'

'You got it. Your own original lady love. And Freddie confided in his wife.'

'Who confided in you? Why would she do that? According to Liane, she's become a Nazi herself.'

'You've seen Liane?'

'I have spent a week with her, recently.'

'Just like that? Shit! You were with her when that train went up?'

'Yes.'

'Fuck the shitting cows! I wish I'd been there. How is she?'

'She's fine. You haven't answered my question.'

'Well, the fact is that, what with Liane blowing up the Germans, and her parents being arrested, and Amalie drowning herself, and Pierre on the run, Madeleine is starting to feel like a lump of shit. She just wanted to *do* something. So she told me what Helsingen had told her.' She looked at Rachel. 'That has got to be an absolute secret. If it ever came out, she'd be for the high jump.'

James also looked at Rachel, who waggled her eyebrows.

'You don't reckon what she told me is worth knowing?' Joanna asked. 'I know you don't go much for Stalin. Neither do I. But surely it's better to have him with you than against you, and if you tipped him off about the German plans, he'd have to be grateful.'

'I agree with you. If what you have told us is true, and not just something you've made up.'

'Why should I do that? Why should I risk my life coming here? I told you, I know you guys are out to get me. So I took the risk because I thought I had some pretty important information.'

'Or you worked out that supplying us with some important info, true or not, could get us off your back.'

'Oh, for Christ's sake. Okay, I didn't like your training methods. I didn't like that Colonel Marsham, and I didn't like any of my roommates. So I fucked off. That doesn't mean I don't want to work for you guys. And if you let me loose to rub shoulders with Madeleine, who knows what else I can do for you?'

Again James looked at Rachel.

'I think we could give it a whirl, sir,' Rachel said. 'At least put it to the brigadier. If there's anything in it, it might even get us our jobs back.'

'And mine,' Joanna said enthusiastically.

After they had seen the brigadier, James took them both out to dinner.

'Do you think he'll go for it?' Joanna asked.

'If he wasn't going to, he would not have reinstated me,' James said. 'Or given me permission to continue employing you. As to whether the War Cabinet will go for it, or Stalin will believe it if they do, that's another matter.'

'If they don't, they need their heads examined. The champagne's on me.' She raised her glass, and smiled at Rachel. 'Here's to the three of us. Onwards and upwards.'

'I'll drink to that,' Rachel said.

'There's another, more important toast,' James said. 'The de Gruchys.'

'Shit, yes,' Joanna agreed. 'They sure are one fucked-up family. Those poor old people, Pierre, Liane . . . Boy, I'd give a lot to be with her right now.'

'Maybe that could be arranged,' Rachel suggested.

'Of them all,' James said, 'I feel sorriest for Amalie.'

'Amalie?' Joanna asked. 'At least she can't suffer anymore. She's dead.'

'Amalie is alive, and with Liane.'

'You joke.'

'I saw her, only a couple of weeks ago.'

'Well, fuck me. But that's great news. So why are you more sorry for her than any of the others?'

240

'You don't reckon it's rough to lose your husband, to all intents and purposes within five minutes of getting married to him?'

'Yeah. I guess that's grim.'

'And then . . . Do you know what the Gestapo did to her? Not once, but twice.'

'Tell me.'

'It's not dinner-party conversation. The fact is that she's suffered like hell, and I don't see what she has to look forward to. So, here's to Amalie. May she find happiness, one day.'

Liane and Amalie lay together on the slopes of the hill and watched the plane circling above them. It was several thousand feet up, and obviously could not make out the two figures nestling in the long grass. But it was keeping an eye on things. The search might have been called off, but the Vichy government understood that another guerilla exploit might well bring a savage Nazi response.

'Are you sorry you did not go with him?' Amalie asked.

'I would have liked to go with him,' Liane said. 'And that is the first time I have thought that about any man. But I would not have been happy. I can only be happy here, fighting for France.'

'But will you ever see him again?'

'Oh, yes. I feel it in my bones. And in my heart.'

Amalie sighed, and Liane squeezed her hand. 'But you, my sweetest angel—'

'Listen!' Amalie said.

'Liane!' a voice was calling from lower down the hill. 'Liane! Your brother is here!'

'Pierre!' Both women scrambled to their feet. Liane led the way down the hill. 'Oh, Pierre! Thank God you got here. But . . .' She stopped running as the three men approached. Etienne, Pierre, and . . . The third man was smaller than the others, and wore a thick black beard. 'Oh, my God!'

'Henri?' Amalie asked. '*Henri!*' she shrieked, and resumed running into his arms.

Pierre came forward to embrace Liane. 'But how?' she asked.

'It is a long story. It seems he could not get back to Dieppe as he intended: the Germans got there first. So then he found his way across France into Vichy. He knew that to re-enter the occupied territory would be to commit suicide, and he had learned what happened to his parents; he thought that Amalie had also been deported to Germany. So he got himself a job as a street cleaner, and, well, like so many of our people, just waited for something to turn up. I was what turned up. I was asked by some people who gave me shelter which regiment I had served with, and when I told them the Motorized Cavalry, they mentioned that there was a Jewish man in the next village who had also served in that regiment. I could not believe my ears. Nor could he his eyes, I am sure.'

Liane decided not to comment on the dangers of so willingly confiding the events of his past to complete strangers; he seemed to have got away with it. 'And so you brought him here.'

'When he heard what I told him about you and Amalie being in the mountains, he was desperate to come. Do you think I did the wrong thing?'

'Of course not. Look at them. Amalie is smiling. Do you know that this is the first time Amalie has smiled since the night before her wedding? I am so happy for them.'

'But what is going to become of them? Of us?'

Liane held his hand as they walked towards the encampment. 'With the help of our friends, of James, we're going to go on fighting. Until we win.'